Christmas in Dixie by Jeanie Smith Cash
Holly Davenport is shocked when she receives a letter in the mail informing her that not only is she adopted but she is an identical quadruplet as well. When she goes to Monticello, Georgia, to get some answers, she has a severe appendicitis attack and winds up in the hospital in the capable hands of handsome Dr. Grayson Brockman. Hurt by her adoptive family's concealment of her adoption, she has plenty of time to consider her options. Can Grayson convince her to stay in Georgia, or will she return home to her adopted family?

Nick's Christmas Carol by Rose Allen McCauley
Carol Peterson, an adopted only child, has always wanted a large, close-knit family. When she hears from a lawyer that she is one of four identical quadruplets, she rushes to his office. Disappointment sets in when he won't reveal any further details until her twenty-fifth birthday, which is almost four months away. But Nick Powers, a man from Carol's past who works in Monticello, Georgia, helps keep her mind and time occupied while she waits. They combine forces to make Christmas a happier time for others, but will they find their own Christmas happiness?

Starry Night by Jeri Odell
Starr Evans grew up in Southern California and loves the surf, sea, and sand. Camden Brockman was raised in Georgia and has deep roots in the soil of the South. But when he arrives in LA to assure her that his letter and the news of her adoption isn't a scam, their attraction is undeniable. Can a free spirit from Los Angeles and a southern gentleman from Georgia find enough to build a life on and a place to do it together?

Loving Stetson by Debra Ullrick
Noel Brady always knew she was adopted. What she didn't know, however, was that she was a quadruplet. When a letter from an attorney in Georgia informs her of that fact, she shares the news with her father's ranch hand, Stetson Laramie. She is in love with Stetson, and she's certain he cares about her, too, but something is holding him back, and the lawyer's letter seems to push him further away. When he reveals his secret past to her, will Noel continue loving Stetson?

CHRISTMAS
BELLES OF GEORGIA

FOUR-IN-ONE COLLECTION

JEANIE SMITH CASH
ROSE ALLEN McCAULEY
JERI ODELL
DEBRA ULLRICK

BARBOUR
PUBLISHING

College of the Ouachitas

ISBN 978-1-61626-480-2

Published by Barbour Publishing, Inc., P.O. Box 719, Uhrichsville, OH 44683, www.barbourbooks.com

Cover design: Kirk DouPonce, DogEared Design

Our mission is to publish and distribute inspirational products offering exceptional value and biblical encouragement to the masses.

ecpa Member of the
Evangelical Christian
Publishers Association

CHRISTMAS IN DIXIE

Jeanie Smith Cash

Dedication

To Jesus my Lord and Savior, who made this all possible.

To my own special hero, Andy.
You are always there for me, and I love you very much.

To my wonderful family for their love and support.

I'd like to thank my critique partners:
my sister, Chere Snider, and my friend, Delia Latham.
I appreciate and love you both. I'd also like to thank
Rose Allen McCauley, Jeri Odell, and Debra
Ullrick for writing with me, and especially Rebecca
Germany, our editor, as well as everyone at Barbour,
for their time, patience, and hard work.

Be kind and compassionate to one another,
forgiving each another, just as in Christ God forgave you.
EPHESIANS 4:32

Chapter 1

Holly Davenport rushed in the door of the beauty shop in Mt. Vernon, Missouri, as the clock struck nine. Thank the Lord she hadn't ruined her record. She had never been late in all the time she'd worked for Karen Lawrence, and she didn't want to spoil it on her last day here.

"Hi, Karen. I didn't think I was going to make it. This has been a terrible morning. Everything that could go wrong certainly did this morning."

"What happened?" Karen asked, concerned.

"First the bathroom sink plugged up and ran over on the floor. My cup of hot chocolate boiled over in the microwave. Then I locked my car keys in the house and had to dig in the bottom of my purse for the spare house key, and you know what my purse looks like, so that was quite a task."

Karen chuckled. "Yes, I can imagine."

"It just isn't my morning." She sighed. "When I realized, after everything else that had happened, I'd locked my car keys in the house, I really wanted to stomp my feet and scream. But"—she raised her hands in the air—"that wouldn't be a very Christian way to act on the porch in front of my neighbors, so I restrained myself, but barely." She stuck her purse in a drawer and closed it with her knee.

"Oh, Holly." Karen laughed. "I'm really going to miss you."

"I'm going to miss you, too, but I won't miss having to get up and rush out the door every morning. It will be nice to work at home."

"Yes, you're right about that. But I'd miss seeing the clients and interacting with them every day."

"Yes, I know you would, but I'll be perfectly happy with some peace and quiet, at least for a while. I could certainly do without another morning like this one. Hopefully it gets better as the day goes on." Holly hung her coat on the rack in the back room and changed into her smock.

"I wouldn't count on it." Karen grinned. "Your first client just walked in the door."

Holly groaned. "Ohhh, you're right about that." She had forgotten that Matilda Stratton had an appointment today. Matilda was one of those clients who, no matter how you did her hair, was never satisfied.

Holly pasted on a smile and went to greet the woman. The rest of the day didn't get any better. Every difficult client she had chose today to come in. She glanced at her appointment book later that afternoon and smiled. At least Elaine Fenwick was pleasant, and she was always pleased when she left. She was glad Elaine was her last client. It was a good way to end this awful day.

"Holly, are you about through for the day, or do you have another client coming in?" Karen asked. "I need to go to the bank and make a deposit before it closes."

"Go ahead, Karen. I'll close up for you. Elaine Fenwick is coming in for her nail appointment in about ten minutes, and she's my last client." Holly finished washing her brushes and placed them in a plastic tub. "I can drop the keys by to you on my way home."

"That would be great. What am I going to do without you?" Karen slipped her purse over her shoulder and grabbed her jacket. "Your clients are going to miss you as much as I do. To listen to me you wouldn't think so, but I really am happy for you."

"I know, and I so appreciate you giving me a chance when I was so new at this."

"It wasn't a hardship—believe me. You've been the best employee I've ever had. I'd better go, or I'm going to miss the bank. I'll see you at the house later."

Holly had worked at Karen's Hair & Nail Salon since she got out of high school. She had worked part-time until she received her cosmetology license and then full-time ever since. She would have been through at noon today, but Elaine Fenwick had been her first and most loyal client, and she wanted to do her nails one last time. She'd had a standing appointment with Holly every Monday at three o'clock since the first week Holly worked for Karen.

Karen was a good boss, but Holly's heart wasn't in this job. She had been building her savings so she could quit and write full-time. Her first Christian romantic suspense novel had hit the shelves last week, and she was excited to see it in print. It was the first of a six-book contract she had signed with her publisher. Holly had given Karen notice two weeks ago. She was excited to stay home so she could start working on her second book.

At four o'clock Holly locked up the shop, dropped off the keys with Karen, and drove home. On her way into the house, she grabbed the mail from her box. She unlocked the door and tossed the mail on the entry table long enough to hang up her jacket. After pouring herself a glass of root beer, she grabbed her letter opener and sat on the rust and gold plaid sofa that matched the solid gold rocking chair in her living room.

She laid the mail—all but a large envelope that caught her eye—on her oak coffee table. *What is this?* She turned the envelope over and read the name at the top left-hand corner. Brockman and Davis, Attorneys at Law, Monticello, Georgia. She didn't know anyone in Georgia. Why in the world would she be getting a letter from an attorney's office there? Maybe it had something to do with her book contract.

She slid the letter opener underneath the flap of the envelope and retrieved an official-looking document. Her blue eyes widened as she read it. "Oh Lord," Holly cried. "Please tell me this isn't true. My whole life can't have been a lie."

Holly didn't know how long she sat on the sofa with the letter in her lap. Surely an attorney wouldn't make this kind of mistake.

She was adopted.

Holly glanced at her watch. Five o'clock. She was supposed to meet Beth, her best friend, at six for pizza. But right now both of Holly's parents would be home. She might have to cancel pizza; this couldn't wait.

She grabbed her purse, headed out the door, and climbed into her red Volkswagen bug. She drove the three miles out to her parents' ranch. The home where she had been raised by two people she'd thought were her parents. Had her whole life been a lie? She was so confused, devastated by this news. Why hadn't they told her?

Holly used her key to unlock the front door. She walked through the living room, down the hall, and into the kitchen. She had always loved this room decorated in yellow sunflowers, where she knew her mother, or the woman who called herself her mother, would be fixing supper. It was a warm and inviting room, just like the woman who had raised her. How could she have kept something so important to herself and not shared this information with the daughter she claimed to love so much?

"Holly, darling. What a surprise." Virginia Davenport smiled as Holly walked into the large country kitchen.

"I need to talk to you and Dad," Holly said, her voice flat.

"Darling, what's wrong?" Alarm filled her mother's voice.

Holly knew the devastation she was experiencing had to show on her face.

"Would you ask him to join us, please?"

"Holly, you're scaring me. What is this all about?"

"I'll explain it to both of you together."

A few minutes later Robert Davenport joined his wife and daughter at the kitchen table.

"Holly, what is this all about? You've got your mother all worked up. We can't help if we don't know what the problem is."

"This isn't something you can make right, Dad." The bitterness in her voice was evident even to her. But she couldn't help how she felt. "I received this in the mail today." She slid the letter from the envelope. "It's from Brockman and Davis, Attorneys at Law, in Monticello, Georgia."

Holly noticed the color drain from her mother's face. She almost felt sorry for her. She obviously knew what was coming. "Let me read it to you. But I'll bet it doesn't come as the shock to you that it did to me."

Ms. Holly Davenport,
    This letter is to inform you that you are one of four identical quadruplets born to Janice Lynn Bellingham,

December 25, 1986. Janice expired December 28, 1986, from complications. The four infant girls were given up for adoption. Each child went to a different family. Along with your three sisters, you have inherited one hundred acres of land, which is now being used to farm peanuts, with a large antebellum home from your maternal grandparents, Charles and Emily Bellingham of Monticello, Georgia. There are two stipulations in the will. One, you and your three sisters must spend December 25, your birthday/Christmas day and night, at the plantation house together. Two, you cannot sell the property or home; it has to stay in the Bellingham family. Should you accept your inheritance, each of you will be responsible for a percentage of the taxes, upkeep, and related fees.

Your adopted family is welcome to join you at the house for the holiday, if they so desire.

Sincerely,
Camden Brockman
Attorney at Law

Holly raised tear-filled eyes to her parents. "How could you keep something like this from me? I had a right to know."

"Holly, darling. We are so sorry you found out this way. We planned to tell you. It never seemed to be the right time. We love you so much. Please, you have to believe that. The Lord sent you to us. You're our special little girl and always have been. We've never felt any different about you than we do about Lance," Virginia said. "Daddy and I couldn't love you any more than if we'd given birth to you."

"Your mother's right, princess. The Lord blessed us in a way we could never have imagined the day He brought you into our lives. You're ours; you always have been. We've loved you from the minute we first saw you."

"You shouldn't have kept this from me." Holly grabbed the letter and her purse as she ran out of the house, ignoring her mother's pleas for her to stay so they could work this out. If she stayed, she knew she might say something she'd be sorry for. Hurt and betrayal from the two people she loved most in the world churned in her stomach. She felt sick. Tears fell unchecked down her face as she climbed into her car and drove away without even looking back.

Holly dialed Beth's cell number on her way back to her house. Her friend answered on the second ring.

"Hey girlfriend, what's up? You aren't cancelling on me, are you?"

"Can you please pick up a pizza and meet me at my house?" Her voice caught as she fought more tears.

"Of course I can, but what's wrong, Holly?"

"I'll explain when you get here." She lost the battle, and more tears coursed down her cheeks. She could hardly talk for them.

"Holly, don't cry. It's going to be all right. I'll be there as soon as I can get the pizza." Silence filled the line for a moment, and then she said, "I love you, you know that, right? Whatever it is, we'll deal with it together."

"I know. I love you, too. See you in a few minutes." Holly closed her cell phone and pulled into her garage. As soon as she got inside the house she called the airport and booked a flight to Monticello, Georgia, for early the next morning. This attorney must have more information than he'd given her in his letter. She needed to talk to him in person. *Thank You, Lord, for allowing me to get a flight on such short notice.*

While she waited for Beth, she packed her bags so she would have everything ready to leave the next morning. She'd just snapped the last one closed when she heard a knock on the front door. Holly opened it for her friend. Beth set the pizza on the coffee table and pulled Holly into her arms for a hug. "Okay, now tell me what's wrong."

Holly handed Beth the letter she'd received in the mail. Beth looked at it, glanced at Holly, and then sat down next to her on the sofa and read the letter. Her gasp revealed she was as shocked at the news as Holly had been when she'd read it earlier.

"Oh Holly. I can't even imagine what a shock this is. No wonder you're so upset. Have you talked to your parents about it?"

"Yes. They said they planned to tell me, but it was never the right time. They said they couldn't love me more if I'd been born to them. I told them I had a right to know, and I walked out."

"I'm so sorry. I wish there was something I could say or do to make this easier for you."

"I don't think anything can make this better, Beth. My whole life has been a lie." Holly sobbed. Beth put her arms around Holly and held her while she cried.

"It's going to be all right. Somehow this will all work out, sweetie." Beth began to pray. "Lord, You know how devastated Holly is over this news. We know You have a plan. Please comfort my sweet friend, and lead her in the right direction in this matter. Thank You, Lord. In Jesus' name we ask, amen."

"Thank you, Beth. I couldn't ask for a better friend."

"Nor could I. How many times have you been here for me? That's what friends do for each other."

"Thank you." Holly gave Beth a shaky smile, hugged her, and then got up from the sofa. "Let's eat, I'm starved."

"Sounds good to me, and while we eat you can tell me your plan, because I know you have one." She smiled back.

Holly served the pizza and soda, sat again beside her friend, and thanked the Lord for their food. "I booked a flight to Monticello, Georgia, in the morning. I have to talk to that lawyer, the one who sent me the letter."

"I can understand that, but please be careful. And promise you'll call me as soon as you get there and know something. If Callie wasn't going to be induced tomorrow morning I'd come with you."

"I know you would, but you need to be here when your little niece is born." Holly grinned for the first time since she'd received that letter. "I know how excited you are about being an aunt for the first time."

"Of course I am, but if you need me, I'll come tomorrow evening."

"I know that. But I'll be fine. You enjoy your little niece, and I'll be back in a couple of days."

Beth left after helping clean up. Holly promised she'd call her when she got to Monticello. Even though it was only nine o'clock in the evening, Holly got ready for bed. She knew she wouldn't get much rest tonight, but she climbed under the covers and stared at the ceiling until morning.

Chapter 2

Early the next morning Holly called for a taxi. Twenty minutes later it picked her up and took her to the airport. The driver dropped her off at the door of the terminal in Springfield at 5 a.m. Holly went through the double doors and up to the counter to check her bag. She went through security without any trouble since she was only taking her laptop and purse on the plane. Her flight left at 6:55 a.m., and she wanted to be ready to board on time.

Her stomach felt a little queasy. She'd only eaten one slice of pizza the night before, but she figured the cause was more likely from stress. Maybe if she ate something light she'd feel better. Holly ordered a bowl of cold cereal and found a place to sit. About halfway through her meal she began to feel worse, rather than better, so she dumped the remainder in the trash. Before she had a chance to sit back down they called her flight. Carrying her purse and laptop, she boarded the plane that would take her to Atlanta, Georgia, where she had rented a car to drive to Monticello. As the plane taxied out onto the runway, the discomfort in her stomach became a dull ache in her right side. No matter how she shifted in her seat she couldn't get comfortable.

One of the flight attendants stopped next to her seat and asked, "Miss, are you okay? Can I do something to make you more comfortable?"

Holly knew her shifting in her seat several times had attracted the young woman's attention. "No thank you. I'll be okay."

"If you need something, let me know."

"I will, thank you."

Her plane taxied into the Atlanta airport right on time at 10:35 a.m., and Holly retrieved her luggage and then went in search of her rental car. The pain in her side seemed to be getting worse. She loaded her luggage in her car and drove out of the rental company's parking area. Google map in hand, she found her way onto the freeway. The first fast-food restaurant she came to, she took the exit and went through the drive-through. It was only 11:20 a.m., but she ordered a Sprite hoping it would settle easy on her stomach. Then she parked in one of the spaces long enough to take two Ibuprofen tablets.

Please, Lord, I pray these will help the pain in my side. I can't imagine what is causing it, but I know You know. I'll leave this in Your hands and ask that You'll please take care of me. In Jesus' name I ask, amen.

She wanted to call Beth just to talk to her, but she was with her sister at the hospital, and Holly wouldn't put a damper on her excitement by telling her she didn't feel well. Beth would just worry.

Back on the freeway, she drove to Monticello, Georgia, and took the exit the map indicated. Once she got into town she drove directly to Mr. Camden Brockman's office. She parked her rental car in one of the spaces and went inside. Holly approached a desk where a young woman was sitting behind the counter. Printed on her name tag was BEVERLY DAILEY. She was an attractive young woman with dark hair and wore a navy-blue skirt and jacket. Typical business attire.

"Good afternoon, may I help you?" Beverly smiled.

"I hope so. I received this letter." Holly pulled the

envelope out of her purse, retrieved the letter, and handed it to the receptionist. "It's from Mr. Camden Brockman. I just flew in from Missouri, and I was hoping I could speak with him if possible."

"If you'll have a seat, Ms. Davenport, I'll see when Mr. Brockman might be available to see you."

As Holly took a seat in one of the plush pale-blue chairs, someone walked in the door and took a seat across from her. She glanced up and noticed a man dressed in a dark-brown suit and tan shirt, with a brown and tan print tie. His clothes were obviously expensive and complemented his coloring. He was quite attractive with dark wavy hair combed neatly. He looked over at her, and for a moment she couldn't look away. His eyes were the most beautiful green; she'd never seen eyes quite that color before. There weren't many men who caught her attention like this. He smiled, and she realized she was staring. Heat filled her cheeks as she looked away.

Pain worse than before sliced through her side, and she gasped, nearly doubling over.

"Are you all right?" The man asked from across the room.

When Holly could catch her breath, she said, "Yes, thank you. I'm fine." She shifted in her chair to try to relieve the pain. She certainly wasn't going to tell this stranger that it felt like a knife was stabbing her. What could be causing her to have such a pain in her side? Before she could think too much about the answer, the woman named Beverly called her name and said, "Mr. Brockman can see you now, Ms. Davenport."

"Thank you." Holly slowly stood, and the pain in her side increased. She hesitated, hoping the pain would subside, but that didn't happen. She walked to the door, where the young woman was waiting to escort her back to Mr. Brockman's office, making an effort to hide the pain.

As she passed by she glanced at the man sitting in the chair. Those gorgeous green eyes held obvious compassion and concern. He smiled and nodded his head as she followed the young woman through the door. Surely she was mistaken. He didn't even know her.

"Dr. Brockman, I'll let your brother know you're here." Beverly addressed the man in the waiting room as they walked through the door.

He was Mr. Brockman's brother? A doctor and an attorney in the same family. No wonder he wore expensive suits.

They walked into Mr. Brockman's office, and he introduced himself. "Hello, Ms. Davenport." He offered her his hand. "I'm Camden Brockman. Please have a seat. What can I do for you?"

"I received your letter yesterday, and I was hoping to get some answers." Holly set her purse in the chair behind her. Not sure if the pain in her side would allow her to bend over enough to sit in the chair, she decided not to try it.

"I realize you've traveled a long way, Ms. Davenport, and I'm sorry, but I'm not at liberty to share any further information with you at this time."

Holly couldn't believe this. "Mr. Brockman, please. This letter has been devastating to me. I didn't even know I was adopted until I read it yesterday afternoon. This has turned my world upside down. And now you're telling me you can't even give me any information or answer my—?" She cried out and doubled over in pain.

21

❄

Dr. Grayson Brockman sat waiting for Camden. The attractive young woman who had gone in to see his brother concerned him. Her beautiful blue eyes held obvious pain, though she tried to hide it. Did it have anything to do with the reason she had come to see his brother?

It had been a while since a woman attracted his attention, but there was something about this one. He didn't know if it was the vulnerability he sensed or the pain in her eyes. He didn't even know her, but something about her made him want to protect and reassure her. He glanced up as Beverly came into the room, interrupting his thoughts.

"Dr. Brockman, your brother needs you in his office right away." She dialed the cell phone in her hand, and he heard her say, "We have an emergency, and we need an ambulance," as he rushed through the door toward Cam's office.

The young woman he'd seen in the outer room lay on the carpet, and his brother knelt on the floor beside her.

"Cam, what happened?"

"I'm glad you're here. I don't know what happened, Gray. She just doubled over in pain and collapsed."

Grayson thrust his car keys at his brother. "I need you to go out and get my bag." He knelt beside the young woman and took her pulse while he waited for his medical bag. She grimaced in pain, her skin pale and clammy to the touch.

"Easy, hon. I'm a doctor. An ambulance is on the way, and we're going to help you."

"Do you have any idea what's wrong?" Camden handed Grayson his medical bag.

"I won't know for sure until I get her to the hospital

where I can examine her properly. What's her name?"

"Holly Davenport."

"Ohh, I hurt so bad! What's wrong with me?" Tears spilled down her cheeks.

"Where do you hurt?"

She placed her hand between her navel and her right side. "Here."

Grayson touched her cheek and glanced up at Camden. "She definitely has a fever."

Before Grayson could say any more, the paramedics came in with a gurney, and he introduced himself. They lifted Holly onto the wheeled bed, and Grayson rode with her to the hospital. He did a quick exam in the ambulance. He figured it was appendicitis, but he didn't want to say for sure until he had a CAT scan.

Grayson comforted the young woman as the paramedic prepared to place an IV. Scared and in pain, her lavender blue eyes appeared huge in her small face. She flinched, gasping as the needle penetrated her soft skin.

"Easy now." Grayson took her hand. "The worst is over."

When they arrived at the hospital, Grayson followed the paramedics as they rolled Holly down the corridor to emergency and took her into one of the exam rooms. Together they moved her onto one of the beds and then rolled the gurney out into the hall.

Grayson thanked the paramedics and stepped to the phone to order a CAT scan. When he came back into the room, the nurses had changed Holly into a gown.

"May I call you Holly?" Grayson asked.

"Yes."

"Holly, I've ordered a CAT scan, a CBC, and blood

panel. A CAT scan is on the order of an X-ray, and a CBC and blood panel are blood tests. They should tell us what's causing the pain in your side. As soon as we get some answers we'll try to make you more comfortable. Are you allergic to anything?"

"Not that I know of." She grabbed hold of his hand. "Please, don't leave me. I'm so scared."

"I'm not going to leave you. Is there someone we can call for you, a family member or a friend to be with you?"

"I don't know anyone here. I just flew in from Missouri this morning. Ohh," she cried out suddenly. "I feel sick!"

Grayson grabbed an emesis basin and placed it under her chin. When she was through, he handed the basin to the nurse. She gently bathed Holly's face with a cool cloth and gave her a sip of water to rinse her mouth.

When a young orderly came in to take Holly for the CAT scan, she once again took hold of Grayson's hand. "Please, Dr. Brockman, will you go with me?"

"Grayson, and it'll be all right. I'll walk down with you." He didn't know why he'd given her his first name or why he had agreed to go along with her. He should be grabbing a sandwich while she was gone. If this was what he suspected, he'd be assisting in surgery for the next couple of hours. But he felt her fear, and if it would give her some comfort knowing he was there close by, what could it hurt?

Holly cried softly, tears seeping from her eyes and onto the pillow, as she waited for the scan to be completed. It bothered him that she was in pain. A nurse brought him the results of Holly's blood work while he waited for the CAT scan. As soon as the results were ready he stepped into the room with the technician and found exactly what he'd expected to find.

He walked over to the bed. "Holly, you have appendicitis, and we need to take you to surgery immediately. But first, Mary"—he indicated a young woman standing next to him—"needs you to sign some forms giving your consent for surgery."

"Surgery?" Her blue eyes reflected her alarm.

"I know that sounds scary, but it'll be all right. I'll be assisting the surgeon, so I'll be right there with you all the way through it. Are you sure there isn't anyone you want us to call for you?"

❄

Holly was scared, and she hurt so badly, but surgery? She'd never even been in the hospital, much less faced anything like this. Even under the circumstances and the fact that she was still upset with her parents, she wanted her mother. "Can I call my parents, please?"

"Of course, but do it quickly. We need to get you prepped for surgery right away."

"Thank you." Holly gave him her parents' phone number, and he dialed it for her and handed her the receiver. She waited as the phone rang, and then she heard her mother's voice on the line.

"Mom?"

"Holly! Oh darling, we've been so worried. Where are you? We've called several times but you didn't answer."

"I know. I turned off my cell phone. I'm in Monticello, Georgia. Mom, I'm in the hospital."

"Hospital! Holly, oh my goodness, what's wrong? Are you hurt?"

"I had an appendicitis attack, and I'm going to have to

have surgery right away. I'm so scared, Mom."

"Oh honey! I'll call your father, and we'll leave as soon as he gets here. What hospital are you in, and when is the surgery?"

"Grayson, what hospital am I in?" He told her the name. "I'm in Jasper Memorial Hospital. Dr. Grayson Brockman is my doctor, and I'm going into surgery right now. Mom, please call Beth and Lance."

"I will, darling. Is the doctor there where I can I talk to him?"

Holly put her hand over the phone and asked, "Could you talk to my mother for a minute? She's very upset. Maybe you could reassure her."

"Certainly. What's her name?"

"Virginia Davenport." Holly handed Grayson the receiver. He placed it on speaker phone so Holly could hear the conversation. "Hello, Mrs. Davenport, this is Dr. Grayson Brockman."

"Is Holly going to be okay, Dr. Brockman?"

"Yes, she'll be fine. We'll take good care of her."

"My husband and I will catch the next flight out, but it'll be this evening before we can be there."

"I'll stay with her, Mrs. Davenport. She won't be alone. I'll have my nurse call you when Holly is out of surgery, if you'd like."

"Thank you, Doctor. I'd appreciate that." She gave him her cell phone number.

Holly took the phone back.

"Darling, we'll catch a flight and be there this evening."

"Okay, Mom. Be careful, and I'll see to you tonight."

"We will. You don't worry about us; you just worry

about getting well. I love you, and so does your dad. Don't be afraid. We'll be praying, and the Lord will be with you through the surgery."

"I love you and Dad, too, Mom, and thank you for your prayers." Holly handed the phone to Grayson. She hoped she'd make it through this and that she'd have a chance to see her parents again. She didn't know when she'd ever been so scared.

"It's going to be okay." Grayson motioned for the nurse at the door to come in.

Holly watched her as she administered something into the IV tube. She glanced up at Grayson, but before she could ask he explained, "This will take the edge off of the pain and relax you a little. I have to leave for a few minutes, so I can scrub for surgery." He must have sensed her panic at his words, for he quickly added, "I won't be gone long."

When he started to walk away Holly grabbed hold of his hand in a panic.

"It's okay. Don't be afraid. I'll be in with you shortly. Try to relax and let the medication take effect."

Holly nodded and let go of his hand. As he walked out the door she felt alone and frightened. She didn't even know this man, but there was something about him that put her at ease. She wasn't quite so afraid when he was there with her.

A little while later, a man who introduced himself as an anesthesiologist asked her some questions. He explained that he would be placing her under the anesthetic and monitoring her through the surgery. Right behind him the surgeon came in and introduced himself. He explained to her that he would be performing her surgery. Grayson would be assisting him and then taking care of her follow-up treatment. It wasn't long after he left that two surgery nurses came in and introduced themselves.

Please, Lord, Holly prayed. *Help me to survive this.* She closed her eyes, and tears slipped down her cheeks as the nurses rolled her through the double doors into surgery.

Chapter 3

Holly, I'm here." A familiar deep voice came from the other side of the room. She turned her head relieved to know he was still there. He was sprawled in a chair too small for him to possibly be comfortable, yet he'd stayed just as he'd said he would.

"The surgery went well. It's going to take a little time, but you're going to be fine."

She tried hard to keep her eyes open, but her lids were too heavy. She felt him take her hand in his. "It's going to be all right, Holly. You can go back to sleep."

"You won't leave me, will you?"

"No, hon. I'll be right here when you wake up."

She didn't remember, but she must have gone back to sleep because when she woke up again, she was in a bigger room. Grayson was in a chair beside her.

Holly gasped as she tried to shift in the bed, and a searing pain shot up her side. He gave her a sympathetic look. "Easy, it's going to hurt when you move for a while."

"It really hurts." She frowned.

"I know," he soothed. "We'll increase the pain meds, and that'll help ease it some."

He pushed the intercom button on her bed and spoke briefly with a nurse. He reached for her hand again, and it felt nice when he gently squeezed her fingers. A few minutes later a young nurse came in and shot something into Holly's IV tube with a syringe. The pain eased, and she went back to sleep.

29

Holly awoke with her side throbbing again. Her mouth felt like the Sahara Desert, and she could hardly swallow. She tried to shift her weight again and cried out in pain.

"Easy, it's all right." Grayson stepped up to the bed and brushed the hair back from her face.

"You stayed with me."

"Yes, I told you I would."

"Why do I hurt so bad?"

"Your appendix ruptured, and we had to make a larger incision to repair the damage." He pointed to the area above the sheet. "You have sutures and bandages that will have to stay in for a few days until the incision heals. That's what's causing your pain." He spoke gently as he explained the surgery to her.

Holly looked up at him. He was not only gorgeous but also kind and gentle. She thanked the Lord that if she had to go through this, that He had sent this man to take care of her.

"What time is it?"

He glanced at his watch, and she noticed he was still dressed in green surgery clothes. They were just like the ones she'd seen the doctors wear on TV. That was the only thing she had to compare it with since this was her first experience with a hospital and surgery.

"It's six o'clock in the evening." He pushed the intercom and ordered her pain meds.

She glanced around the room. "Do you know what happened to my laptop and my purse?"

"They're in the closet over there." He indicated a narrow door across from them. "My brother stayed in the waiting room during your surgery. Once you were settled in here, he brought them up and checked to see if you were doing okay before he left."

"Would you please thank him for me?"

"Yes, but you'll get the chance to see him. I guarantee he'll be back up to check on you."

"Could I please have some water?"

The nurse came in, interrupting their conversation to administer pain medication.

After she left Grayson grabbed a cup from Holly's table and gave her a few ice chips with a spoon. "No water for a little while yet, but this will help."

"Thank you." She yawned and went back to sleep.

Holly woke up a while later and looked over at Grayson. "Are my parents here yet, and have you heard from Beth? She's my best friend."

"Not yet, but they should be any time. They called from the airport a little while ago to check on you. I understand Beth and your older brother are coming with them."

"That doesn't surprise me. Beth said she'd come if I needed her, and Lance is very protective. He always has been. He takes being an older brother very seriously." She smiled and had hardly finished explaining about her brother when he walked in the door.

"Lance!" Holly cried as her brother came in with her parents and Beth following.

"Hey there, sunshine, what's all this?" He shook his head. "I leave on vacation for two weeks, and while I'm gone you get yourself in quite a fix." Her brother leaned over and kissed her forehead.

Holly made a face at him. "Grayson, this is my brother, Lance, my parents, Robert and Virginia Davenport, and my very best friend, Beth."

Grayson stood and shook their hands. "It's nice to meet you."

"Dr. Brockman, we can never thank you enough for taking care of our little girl," Robert said.

"I'm not a little girl anymore, Dad," Holly said.

"You'll always be our little girl, princess." Her father smiled gently. "How are you doing?"

"It hurts when I move, but Grayson tells me I'll be okay."

Grayson waited until she was through to answer. "It's going to take a little time to recuperate. Her appendix ruptured, sending infection into her system. We found an abscess, which we had to drain before we could complete the surgery. She'll be on antibiotics for a while."

"When will she be able to travel, Dr. Brockman, so we can take her home?" Holly's mother asked.

"She'll be in the hospital for at least a week or two depending on how she gets along, but she won't be able to travel for six weeks after her surgery date."

Holly noticed her parents exchange looks. She knew they had a business to run; there was no way they could stay here that long. Lance had to be back at his job as well, and so did Beth.

"You don't have to worry. I can go to a hotel for the four or five weeks after I'm released. I know you need to go back. I'll be fine." Holly assured them.

"Who's going to take care of you, Holly?" Her mother asked.

"I can take care of myself." She yawned. "I've been doing it for a while now."

"I'll work something out to stay with you, Holly," Beth

said. "I can take care of you."

"No, Beth. I appreciate it. But you need to go back, too. You have a new job. In fact I'm surprised you could get off to even come at all. You won't get into trouble will you?"

"No, but even if I had I would have come anyway. My boss is very understanding. I explained the situation to him. He let me borrow a week's vacation from next year since I haven't been there long enough to have vacation yet."

Holly noticed the smile Lance gave Beth. Was there something going on between them? "Does that surprise you?" She'd have to have a talk with her best friend when they had a minute alone, but nothing would make her happier.

"No," Holly answered and hugged Beth as she leaned over the bed to reach her.

"You would do the same for me." Beth squeezed her hand as she stood at the head of Holly's bed.

"Yes, I would." Holly gave her a sleepy smile. "But I don't want you to get in trouble. Especially since your boss was so considerate. You don't want me to worry about you, and I will if you don't go back. I'll be fine."

"No, you're right. I don't want you to worry. You need to concentrate on getting well."

❄

Holly obviously loved her family and her friend, but Grayson could sense the tension between Holly and her parents. "We'll work this out when the time comes. It's getting late, and Holly needs to rest. I'm sure you're tired as well. Why don't you get some rest and come back in the morning?"

Holly's parents, her brother, and Beth kissed her good night. "We'll see you in the morning, honey," her mother said as they walked out the door. Grayson stepped out into the hall with them for a moment.

"Is she doing okay, Doctor?"

"Yes, Mrs. Davenport. It's going to take time for her body to heal, but she'll fully recover," Grayson explained.

"Thank you, Doctor. We appreciate you taking care of her. We'll be back in the morning. I presume Holly gave the hospital her insurance information, but if there is a balance left, we'll take care of it. I want to be sure she gets the care she needs."

"She did give the hospital her insurance information. You don't have to worry; she'll get the care she needs."

Robert and Lance shook Grayson's hand before they left.

Grayson walked back into Holly's room. He studied her for a moment before she realized he was there. What was it about this young woman that was different from others he'd known? He'd dated his share of women, but never before had one touched his heart. There was something about Holly that was different from the rest. He'd been attracted to her from the moment their eyes had met in Camden's office.

"Thank you for coming back." Holly opened her eyes and looked up at Grayson as he sat down beside her bed.

"I just walked out into the hall to reassure your family that you'd be okay."

"Thank you for that. I appreciate it."

"Beth made me promise I'd tell you she'd see you in the morning. If you need her in the night, just call, and she'll be here to stay with you."

Holly smiled. "We've known each other since kindergarten. Friends don't come any better than Beth—believe me."

34

"It's nice to have a friend like that." Grayson sat down in the chair beside her bed and took hold of her hand. "Holly, you could cut the tension in the air between you and your parents. I won't pry, but I'm a good listener if you find you need someone to talk to."

Tears welled in her beautiful blue eyes. She tried to blink them away, but one made a trail down her cheek in spite of her efforts. Grayson reached for a tissue and wiped it away. "It's a long story." Holly's eyes closed, and she frowned. "I'm so tired."

"Sleep, hon. We'll talk tomorrow."

"Are you leaving?"

"No, I'll be right here for a while. You sleep."

Holly sighed. "But you can't be comfortable in that chair. I know you're tired, too."

"You don't worry about me. I'll stay for a while, and then I'll be in the doctor's lounge if you need me. I have a critical patient I need to be here for tonight."

Grayson pushed the intercom and ordered her pain meds. The nurse came in a few minutes later and administered them into Holly's IV tube.

"Now that should help you relax. Try to go back to sleep."

" 'Kay, thank you. Night."

Grayson smiled. Holly was asleep almost before she could finish her sentence. Now he'd run down to the doctor's lounge, take a shower, shave, change clothes, and try to catch a nap.

After catching a few hours of sleep, he went to check on his critical patient, who was still holding his own. So Grayson went to check on Holly. When he walked into the room, she was awake.

"What's the matter, hon? Are you hurting?"

"I can't seem to get comfortable."

"I don't want you to be in pain." He called for more pain meds, and in a few minutes the nurse brought them in, and Holly went back to sleep.

Grayson wasn't that fortunate. When he went back to the doctor's lounge, he lay on the couch thinking until the sun made an appearance through the curtain and lightened the room. The more time he spent here with Holly, the more attracted to her he became. Even if he was interested in pursuing a relationship with her, he had to keep a professional perspective while she was his patient in the hospital. He'd stay until he was sure his critical patient was going to make it. He didn't mind spending his day off at the hospital when he was needed. But once the patient became stable he'd go home tomorrow and get his head on straight where Holly was concerned.

Before Grayson went home that morning, he stepped into Holly's room to check on her. The nurse was in the process of getting her up for the first time. He waited while the nurse helped her sit up in the bed. It would be rough the first time she got up to walk. She gasped as she sat up and slowly slid her feet to the floor. "Take your time, and sit here on the edge of the bed for a minute," Grayson said. "How do you feel?"

"It hurts, but I think I'm okay."

"It'll get a little better each time," he assured her.

Grayson wrapped his arm around Holly's waist, and the nurse held on to her other arm as they slowly slid her off the bed and helped her to stand. As soon as her feet hit the floor, she swayed. Grayson caught her before she could fall and held on to her until she got her balance.

She slowly walked to the door and back. She didn't complain, but he knew every step hurt, and by the time they made it back to bed, she was exhausted.

Once she was settled under the blankets, the nurse took her vital signs and read them to him.

"You did well for your first time." Grayson smiled.

While the nurse helped Holly to take a sponge bath, Grayson did his hospital rounds.

❄

Holly appreciated Grayson checking on her in the night. He was a caring person. No wonder he made such a good doctor. The more time she spent with him, the more attractive she found him, but she knew he had responsibilities, and she wasn't one of them. She could take care of herself, and she needed to start by looking into a hotel room. The hospital would be discharging her in a few days, and she needed to have somewhere to stay.

Her phone rang, and when she answered, she wasn't surprised it was Beth. "How are you feeling this morning?"

"I think I'll feel better once I'm able to take a real shower. The sponge bath I took helped, but it isn't the same. Since that's my only option for now, I guess it will have to do." She sighed.

"You don't want to rush it. I'm sure it won't be long until you can have a shower. We'll be over in a little while, but I wanted to check on you."

"I'm glad you did. It makes me feel better just talking to you. Now I have a question. Is there something going on between you and Lance that I should know about?"

Beth chuckled. "I should have known you'd pick up on

that. I like your brother very much, as you already know. He asked me to go out to dinner when we get back."

Holly could hear the excitement in Beth's voice. "That's good news." Beth had been attracted to Lance for a while. "You know there isn't anyone I'd rather see my brother with than you."

"Well, let's not jump the gun. It's just dinner. We'll see if it goes any further."

"If my brother has any sense, it will. Beth, thank you for coming, I know it was a hardship for you, and I appreciate it. I'll be praying about you and Lance."

"Thank you, and you know I wouldn't want to be anywhere else."

"Yes, I do, and it means a lot. How are Callie and the baby doing?"

"Great! Little Amy is so beautiful. I never knew how attached you could be to a little baby. She's so special."

"I'm glad that everything went well. I'll look forward to seeing her when I get back."

❄

Holly's parents, brother, and Beth came in and visited with her for the next week. They deliberately stayed away from the subject of her adoption, and Holly assumed Grayson had told them not to upset her. Grayson stopped by her room every morning after he did rounds to check on her before he headed to his office. Then he came by to see her in the evening on his way home, but he didn't stay long since her family was always there with her.

Camden came in with Grayson to see Holly on Friday evening. Her family was there, and she introduced him to everyone.

"Mr. Brockman is the attorney who sent me the letter about my adoption." Holly addressed the subject everyone had been avoiding. "He knew my grandparents. His firm did the adoption papers when my sisters and I were adopted out to four different families.

"Mr. Brockman, why were we separated? Wasn't there even one family who would have taken all four us and raised us together?"

Camden walked over to the bed. "Holly, our firm didn't have anything to do with that part of your adoption. My father was head of the law firm at that time, and this was his case. He just drew up the paperwork as his clients requested."

"So you're telling me it was my grandparents' wishes that we be separated and never even know we had sisters?"

"I can tell you that your grandparents loved you very much and thought they were doing what was best for you at the time. They didn't want you to be separated. In answer to your question—no, there wasn't a family who could take all four of you. I'm sorry, but I'm not at liberty to tell you any more at this time."

"I know. I have to wait until the twenty-sixth of December to find out anything else."

"I would answer all of your questions if I could, Holly, but I'm bound by an oath to honor my client's wishes."

Chapter 4

Holly's mother walked over beside her. "Darling, Mr. Brockman isn't at fault here."

"I know. I don't have any choice but to wait for my answers, just as my sisters and I didn't have any choice in being separated at birth."

"You will answer her questions on December twenty-sixth, though, won't you, Mr. Brockman?" Beth took hold of Holly's hand.

Camden nodded but addressed his answers to Holly. "When you and your sisters meet with me on December twenty-sixth in my office, you will receive the answers to all of your questions. Now I had better go. I'm glad to see you're doing better, Holly. It was nice to meet all of you. I hope you have a safe trip home."

"Thank you, Camden. I really do appreciate the flowers and all you have done for me. I know this isn't your fault. I'm just upset over the circumstance, not at you personally."

"Thank you, Holly. I do understand how you feel, and believe me I wish I could tell you everything. I feel bad that you have to wait, but I don't have a choice. Good evening." Camden nodded and left.

"Holly"—Grayson glanced at her monitor—"I think you've had enough excitement for one day. You need to rest." Grayson waited while Holly said good night to her family and Beth.

After they left he walked over beside the bed. "Your blood pressure is up a bit, but that's to be expected when you get as upset as you are." He pushed the intercom and asked the nurse to bring in something Holly didn't recognize.

"What did you ask her for?"

"Something to help you sleep. You need to calm down, and I want you to rest."

"I'm so frustrated, Grayson. I can't believe my whole life has been a lie, and nobody will give me any answers." Tears coursed down her cheeks. "I didn't even know I was adopted until I received that letter in the mail from your brother. He told me I have three identical sisters and that we had all been adopted."

"Don't cry, honey. I can't even imagine what a shock that had to have been. Did your parents say why they didn't tell you that you were adopted?"

"Just that they loved me very much and that they had planned to tell me, but the right time never came up. How could something like this not come up? I had a right to know."

Grayson handed her some tissue. "I don't know the answers, honey. But I can see that your parents love you. Maybe they were afraid you'd feel different about them if they told you. So they kept putting it off, and then it was too late when you received the letter."

"Maybe you're right. I do love them, Grayson. They have been so good to me. I couldn't have asked for better parents or a better brother."

"Well then, maybe you have the most important answers. The Lord placed you in this family for a reason. We don't always understand why things happen the way they do, but we know He doesn't make any mistakes."

"You're right. He doesn't. Thank you for reminding me of that."

"You're welcome. Now the nurse is here to give you your meds. I want you to relax and try to get some sleep. I'll see you in the morning."

"Okay, good night."

❄

Saturday morning Holly's parents, brother, and Beth came to spend the day with her. She was sad that they had to leave that evening, but they had been there for seven days, and she knew her parents had stretched the time. They should have gone home last Sunday.

"Holly, we hate to leave you here." Her mother dabbed at her eyes with a handkerchief.

"I'll be fine, Mother—don't worry. I'm doing better now. I can take care of myself, and I'll be back home soon."

"Do you want us to see about getting you a hotel before we leave?"

"No, but thank you, Mom. I don't know yet when I'll be released. I can take care of it when I have a date. I'll be fine."

"I'll call you every day to see how you're doing," her mother assured her.

"I'll be checking on you, too." Lance kissed her forehead. "If you need anything, you let me know. You promise?"

"Yes, I will." Holly smiled up at him.

"I'll stay if you want me to," Beth said, her eyes filling with tears.

"I know you would, but you need to go home. I'll be fine."

"I'll call you every day, and if you need me, you just let me know, and I'll come back."

"Okay, I will—I promise. Now stop worrying."

They each gave her a kiss and hug before they left to

catch their flight home.

Exercising her independence had been easy when her family and best friend were there, but now that they were gone she wasn't feeling very brave. She was scared. What was she going to do? The thought of being alone in a hotel room in a strange city wasn't very appealing.

Lord, You know my situation. I'm scared and alone. Please help me to know what to do, and provide a place for me to stay that will be safe. And Lord, please take my parents, Lance, and Beth home safely. Even though I'm upset with Mom and Dad, I love them. In Jesus' name I ask, amen.

❄

Grayson was getting ready to leave his office for the day when his phone rang. He answered and heard his brother's voice on the other end of the line. He had sent flowers and had come by to see Holly twice, and Grayson had received a call from him at least once a day since Holly was taken by ambulance from his office.

"Gray, how's Holly doing?"

"I went by to check on her this morning. She's progressing, but with that kind of infection it takes a while. I'm just getting ready to go over to the hospital to check on her again. I'll probably release her tomorrow, but she'll be taking her IV home with her. She'll need antibiotics for at least another four weeks."

"Where's she going to go? She doesn't know anyone here," Camden said, concern evident in his voice.

"I have that worked out. Don't worry."

"Before you go to the hospital, can you come by my office? I have something I want to discuss with you before you go to see Holly. It'll only take a few minutes," Camden assured him.

Grayson glanced at his watch. It was 4:45 p.m. "All right. I'll be there shortly." He hung up the phone and grabbed his jacket as he walked out the door, pausing only long enough to make sure it was locked. He pulled out of the parking lot and headed to Camden's office, wondering what was so important that his brother felt he had to talk to him before he went to see Holly.

Camden opened the door before Grayson even knocked. He was obviously waiting for him. "Come on in." Grayson stepped inside and followed his brother through the waiting room, down the hall, and into his office. When they walked in, to his surprise an older woman sat waiting in one of the chairs across from Camden's desk. She was an attractive lady and very well dressed.

"Grayson, I'd like for you to meet Mrs. Emily Bellingham. Emily, this is my brother, Grayson Brockman. He's Holly's doctor."

"It's nice to meet you, Mrs. Bellingham. You know Holly?" Grayson was confused. "Are you from Missouri? Holly said she didn't know anyone here in Monticello."

"Sit down, Gray, and we'll explain, but first it's very important that what we're going to share with you be kept confidential between the three of us." Camden poured them a cup of coffee and then sat in his desk chair.

"All right, what's this all about?"

"Emily is Holly's grandmother. She and her husband have been our clients for several years. Dad handled their affairs until he retired, and I've now taken over as their attorney. After you read this letter, which is a copy of the one sent to Holly and her three sisters, I'll let Emily explain her situation to you."

Grayson frowned as he read the letter. He laid it on Cam's desk and glanced up at his brother. "This is the letter Holly was talking about when you were in her room the other night?"

"Yes."

"Mrs. Bellingham, were you aware that until she received this letter, Holly didn't know she was adopted?"

"No." Emily sighed. "I never even considered the fact that the girls might not have been told of their adoption. I figured their parents would tell them when they were old enough to understand. I regret that she had to find out this way."

"The letter is the reason Holly came to see me the day she collapsed in my office," Camden said. "Which as we know now came as quite a shock to her."

"Yes, and I'm afraid it's caused a lot of tension between Holly and her parents," Grayson added. "It was quite evident when they were here to see her after her surgery."

"How is she doing, Dr. Brockman? Is she going to be okay?" Emily asked anxiously.

"Grayson please, and yes, she's recovering. It will take several weeks before she'll be back to normal. She'll need antibiotics intravenously for a while to completely fight the infection."

"Well, that's a relief! I've been so worried." Emily shifted in her chair. "Grayson, I wanted to keep the girls and raise them, but my husband was convinced we were too old to raise four infants, that they would be better off adopted by a young couple. I didn't like it, but I had no choice. So I agreed with the stipulation that the will you just read about would be drawn up and we'd both sign it. Had my husband lived, we would both be living in the house I will be moving into soon, but the good Lord saw fit to take him home a year ago." Tears welled in her blue eyes, which were the same unusual lavender blue as Holly's, and she dabbed at them with a frilly handkerchief.

"The girls don't know that I'm still living. I didn't want them to know until they all arrive to spend their twenty-fifth birthday together on Christmas Day at the plantation they've inherited. I wanted it to be a surprise. I can't wait to see them," Emily explained. "But now I am concerned. If Holly isn't able to return home to her parents, where will she stay until she completely recovers? I could take her home with me; her health is more important than keeping my secret."

"I already have that worked out, Mrs. Bellingham, so you don't need to worry. Your secret is safe."

"Please call me Emily. Where will she be going to recover?"

He'd only known this lady for a few minutes, but it was obvious to Grayson that she loved her granddaughters and had their best interests at heart. But he shook his head. This has to have been quite a shock to Holly. Grayson would keep this secret. But he didn't like it. Holly had a right to know this information.

"She'll be staying at my home. I have a live-in house-keeper who has agreed to help take care of her."

Camden frowned. "Grayson, are you sure you want to do this?"

"Quite sure. She has to have her IV monitored. I'll take care of that in the morning before I leave for work and again in the evening when I get home." He glanced at Camden and then back at Emily. "Our sister also lives with me. She's an RN who does home care; she will check on Holly in between her other patients and administer her afternoon doses of medication. Our mother is a retired RN and lives just down the road, and she is a mother hen." Grayson looked at Camden, and they both chuckled. "Mom will also stop in from time to time to see her. She will be well taken care of, Emily. I assure you that you needn't worry."

"It's very nice of your family to agree to do this for my granddaughter, and I do appreciate it. If I can help financially or with her hospital bill, please let me know."

"I know Holly has insurance—she gave her information to the hospital when we brought her into the emergency." He stood and gave the woman a nod. "It was nice meeting you, Emily, but now I need to go to the hospital."

"It was nice meeting you, Grayson. Thank you for taking care of my granddaughter. I do regret that Holly found out she was adopted in this manner. That was not my intention, I assure you. I would never do anything to intentionally hurt any of my granddaughters."

"I'm sure you wouldn't. It's just an unfortunate set of circumstances, but Holly *is* hurt over it, and this has certainly caused hard feelings between her and her adoptive parents, which I hope can be rectified. It's obvious to anyone who's around them that they love her very much."

"I'll be praying about that and for Holly's complete recovery," Emily said.

"That's the best thing we can do at this point."

"I appreciate you coming, Grayson. I had to know Holly would be taken care of."

"I will keep your secret, Emily, because I agreed to. But

I want you to know I do so very reluctantly. I feel Holly has a right to know, but that's your decision, not mine. Now I must be going. Camden." Grayson nodded to his brother and said good night as he walked out the door.

❄

"Hello, Holly," Grayson said as he walked into her room a little while later. "How are you feeling tonight?"

"Better, thank you. I got up and walked partway down the hall this afternoon by myself." She smiled.

"That's good, but don't go too far, just a little ways at a time. I don't want you to overdo it."

"You don't have to worry about that. I barely made it back to bed. Why don't I have any energy?" She sighed. "Normally I walk two miles every morning. I sure couldn't do that now."

"You're recuperating from surgery. You'll get your strength back, it'll just take a little time. And speaking of recuperating, I have something I want to talk to you about."

❄

She frowned, wondering what was wrong. Grayson seemed so serious. "What about?" she asked softly.

"You're doing well, and you're tolerating food okay. I plan to release you tomorrow, and I want you to stay at my place until you're back on your feet."

"I can't stay with you! I appreciate the offer, but it wouldn't be right." Holly was shocked that he would even suggest it.

"I have a live-in housekeeper, and one of my sisters lives with me as well, Holly. It'll be fine. You don't know anyone here, and there is no one to take care of you."

Well, at least that made her feel better to know he wasn't

suggesting she stay at his home with just the two of them there. "I'll go to a hotel, and I can take care of myself."

"You can't take care of yourself right now. Plus, you'll need antibiotics administered through your IV for at least three to four more weeks. A ruptured appendix is serious, Holly. It's nothing to fool around with. My sister is an RN, and she does home-care nursing. She can administer your medications when I'm not there. My parents live just down the road from me, and my mother is a retired RN. If you stay at my place, we can see to it that your medication is administered. I've already spoken to my sister and to my mother. They're willing to help."

Holly had to admit—at least to herself—that she was tempted to take him up on his offer. She didn't relish staying alone in a hotel in a strange town. Still, she didn't want to take advantage of Grayson's kindness.

"I can't begin to tell you how much I appreciate all you've done for me. It's so nice of your mother, sister, and housekeeper to want to help, and for you to continue to want to help me, but I'm not your responsibility, Grayson. I know you have other things to do besides taking care of me. I'll be fine at a hotel."

"You can't go to a hotel by yourself, Holly. Either you stay at my place or you go to a rehabilitation hospital for the next few weeks. I believe you'll be more comfortable at my place. I have four guest rooms, so you'll have a room of your own there. You have to continue these antibiotics." He pointed to her IV. "You can't do that yourself. You have to have someone who is trained to administer them for you for the next couple of weeks."

She shook her head. "I don't want to take advantage of

your generosity, Grayson. You've done so much already."

"You aren't taking advantage, Holly. You need someone right now, and we want to help you. As my mother would say, it's the Christian thing to do. When I talked to her earlier she offered to take you to her house, but they only have three bedrooms, and my younger brother and sister are still living at home. Cindy is in college, but she comes home part of the time. You would have to sleep on the sofa. I have plenty of room, so the logical thing would be for you to come to my place."

Holly thought about it for a few minutes. It probably wasn't wise on her part. She was going to get hurt; she already had feelings for Grayson, and he was only being nice to her because she was his patient. But then again, maybe he did feel something for her. If she were just a patient to him, surely he would have let her go to the rehabilitation hospital, wouldn't he? No, she didn't think he would. He was a really good, compassionate doctor, and patients with her circumstances didn't come along every day. If she couldn't go to a hotel, she'd rather be at Grayson's. She flushed in embarrassment when she glanced up and remembered he was waiting for an answer.

"I'm sorry, Grayson. My mother is always accusing me of woolgathering when she's talking to me and my mind wanders. I guess that's what I was doing. I'll go to your house, but only until I can take care of myself, and then I'll stay at a hotel until I'm able to go home."

Chapter 5

The following morning Grayson came into Holly's room. "Are you ready to get out of this place?"

"More than ready." Holly smiled. "Not that everyone hasn't given me excellent care, because all of you have. But it's the first step to being able to get back to my life."

"Speaking of getting back to your life, what will you be getting back to? We never discussed what you do for a living."

"I'm a published author." She sat up on the edge of the bed.

"An author!" Grayson raised one brow. "That's interesting. What do you write?"

"I write Christian romantic suspense novels. My first book hit the shelves the week before I came here, and I have a contract for five more." She grinned. Even lying in a hospital bed, she couldn't help being excited.

"Well, you're obviously talented, or they wouldn't be interested in contracting that many books with you."

"Thank you. I hope they sell as well as my editor thinks they will."

"It's her business to know what will sell. If she wasn't confident in you as an author, she wouldn't have signed a six-book contract with you."

"I hope so. Would you happen to know where I can find my clothes?"

"They're right there in the closet, along with your laptop

51

and purse." He indicated the narrow doors across the room. "I'll go sign your release papers while the nurse helps you get dressed, and then we'll be ready to go."

In the car on the way to Grayson's house, Holly glanced out the window. "Oh look! There's the restaurant some of the nurses were talking about the other night. Big Chic's. They said the chicken is excellent."

"They're right. Big Chic's is one of my favorite places to eat. Do you like chicken?"

"I love chicken." She grinned.

"This is the historic district of Monticello. When you're back on your feet, I'll take you there for dinner if you'd like to go."

Holly glanced over at Grayson. Was he saying he wanted a relationship with her? *It's just dinner, Holly. That doesn't constitute a relationship, so don't jump to conclusions. You'll just end up getting hurt.*

"I'd like that," she said softly.

❄

"We'll plan on it, then." Grayson found his day a little brighter at her answer. He thought about her before he went to bed at night, and she was the first thing on his mind in the morning when he woke up. He glanced at her, and their eyes met. She had the most unusual blue eyes. Beautiful eyes. He'd never seen anyone with that color before except for her grandmother.

"My younger brother will no doubt be over to see you when he realizes you're an author."

"You have another brother besides Camden?"

"Yes, and two sisters. My older sister I told you about lives with me."

"What are their names, and how old are they?"

"Gabriel is my youngest brother—we call him Gabe. He's twenty-two. Cindy is my youngest sister, and she's twenty. Cam is twenty-seven. I'm the oldest at twenty-nine. Our sister, Courtney, is twenty-five. Gabe and Cindy still live at home. They're both in college."

"Is Gabe a writer?"

"He wants to be. He's majoring in journalism. He just sent his first book proposal to a publisher, so we'll see what happens."

"That's great. We'll have something in common then. Courtney's the RN?"

"Yes."

"What is Cindy studying to be?"

"A high school teacher."

Grayson glanced over at Holly and smiled. "I don't believe you'll have to wait long to meet them. From the looks of the cars in my driveway, they're all here to greet you."

❄

Grayson parked in front of a large ranch-style home with log siding and green shutters. It sported a large front porch with several steps leading to the front door, which matched the shutters and trim in color. Holly glanced out over the pasture and noticed several cows and a few horses. A ways back from the house sat a huge barn.

Grayson came around to Holly's side and lifted her from the car as if she weighed about ten pounds. She frowned. "I can walk, Grayson."

"I don't want you climbing stairs just yet. I'll carry you to the front door, and you can walk from there."

Holly glanced around as Grayson carried her up the

steps onto a wide front porch with a swing hanging at one end. It looked inviting. Holly hoped for a chance to enjoy it while she was staying here. She'd love to share the swing with Grayson but doubted that would happen. She had definite feelings for him and had hoped he'd feel the same about her.

The only time he had even mentioned anything personal was when he asked her about Big Chic's, and Holly was sure that had only been polite conversation. He probably didn't mean he'd actually take her there. She needed to get out of her dream world into the real one and concentrate on getting well.

Her book wasn't going to write itself. She was already two weeks behind. If she didn't get her head on straight and get back to writing, she wouldn't make her deadline. She couldn't let that happen, so she had to start working on it first thing in the morning.

"Are you okay?"

Grayson's voice interrupted her thoughts, and she realized she'd been woolgathering again. "Yes, I'm just a little nervous."

"Don't be. You'll like my family." He smiled. "They'll make you feel right at home."

She returned his smile. "You have a nice home. It's beautiful out here."

"Thanks. I like it. I had it built about a year ago. My parents have a place just down the road to the left of mine, and my grandparents are on the other side of them. Cam built his home on the other side of mine. We're all on the same property, about a quarter of a mile apart." Grayson set Holly on her feet as they reached the porch. She walked the few steps to the door, which opened before Grayson had a chance to reach for it.

"Hello, darling." A woman Holly knew must be Grayson's mother hugged him as they walked inside. Behind her, a young woman waited to give him a hug. Holly grinned when a young man hugged him as well.

"Mother, Gabe, Courtney, and Cindy, this is Holly Davenport. Holly, this is my mother, Eloise, my brother, Gabriel, and my sisters, Courtney and Cindy."

"It's very nice to meet all of you." Holly smiled and started to shake their hands, but Grayson's mother pulled her into a gentle hug, and the other two women followed suit, careful not to hurt her.

"We're a hugging family, Holly. I hope you don't mind, and please call me Ellie." She smiled.

"No, not at all." Holly smiled back, thinking she was going to like this family. She had barely stepped into Grayson's house, and already she felt welcome.

"Okay, now that the introductions are over, Holly needs to get off her feet." Grayson placed his hand at the small of Holly's back and guided her into a big living room. A rock fireplace covered the entire back wall. A large chocolate-brown rocker and a matching recliner sat across from a sectional all made of what appeared to be real leather. The blazing fire gave the room a warm and cozy feeling. Holly felt comfortable here in Grayson's home, with him and his family.

"I placed a pillow and blanket here on the sofa for you, Holly." Grayson's mother smiled.

"Thank you, Ellie. That was very thoughtful of you." Holly slipped her shoes off and lay on the sofa. She couldn't believe how tired the trip home from the hospital had made her.

She fell asleep, and when she awoke she heard Grayson and his family talking softly across the room. When she sat up, she noticed that it was dark outside.

"I'm sorry. I guess I was even more tired than I realized."

"There's no need to apologize. You need to rest." Grayson sat down across from her.

"We brought supper." Ellie brought a tray and placed it across Holly's lap.

"Thank you, this looks and smells delicious."

Grayson handed her a glass of milk. "Believe me, it is. No one makes chicken and dumplings like Mom."

"You're right about that," Gabe, Courtney, and Cindy chorused.

"Thank you, but you're prejudiced." Ellie smiled.

"No, just honest." Gabe laughed. "We've eaten them at other places. We know what's good. The only ones that can even come close are Granny's."

Holly enjoyed the evening visiting with Grayson's family. His father, Pierson, stopped by for just a few minutes on the way home to pick up Ellie. Grayson introduced him, telling Holly his dad was an attorney. Camden had taken over the office when his dad retired. She liked him right away. He seemed to be a warm and kind man.

The next morning Holly heard a soft knock on her bedroom door. Grayson had insisted she stay in the master suite. Since he didn't want her climbing the stairs, he took one of the guestrooms on the second floor.

"Come in." Holly sat up in bed and slipped into her robe.

"Good morning, Holly." Martha, Grayson's housekeeper,

smiled. "If you're ready, I'll help you into the living room. Grayson is waiting to administer your medication before he leaves for the office."

Grayson met them in the hall. "I'll get Holly settled, Martha, if you want to fix her some breakfast."

"That will be fine. Holly, would you like bacon, eggs, and toast this morning?"

"Oh, just toast and orange juice would be fine, Martha. I don't usually eat a big breakfast."

"I'll have it ready in a few minutes."

"Thank you," Holly called, but Martha had already left the room.

"I feel bad that she has to wait on me."

"She doesn't mind—I assure you." Grayson took her vitals and administered antibiotics into her IV tube. "She says it's her motherly instincts; she enjoys having someone to take care of. Now that her children are all grown and moved out on their own, she misses having them there."

"What happened to her husband?"

"He died of a heart attack a few years ago, just a year after her last child got married. I advertised for a live-in housekeeper when I was starting my residency, and she answered the ad. She's been with me ever since. Even though I'm a grown man and a doctor, she still considers me a child who needs caring for, and she will you, too." He chuckled.

"I really appreciate this, Grayson. I could have gone to a hotel, but you're right, it wouldn't be as nice as being here in your home."

"I'm glad you're comfortable here. Now stop worrying, and try to rest. My mother will be here around one to administer your meds again. I'll see you tonight."

"Okay. If you don't mind, hand me my laptop before you leave. I'm going to work on my book."

"Here you go." Grayson laid her computer on the table beside her and plugged it into the wall to charge the battery.

"Thank you."

"Working a few hours at a time on your book is fine, but I want you to walk to the bedroom and back at least twice. And I want you to rest for a couple of hours this afternoon."

"Yes, sir." She saluted and grinned. "I hope you have a good day."

He shook his head and laughed as he walked out the door. Holly watched him go. She knew it was too soon to care about him so much, but she just couldn't seem to help it. Grayson was so good to her, but she knew it was only a doctor-to-patient relationship on his part, and that scared her. She was falling hard, and she was going to get hurt.

Martha brought her breakfast, and once she was finished, she opened her laptop and started working on her book. She set it aside twice and made the trip to the bedroom and back, with the housekeeper walking alongside her.

The morning passed quickly, and she was surprised when Ellie sat down beside her.

"Hi, Holly. Working on your book?"

She nodded. "I only have thirty days until my deadline. I didn't do much on it the two weeks I was in the hospital, so now I need to make up for lost time." Closing the computer, she set it aside and smiled at Grayson's mother. "How are you today?"

"I'm fine. The question is, how are you feeling?"

"I'm still pretty sore," she admitted. "But otherwise, I feel good. Grayson says I'm doing fine."

"Good. Well, let's get this antibiotic taken care of. Courtney got held up, so she called and asked me if I could take care of it today."

"I really appreciate you coming over to do this for me, Ellie."

"Honey, I don't mind at all."

After Ellie left, Holly decided to take a nap. She was tired, and she knew that when Grayson got home that evening, he would ask her if she had rested.

When Holly woke up from her nap, she glanced at her watch and realized she'd been asleep for two hours. Just as she sat up and turned her laptop back on, she heard a soft knock on the door. Martha answered and let Gabe in.

"Hi, Holly. I hope I'm not disturbing you." Grayson's younger brother came in and sat across from her.

"Not at all, Gabe. I'm glad to see you. I can use the company. How was school today?"

"Great! In my writing class, we had an author come in and speak. She gave us the basics of what happens after we submit a proposal to a publisher. It was very interesting to me, since I'm waiting to hear back from a publisher on my own proposal."

When he grinned he looked so much like Grayson that Holly had to smile. "It is exciting. It hasn't been that long. I remember when I was at the point where you are now in my writing."

"How many books do you have published?"

"My first one just hit the store shelves about three weeks ago. I have a contract for five more. I'm working on the second one now, so I'm not that far ahead of you." Holly smiled at his enthusiasm.

"Oh man, I'd love to read your book. Grayson says you're a suspense author. Where can I find it?"

"Well, it just so happens. . ." She grinned. "If you'll hand me my case right there"—she pointed to her briefcase on the floor by her chair—"I have a couple of copies with me, and you can have one of them."

"Oh, Holly. That's really nice of you, but you don't have to give me one. I'll be happy to buy it, because I really do want to read it."

"No, I want you to have it. I'd love to have your honest opinion when you've finished reading it." Holly handed him the book.

"Will you sign it for me?" He handed it back to her.

"Sure, I'd be happy to." She fished an ink pen out of her briefcase, signed the book, and handed it back to him. "I hope you enjoy reading it."

"I'm sure I will, and I can't wait to get started. I'd better get going, though. Grayson warned me not to tire you." He started out but turned back after a couple of steps. "Would it be okay if I come back to see you again after school?"

"You're welcome to come by any time. I enjoyed visiting with you."

"Thanks, Holly. I'll see you later, then." He grinned and waved as he left.

Holly smiled. He was so cute! She had really enjoyed her time with him and hoped he did come back again.

That set the pace for the next few weeks. Grayson administered her medication in the mornings and evenings, and his sister or mother came by to give her the second dosage in the afternoon. She liked Grayson's sister, Courtney. She spent at least a couple evenings with her and Grayson.

When he had to work late, Courtney kept her company. Holly liked his mother, too. She was such a warm person—she'd put Holly at ease from the moment she'd met her.

Gabe came by at least three days a week after school. The young man had loved Holly's book, and they discussed it as well as the manuscript he had sent to a publisher.

Chapter 6

Grayson came in that evening with a pizza. "Martha stopped at the supermarket, and Courtney has a dinner engagement with a friend. They'll be back in a couple of hours, so I brought supper and a movie. I heard you mention to the nurses that you'd like to see *Letters to Juliet*."

She grinned. "Well that was nice of you. I would love to see that movie, and pizza is one of my favorites. So you win all the way around."

"I hope so, Holly. I'd like to be a winner in your eyes." He smiled, gazing directly into her eyes.

Holly paused, wondering at the intimate tone in his voice. She swallowed. If she thought back over the last few weeks since she'd been staying in his home and was honest with herself, she had to admit there had been subtle hints leading up to his comment. She had been afraid to acknowledge them, in fear that it was her imagination due to her feelings for him.

He didn't make any more comments on that subject for the rest of what became a very nice evening. When Martha came, she popped them some popcorn, which they enjoyed as they watched the movie together.

When Holly yawned, Grayson said, "I think it's bedtime." As he walked with her to her bedroom door and placed a kiss on her forehead, they heard Courtney come in.

"Hi, guys, I had a great evening, but I'm glad to be home. It's been a long day. How are you feeling, Holly?"

"I seem to improve some every day." She smiled.

"Great. Well, I think I'll go take a shower. Good night." She went down the hall to the bathroom.

"Sleep well, Holly. I'll see you in the morning." Grayson smiled.

"Okay—good night." She touched her fingers to her forehead where he'd kissed her and then closed the door. She got ready for bed and climbed under the covers, only to lie there thinking.

Even if Grayson had feelings for her, how could it ever work out? Her life was in Missouri, and his was here in Georgia. He had his practice established here, and Holly's family and life were back home. Of course she was probably worrying for nothing. One comment and a kiss on the forehead didn't mean Grayson wanted a relationship with her. She needed to stop dreaming about something that would probably never happen and concentrate on getting well so she could go home where she belonged. It was time to try to work things out with her parents and get on with her life. Her heart ached at the thought, but that was how it had to be.

When Grayson came in the next evening, he said, "Mom's birthday is on Thursday, Thanksgiving Day. We're going to combine the two and give her a party at their house that afternoon. We'd like for you to join us."

"I appreciate that, Grayson. I'm sure I would enjoy it. But that's three weeks away, and I've already been here two months. I thought I'd be off of these antibiotics by then, and I could go home for Thanksgiving."

"Your tests came back normal. I got the results this afternoon from the panel I took this morning before I left for the office. I'm going to remove your IV, but—I'd still like for you to stay," he said as he removed the IV from Holly's arm. "There, all done."

"Why do you want me to stay, Grayson?" Holly waited anxiously to hear his answer.

Grayson sat down beside her on the sofa. "I didn't feel comfortable sharing this with you, Holly, as long as you were my patient. Now that your IV is out and you no longer need my services as your doctor, I can tell you that I care very much for you. I want you to stay here so we can pursue these feelings. Can you honestly tell me that you don't feel something for me as well?"

"No, I can't, because I do have feelings for you. But Grayson, your life is here, and mine is in Missouri."

"Well, let's take this one step at a time. If this relationship is the Lord's will—and I believe it is—He'll work that out for us." Grayson took her hand in his. "Now will you stay and spend Thanksgiving with us and give this relationship a chance?"

Holly studied his face for a moment before she answered. *Lord, please help me to know what to do. I don't want to make a mistake.* In that moment a scripture came to mind. Psalm 37:4. "Take delight in the LORD, and he will give you the desires of your heart." *Thank You, Lord.* "Okay, I'll stay, at least for Thanksgiving and your mother's party."

"I'll let her know. She'll be as pleased as I am. Now that you're going to be able to go out, would you like to go to dinner tomorrow night?"

"I'd love to. It will be so nice to get out of the house for a change. Not that I don't love your house and appreciate you letting me stay here."

"I know what you mean. I can imagine you have a strong case of cabin fever by now. If you like Italian food, Marco Ristorante Italiano is the best Italian food in the area."

"Yes, I love Italian food."

❄

The next evening Grayson stopped in front of Marco's. He came around to her side and opened the door for her. Placing his hand at her waist, he guided her in the door of the restaurant. They were seated in the back at a table in a quiet corner.

The waiter handed them menus and took their drink order. After he left, Grayson asked, "How is your book coming along?"

"It's coming along quite well, I'm halfway through."

"Gabe isn't driving you crazy, is he?"

"No, not at all. I like Gabe. I enjoy his visits."

The waiter returned. "Are you ready to order?" Grayson asked.

"I'll have ravioli," Holly replied and then waited quietly while Grayson ordered.

"I'll have the lasagna."

The waiter took the menus, smiled, and left.

"I appreciate you spending so much time encouraging Gabe and answering his questions. Mom said instead of hanging out with some of his friends who are questionable, he's spending time with you. She and my dad are grateful. About a year ago Gabe stopped going to church when he met a couple of young guys who spend too much time at the local bar. So far Mom said she's never seen any signs of Gabe drinking, but I was afraid it was just a matter of time before he got dragged into that scene. Mom said she hasn't seen them around since he started spending his afternoons with you."

"Well, I'm glad if I could make a difference. I don't know whether you realize it, but from the questions he's been asking me since he read my book, I don't think Gabe knows the Lord."

"Mom's tried, Dad's tried, Cam, Courtney, Cindy, and I have tried to talk to him about his relationship with the Lord. He won't discuss his feelings with any of us, so if he's opening up to you, that's a good thing."

When they were finished with their meal, Grayson paid the check, and they left.

"Thank you for dinner, Grayson. You were right—the food was delicious, and this was a lovely evening." As Holly handed him her coat so he could hang it in the closet, she yawned.

"It was my pleasure, and now I think it's bedtime. You did pretty well for your first time out, but you're tired, and I don't want you to overdo it."

"I am tired. Good night."

"Good night, sweetheart. Sleep well." Grayson kissed her on the forehead again and walked her to her door. "Would you like to go to church with us tomorrow?"

"I'd love to."

"Okay, then. I'll see you in the morning."

❄

Holly enjoyed the service. Grayson's pastor gave a good sermon that kept her attention. She noticed that all of the family was there except Gabe, and of course Cindy was too far away at college. This was a Christian family. Gabe had been raised in church the same as the rest of them. She wondered why he hadn't accepted the Lord. She had really become close to Gabe during their time together, and she was concerned about him. *Please, Lord, if it's Your will for me to reach Gabe, I pray that You'll give me the opportunity to witness to him and the right words to say to bring him to You.*

When they were on their way home after lunch, Holly said, "I really enjoyed the service and having lunch with you and your family. You have a good pastor, and he preaches a good message."

"I think so. He's been with us for about two years, and the congregation has nearly doubled since he's been here."

"I can see why. I'm sorry Gabe wasn't there."

"Mom said she quit asking him. It causes an argument every time she mentions it. She's decided it would be better to pray for him instead. Hopefully he'll come back one of these days."

"He will, Grayson. I fully believe what the Bible says in Proverbs 22:6—'Start children off on the way they should go, and even when they are old they will not turn from it.'"

"I do, too, Holly, and I'm banking on that."

❄

Thanksgiving morning dawned cold and dreary. Holly was glad her parents had shipped her some clothes. They had only brought her a couple of outfits when they came to the hospital to see her, because they hadn't realized she would have to be here this long. She glanced in the mirror one last time before leaving her bedroom. Grayson stood by the fireplace waiting for her. He was dressed in green cords and a brown tweed sweater over a green turtleneck that matched the color of his eyes. His dark hair had been combed in the same neat style he always wore, and the wonderful scent of his cologne nearly took her breath away.

Holly glanced down at her brown cord pants and green sweater with fall leaves on the front and hoped she looked all right. She walked over to him. "Good morning. You look nice."

His eyes swept over her from head to foot, and he smiled. "So do you. I like your outfit."

"Thank you."

"Are you ready?"

"Yes, I just need to get my coat."

Grayson held her green jacket while she slipped into it, and then she grabbed her dark-brown purse, which matched her boots.

"Is that a cake?" Holly asked as Grayson grabbed a square pan from the coffee table.

"Yes, it's chocolate and my favorite." He grinned. "Martha baked it for us to take to Mom and Dad's so we'd have something to contribute to the meal."

"That was nice of her. I love chocolate cake." She grinned back at him.

"It's one of the many things that I love about the holidays, seeing family and good food."

They laughed as they went out to the car.

It didn't take long to drive down the road to Grayson's parents' home. He pulled up in front of a house similar to his in style, except it was used brick instead of log.

As they reached the porch, the door opened, and Ellie greeted first Grayson and then Holly with a hug.

She smiled. "Come on in, and make yourselves comfortable. Holly, it's good to see you up and about."

"Thank you, it's good to be out, too. I was getting cabin fever."

"I can imagine you were."

Grayson's dad took hold of her hand. "I'm glad that you're feeling better and able to join us today. Come over and sit by the fire where it's warm. How about a cup of warm apple cider?"

"That would be nice. Thank you, Pierson." Holly sat in the chair by the fire, and it did feel good after being out in the cold.

"Holly," Grayson said as he joined her, "these are my grandparents, Spencer and Roselyn Brockman. Papa and Nana, this is Holly Davenport."

Roselyn hugged her. "Hello, Holly, it's so good to meet you. We've heard a lot about you."

"All good things, I assure you, my dear." Spencer chuckled as he shook her hand.

Grayson's mother called that dinner was ready, and they all gathered around the table. It was the first time Holly had seen Cindy since Grayson's family had gathered at his house the day Holly was released from the hospital.

"Hi, Holly, it's good to see you. How are you feeling?" Cindy asked.

"Much better, thank you, and it's good to see you, too. How's school going?"

"It's good. I really enjoy my classes. I don't get home as much as I'd like, mostly for holidays and once in a while on the weekends. It's too far to drive for only a couple of days. I don't have that much longer before I graduate, and then I'll be back to stay. I got a position at the high school here in Monticello starting in the fall, so I'm pretty excited about that."

"That's wonderful, Cindy. That should work out well for you."

"Yes, I really dislike being so far away from my family."

"I certainly understand that." Holly smiled. "I don't like being so far away from mine either, and it hasn't been as long as you've been away from yours." She noticed the look Grayson gave her when she made that comment. But it was true. Even though she was upset with her parents, she'd never been away from home before, and she missed them, as well as her brother and Beth.

The dinner was delicious. The love in this family showed as they kidded each other around the table throughout the meal. When they were finished, they sang "Happy Birthday" to Ellie, and she opened her birthday gifts. She loved the jewelry armoire Grayson gave her from him and Holly. It was beautiful. He was such a thoughtful man, and Holly loved him so much. But did she love him enough to give up her family, to live here with him and his family? That was a question she would have to think and pray about. Of course, she might not have to worry about it. Grayson didn't say he loved her. He said he wanted her to stay so they could see where their relationship would take them. After spending so much time with her these last few weeks, he may have decided a permanent relationship with her wasn't what he wanted.

Chapter 7

They finished with dessert, and before she knew it, it was time to leave. Everyone said good-bye and shared hugs.

"Holly, honey, it was so good to have you here with us. Please come back any time." Ellie hugged her good-bye, followed by Grayson's grandmother and Courtney. His father and grandfather shook her hand.

Courtney hugged her. "I'll be home in a little while. I'm going to stay and help mom finish up here. Get some rest—you look tired. It's been a long day."

Holly nodded. "I will. Happy birthday, Ellie! Thank you so much for inviting me today."

"Thank you, honey. We enjoyed having you. We're glad you're feeling better."

Gabe scooted in beside her. "Can I give you a hug, Holly?"

"Sure you can." Holly hugged Grayson's younger brother. "Will you come see me Monday after school? I don't know how much longer I'll be staying." She glanced at Grayson and didn't miss his frown at her words.

Gabe grinned. "Sure thing, I'll be there."

❄

They made their way out to the car, and Grayson opened the door for Holly. He slid in beside her and started the engine. The more time he spent with her, the more he wanted to be with her. He loved her, there was no doubt in his mind, but it was too soon to declare his feelings. He wanted to give her a little more time. He felt almost certain Holly loved him, but he wasn't sure she had admitted it to herself yet, and he didn't want to pressure her. They had spent the last three weeks going to church together, and they had been out to dinner several times. He had enjoyed his time with her, and she seemed to have a good time. Christmas was only four weeks away. He'd give her that time. If things went the way he hoped they would, he planned to buy her a ring and ask her to marry him.

Her comment to Gabe about not being here much longer concerned him. He had to convince her to stay until Christmas and marry him when the time was right. He knew she loved her family and they loved her. They weren't going to be happy about her moving so far away. And would she be happy away from them? That was another question. *Lord, You know how I feel about Holly. Please help us to make the right decision here. I love her, and I want her to be happy. I pray that Your will be done in this.*

At the house, Grayson helped Holly out of her coat and hung it in the closet. "Did you have a good time?"

"Yes, I did. You have a wonderful family, Grayson. They made me feel so welcome. I missed my family, but otherwise it was a very nice day."

Grayson drew her into his arms and placed a brief kiss on her soft lips. He wanted to deepen the kiss, but the timing wasn't right. He would have to be satisfied for now. "I'm sorry your family wasn't able to join us today."

"I appreciated your mother inviting them to come. Although it might have been just as well. I don't know that I'm ready to discuss my feelings with them yet."

"Thanksgiving is a day for families to be together, Holly.

I hope you can come to grips with this and work things out with your parents. I know you love them, sweetheart, and you're not going to be totally happy until you do."

"I do love them, but I still have such mixed feelings. I can't understand why they didn't tell me I was adopted. I can't seem to get past feeling betrayed. They taught me all my life that honesty was very essential, but they weren't honest with me about something this important."

"Sweetheart, as I said in the hospital, I don't have the answers for you on this. Maybe they were afraid it would change the way you feel about them if you knew you were adopted, and they loved you so much they were scared."

"You may be right. I'll have to think about that—and pray, because I'm still very hurt and disappointed in them."

"I'll be praying with you."

"Thank you, Grayson—for everything." She managed a smile. "Good night."

"You're welcome. Good night. Try to get some rest, and I'll see you in the morning."

❄

The weekend was cold and dreary. About three inches of snow covered the ground on Monday morning when Holly got up and went into the living room.

"It's beautiful out." She stood at the window looking out over the property when Grayson joined her.

"Yes it is, but it's not great to drive in." He slipped into his coat.

"No, you're right. Please be careful."

"I will. I'll see you tonight." He gave her a quick kiss and headed out the door.

Holly worked on her book most of the day. Other than

the daily phone call from her mother and Beth, she hadn't taken a break from it. She missed Ellie and Courtney coming in the afternoons, now that Holly didn't need antibiotics anymore.

When Holly's mother called that morning, she asked when Holly planned to come home. It was time to talk to Grayson about it, but her heart ached at the thought of leaving him.

Holly was glad when a knock at the door interrupted her thoughts. Martha answered and let Gabe in.

"Hi, Holly. How are you doing today?"

"I'm doing just fine, thank you. How about you?"

"I'm great!" He grinned.

Holly knew something was up. "Okay, tell me. What's with the huge grin?"

"I sold my book!" He let out a deep laugh.

"Woo-hoo! That's great news!"

"I couldn't wait to come tell you. Thank you for all of your time and answering my questions, Holly."

"Anytime, Gabe. I enjoy your company, and I'm always willing to answer your questions."

"I. . ." He hesitated.

"What's on your mind?"

He took his ball cap off and laid it on the table and then ran a hand through his dark hair.

"Gabe, what it is? You can talk to me about anything, buddy."

Green eyes so like Grayson's met hers. "I want to talk to you about Jesus."

Holly was thrilled. It was the last subject she expected him to talk about. "Okay, what do you want to know?"

"I've been thinking about this ever since I read your book. I've never really understood it before, or maybe I just wasn't ready—I don't know. But you laid it out pretty plain, and I realized you and my family have something I don't have. I know now after reading your story that it's Jesus."

Please, Lord, help me with this. "Gabe, do you believe that Jesus is the Son of God? That He died on the cross to save us from our sins? That He was raised on the third day?"

"Yes, I do."

"Would you like for me to pray with you to accept Jesus into your heart?"

He looked at her for a moment. "Yes, I would."

Holly nodded and took his hands in hers. "Just repeat this prayer after me." She bowed her head and closed her eyes. "Jesus, I know that I have sinned and fallen short of the glory of God. I know that I'm a sinner and need salvation. I believe that You died on the cross for me and rose again. I also know that salvation comes only through You. I believe You are the only true God, and I ask that You would please forgive me, cleanse me from all my sins, and come into my heart as my Lord and Savior. I give You my heart and my life. I will live for You from this day forward. In Jesus' name I pray. Amen."

Holly rejoiced as Gabe's deep voice repeated her prayer word for word to the very end. When they opened their eyes, his shone with a peace she had never seen there before.

He smiled, and already Holly saw a new light of joy in his face. "I'll never be able to thank you enough, Holly. You've changed my life." He gave her a hug.

She hugged him back. "No, Gabe. The Lord has changed your life. I was just a tool He used to accomplish that."

"You're right. I can feel His peace in my heart." He smiled. "But thank you for leading me to Him."

"You're welcome. It's one of the best days of my life, too, Gabe. I also received a real blessing. It's quite a privilege to lead someone to the Lord."

Gabe grinned. "Now, I'm going to go home and make my mother very happy."

❄

Grayson and Holly met the family that evening at Big Chic's to celebrate Gabe's decision for the Lord. They were all thrilled he had finally become a part of the family of God.

"You were right about the food," Holly said as they were driving home after dinner. "The chicken was wonderful. I really enjoyed it and the company."

"You can't beat their chicken."

Holly smiled when she thought about Gabe's mother and dad. They had both hugged her and thanked her for taking the time to get to know their youngest son, for sharing her book with him, which ultimately led him to the Lord. She was excited that her book had been an instrument in reaching Gabe. She prayed it would reach others for the Lord as well.

They arrived at the house, and she knew she had to talk to Grayson about going home.

Chapter 8

Once they were inside Holly decided to put it off. She wasn't ready to say good-bye to Grayson. She'd give him a few more days, but if he didn't declare his feelings soon, she would book her flight home.

"Thank you for a very nice evening," she said. "I'm a little tired. I think I'll go to bed."

"It was my pleasure." He drew her into his arms and kissed her briefly. "Good night. I'll see you in the morning."

She nodded and went to her room. Her parents had been on her mind all evening. Spending time with Grayson's family made her homesick for her own. She spent some time in prayer over her situation and realized that it didn't make any difference whether her parents had given birth to her—she couldn't have been raised in a more loving family. They had given her everything she needed and most of what she wanted throughout her childhood and teen years.

She still wasn't happy that they hadn't told her that she had been adopted, but Grayson was probably right. They were most likely afraid it would change the way she felt about them. But searching her heart, she knew if they'd just told her themselves, it wouldn't have. She couldn't love them any more if they were her biological parents. She decided she wasn't quite ready to talk about it yet, but she would probably go home for Christmas, and she promised herself she'd do it then.

The next morning Holly, Courtney, and Cindy went to the Christmas sales. They didn't stay long, but in the time they were gone they had a great time and found several bargains. She'd never be able to get everything in her suitcase when she decided to go home. She'd have to mail the gifts and most of her clothes. Looking at the calendar she knew she should call the airline and make a reservation, but she wasn't ready yet.

❄

Two weeks before Christmas, Holly woke up with a fever and a sore throat. She usually got up every morning so she could have coffee with Grayson before he left for the office, but this morning she felt miserable, so she stayed in bed. When a knock sounded at her door, she wasn't surprised.

"Holly, are you okay? We were concerned when you didn't come in for breakfast."

"I'll be right there, Martha." Holly got up and slipped into her robe and slippers. She went to the living room and sat on the sofa.

"Are you all right?" Grayson sat next to her.

"I'm okay." Her voice was hoarse, and she knew she wasn't very convincing.

Grayson touched her cheek. "You're burning up." He opened his medical bag and placed a thermometer in her ear.

"Your temp is 102. Does your throat hurt?"

"Yes, I can hardly stand to swallow."

"Open up, and let me take a look." Grayson used a tongue depressor and looked in her mouth and then ran a swab around in her throat. He listened to her chest and checked her ears.

"I'd say you have strep, but this will tell me for sure. I'll have the lab run a culture when I get to the office. Normally I'd have you come into the office to see Jackson, my partner.

But if this is strep, I'll have him write you a prescription for penicillin. The pharmacy will deliver it, and Martha can bring it in to you. It'll clear it up in a few days." Grayson gave her something for the fever. "You need to go back to bed and rest. I'll see you this evening." Grayson kissed her forehead.

Holly nodded and went back to bed.

Martha came into her room a couple of hours later with a glass of water and the medication the pharmacy had delivered. "Grayson called and said to tell you this is strep throat. He wants you to rest and take this medication."

"Thank you, Martha. I appreciate it." With difficulty, Holly swallowed the tablet Martha gave her and then went back to sleep.

❄

That was her routine for the next several days. She was beginning to wonder if she was ever going to be able to swallow without the pain in her throat. She'd never had strep before and hoped she never did again. One minute she was shaking with chills, and the next she was burning up. She didn't know when she'd ever felt so miserable. Grayson brought her some throat lozenges that helped for a little while at a time.

Holly decided it evidently hadn't been meant for her to go home before Christmas. This was the first day she felt halfway decent, and Christmas was just a week away. It would be ridiculous to try to go now. She had to be at the plantation on Christmas day. She would have hardly any time at home if she went now. Besides another airline ticket would be an extra expense she couldn't afford. Grayson had been attentive and kind through her illness, but he hadn't revealed his feelings or asked her to stay. Even though it would break her heart to leave him, after the holidays she would go home.

Friday evening Grayson hauled a Christmas tree through the front door. "You up to helping me decorate this thing?"

Holly grinned. "I'd love to help."

Grayson hung the lights; then they spent the next hour putting on the garland, bulbs, and wooden ornaments Ellie had given him. Grayson said his mother bought each of her children an ornament every year as they were growing up. She gave him all of his when he bought his first Christmas tree after building his house.

"It looks great, Grayson." Laughing, Holly popped some of the popcorn Martha had brought them into her mouth as she watched the lights twinkling on the tree.

"Yeah, it does, doesn't it?" He grinned. "We make a pretty good decorating team."

"Yes, we do. Grayson, is there a taxi service here in Monticello?"

"I believe so. Why do you need a cab?"

"I'd like to go Christmas shopping tomorrow for a little while."

"You can use the Mercedes. I'll take the Escalade tomorrow."

"You have two cars?"

"Yes. The Escalade is a four-wheel drive, and I like to take it when it's snowing."

"Thank you. I appreciate you letting me borrow your car."

"No problem. I'll leave the keys on the table in the dining room."

Holly went shopping the next morning and bought gifts

for her family, Grayson, his family, and her sisters. When she got back to Grayson's house, she wrapped them and placed them under the tree.

She glanced at her watch. Her father would be home for lunch, so she decided to call her parents. She dialed their number, and her mother answered after the second ring. "Mom?"

"Holly, how are you, darling?"

"I'm doing fine, Mom. Is Dad home for lunch?"

"Yes, he's here. Do you want to talk to him?"

"I'd like to talk to both of you, if you can ask him to pick up the other phone."

"Okay, princess. What is it you want to talk to us about?"

"I just wanted to tell you both that I've spent a lot of time in prayer, and I've come to the realization that it doesn't matter to me that I'm adopted. I couldn't love you any more if you were my biological parents. I wish you had told me, but that can't be changed now. I'm sorry for the way I acted. I never meant to hurt you. I hope you can forgive me and we can put this behind us and go forward as if it had never happened. Will you both come and spend my birthday and Christmas at the plantation with me and meet my sisters?"

"Oh, darling, we love you so much, and we would love to come."

"Would you ask Lance and Beth to come, too?"

"We'll all be there. We just discussed this last night when they were here. We were hoping you'd ask us to come. We checked, and we can get there in about twelve and a half hours, so we're going to drive rather than fly this time."

"I'll look forward to seeing you. I miss you so much."

"We miss you, too, darling. We'll see you Christmas afternoon."

"Okay. I love you both."

"We love you, too, honey," they chorused.

Holly felt much better after talking to her parents. Later, she told Grayson about her conversation and how much better she felt.

"I'm glad you worked this out with your parents, sweetheart. It will be nice for them to be here with you for Christmas and to celebrate your birthday."

"Yes, it will." Holly was disappointed that Grayson didn't mention them being together for Christmas or her birthday. Since she'd recovered from strep throat, he hadn't spent much time with her. He came in late, and she'd only seen him for a few minutes before going to bed each night this whole last week. It was pretty clear. He didn't want a future with her.

With her heart aching, she made a decision. After she met with Camden to sign the papers for her inheritance, she would go home with her parents.

Christmas Eve they had dinner with Grayson's family and exchanged gifts. It would have been a nice evening had her heart not been breaking. She didn't want to leave. She loved Grayson and his family. But she had no choice; this was the way it had to be, so she might as well accept it. Holly cried herself to sleep that night.

It started to snow Christmas morning. By the time Holly got up, four inches of snow covered the ground. Grayson came up behind her where she stood at the window and slid his arms around her waist. It was the first time he'd touched her in over a week.

"Come sit with me on the sofa. I have something I want to talk to you about."

Once they were seated, Grayson took both of her hands in his. "Holly, I've waited as long as I can. I stayed away this week because I wanted to give you more time. I didn't want you to feel pressured. But I can't wait any longer. I love you, and I want you to stay here in Monticello with me." He opened a small box and held it out to her. "Will you marry me?"

"Oh, Grayson." Tears filled her eyes. "I love you, too! Yes, I'll stay here and marry you. Nothing would make me happier."

Grayson drew her into his arms, and his kiss left her with no doubt as to the way he felt about her.

"Will you come to the plantation to meet my sisters and spend my birthday and Christmas with me and my family?"

"There's nowhere else I'd rather be, sweetheart." Grayson kissed her again, and then they gathered the gifts and headed out to the car.

As they pulled away from Grayson's house and headed toward the Bellingham Plantation, Holly slipped her hand into his. "I think this is going to be the best birthday and Christmas celebration ever." She grinned. "I can't wait to meet my sisters. The only thing that could have made this day any better is if we could have met our grandparents." Holly pulled her seat belt across her and fastened it securely, anxious to see the antebellum home she and her sisters had inherited.

Jeanie Smith Cash lives in the country in southwest Missouri, in the heart of the Ozarks, with her husband, Andy. They were blessed with two children, a son-in-law, and three grandchildren. When she's not writing, Jeanie loves to spend time with her family, spoil her grandchildren, read, collect dolls, crochet, and travel. Jeanie is a member of American Christian Fiction Writers. She loves to read Christian romance and believes a salvation message inside of a good story could possibly touch someone who wouldn't be reached in any other way.

NICK'S
CHRISTMAS CAROL

Rose Allen McCauley

Dedication

This book is dedicated to two of the most wonderful ninety-four-year-young women I know—Ruth Seamands and Helen Jean Wiglesworth. Their Christian witness and zest for life have been an inspiration to me and countless others. My friends and I all want to be like them when we grow up!

Special thanks to:
My husband, Chester, for all of his encouragement and help, even when it means loading the dishwasher three times in one day!
Becky Germany, Jeanie Smith Cash, Jeri Odell, and Debra Ullrick for taking a chance on me and my writing. And to Margie Vawter for her wonderful editing skills.
My encouragers and prayer warriors—Crystal, Dottie, Kathy, Kim, Connie, Jan, Ann, and Unity Christian Church Rosebud SS class.
My forever friends, whose names are immortalized in some of my characters' names.
Debbonnaire and Jennifer, who helped me brainstorm this story. And my fabulous critique partners who enriched the story— Jennifer, Joy, and Loretta.
My two daughters, Christy and Mandy, who also read the story and gave me encouragement. And my son, Stephen, who now has to read my book because he promised to do so *when* I got published!
My Georgia helpers who answered many questions—Ane and Greg Mulligan, Thomas Smith, Rod Perry, and Scott Smith.
All of my writing friends at LRW, BCW, and ACFW,

with special thanks to Lynn Coleman for making
my first critique so gentle, yet helpful.
The readers whom I hope will enjoy this
book as much as I enjoyed writing it.
And most of all, praise God—Father, Son, and Holy Spirit—
from whom all blessings flow, including this opportunity
to see the writing dream He gave me come true.

God sets the lonely in families.
Psalm 68:6

Chapter 1

Nick Powers parked his battered four-wheel-drive truck by the curb in front of the law firm of Brockman and Davis. His mind had been racing faster than a greased pig at the county fair since he'd received Mr. Brockman's registered letter—the letter whose contents had rocked his world.

Exiting the truck, he pointed a finger at his collie perched atop some feed sacks in the truck bed. "Stay, Shep."

A thump of the dog's tail told him the canine had heard and would obey. Pretty bad when a dog was one of the few you could trust these days.

He entered the lawyer's office and touched the brim of his hat in greeting. "Hey there, Beverly. I've got an appointment with Mr. Brockman at four o'clock."

The woman checked her computer and then looked up over her glasses. "Sure thing, Nick. He'll be with you soon."

"Thanks." Seating himself, he checked his watch. Ten minutes to four. The toe of his right boot kept time to the ticking of the clock on the wall.

A flash of pink caught his eye through the glass-paned front door. Who could that be? Nobody around here would be caught dead in a pink vehicle.

A few toe-taps later, a slender brunette breezed through the door, her pink skirt swishing with every high-heeled step she took. She wasn't from around here, but something about her jogged his brain cells.

Swooshing past him, she stood in front of the secretary's desk. A manicured finger toyed with a pearl necklace. "I know I don't have an appointment, but I have to see Mr. Brockman right away."

"I'm sorry, miss, but he has a four o'clock appointment, and it's his last one for the day. Let me see if I can fit you in on Monday." She flipped a page. "Sorry. Tuesday is the earliest he could see you since Monday is Labor Day."

The girl shook her head, swinging her sleek brown hair with golden streaks from side to side. "That won't do at all. I have to be back in Atlanta for my classes on Tuesday."

Mr. Brockman stepped through his door. Nick began to rise.

The lawyer frowned and then glanced at the secretary. "Is there a problem, Ms. Dailey?"

"No sir. I was just explaining to this lady that—"

The stunning stranger rushed toward the lawyer. "I know I don't have an appointment, but I have to see you. I'm Carol Peterson, and"—she waved a wrinkled envelope in her left hand—"I won't be able to sleep a wink until I find out what this letter from you means."

The lawyer raised his eyebrows. "This is highly un-expected, Miss Peterson, but I will see you for five minutes before my next appointment." He stepped back from the door, motioning her to enter ahead of him.

With a short nod toward Nick, the lawyer followed and then closed the door.

Nick glanced at Beverly, who shrugged her shoulders. He looked back at the door. Something about the woman, now so unsure of herself, reminded him of. . .

His breath whooshed out. *It couldn't be. Not the rich kid*

who made my life miserable that long-ago summer. She always did play to get her way. Whatever it took.

❄

Carol sat in the plush leather chair the lawyer indicated. She crossed her legs and then uncrossed them and forced herself to sit up straight and ladylike the way her mother had ingrained in her.

The lawyer pulled a manila file folder from the corner of his desk and cleared his throat. "I didn't expect you to drive down here so soon, Miss Peterson. As the letter stated, you are requested to be at Bellingham Plantation on December twenty-fifth according to the stipulations of my client's will. You will not be allowed in the house before that date."

"But can't you give me more information about my birth family? Especially the part about my being one of a set of identical quadruplets. I've always wanted a close family with siblings and. . ." She paused and swallowed to control herself. "You can't imagine how important this is to me. I've always known I was adopted, always envied my friends from large families. But to think there are three other girls. Sisters. Who even look like me."

He shook his head. "I'm sorry. I've told you all I am allowed to say until the day after Christmas."

"That's my birthday. Why does it have to be then?"

"Because it *is* your birthday. A special one, correct?"

"Yes, my twenty-fifth." *How does this man know so much about me, yet won't tell me what I want to know?*

"As the letter states, if you don't wish to be separated from your parents on Christmas Day, they are invited to come with you."

I wish. "My parents usually take a cruise over Christmas.

93

I think this year they're going to Panama." *Again.*

"So it won't be a problem for you to be at the plantation on the twenty-fifth? Even to stay the night?"

"No, I'll be finishing my degree from Mercer University on December fourteenth. I plan to wait until the new year to start job-hunting."

"Great college. What's your major?"

"My master's degree is in business to go along with my undergraduate in American history. I've always enjoyed studying the past." *Maybe because I knew so little of my own.*

"I'm sure you'll like the Bellingham Plantation, then. I'll look forward to seeing you on December twenty-sixth."

"I thought the letter said the twenty-fifth?"

"That's when you are to be at the house, but we'll have a meeting here in my office the day after Christmas." He stood.

She arose. "I'm sorry. I shouldn't have barged in like this. I. . .I just hoped to find out something, anything about my sisters."

The man's face melted into a compassionate smile. "And I'm sorry, but you will have to wait a few more months for that information, as per the guidelines set up by my client."

Tears welled in the corners of her eyes. She turned and sped past the secretary's desk and a pair of blue jeans and tan boots.

❄

Nick's nose tickled at the citrusy scent lingering in the girl's wake. She'd sure grown up to be a beauty, but he had too many bad memories from that summer in Atlanta to ever want to cross paths with her again.

The secretary cleared her throat. "Nick, Mr. Brockman

will see you now."

"Thanks, Beverly." He untangled his long legs as he tried to untangle his thoughts.

Mr. Brockman met him at the door with hand extended. "Good to see you again, Nick. Sorry about the interruption." He beckoned toward a chair in front of his desk. "I appreciate your coming in on such short notice."

Wild mustangs couldn't keep me away. Not until I know how my job will be affected. He sat and then pulled the registered mail from the pocket of his flannel shirt. "I need to know how all of *this* will impact my position as manager of Bellingham Plantation. My main concern is—do I still have a job?"

"Yes, you do. . ."

Nick's muscles relaxed for the first time since he'd entered the office.

". . .for the time being."

"What do you mean?" His fingers gripped the chair arms. "Is Mrs. Bellingham not pleased with how the plantation is doing? I know the price on pecans went down last year, but we still showed a profit."

"Nothing like that, Nick. Mrs. Bellingham is moving into a smaller house in town soon."

"But she loves it out there and—"

"I know, but she will no longer own the property after the first of the year, so thought it best to move before the new owners take possession."

I can't believe this. "Why would she have to sell? I thought her husband left her plenty to live on and to keep up the plantation."

"He did, but she was keeping it for..." The lawyer rubbed

his hand over his mouth and down his jaw. "I'm sorry, Nick. I can't tell you any more without breaching confidentiality. I do need you to keep a good watch on the house. We don't want anyone trespassing. And I think there's a good chance the new owners will want someone to run the place, but I can't guarantee it."

"New owners? Could I meet with them and find out what they plan to do?"

"I can't divulge any more information until I meet with the new owners on December twenty-sixth. I suggest you talk with Mrs. Bellingham to see what she can tell you." He smiled. "Try not to worry. You'll be there at least through Christmas."

Nick shook his head in disbelief. Sounded like a very *un-merry* Christmas.

Chapter 2

Wiping tears from her eyes, Carol drove her pink Audi IT Coupe down the quaint streets of Monticello. She wished she could have grown up in a town like this. A town with lots of close family and friends.

An idea pinged in her brain. She pulled over to the curb and dug the letter from her purse and then typed the address into her GPS system. Her pink fingernails tapped on the dash, waiting for the familiar droning voice to lead her to the desired location.

"Proceed point two miles; then turn left onto Bellingham Road."

Way to go, Lola. I can always depend on you, even when I have no one else.

Carol made the turn.

"Drive one point three miles until you reach your destination."

Sweet. I'll be there in a couple minutes. Maybe even see one of my sisters. Her heart danced a rumba.

The car shuddered to a halt at the sight of an imposing black wrought-iron gate. Amid the scrolls and curlicues, an elegant letter *B* gleamed, telling her she must be at the right place. How could she get inside? A six-foot fence spread as far as she could see on both sides.

She eyed a button to the right of the gate and pushed it. Expecting a voice, she startled when the gate began to swing open on its hinges.

Carol jumped in her car and sped through before the gate could shut again. She parked in front of the house and then climbed the steps leading to the white two-story home. After ringing the bell, she waited. No one answered, so she punched it again.

She hadn't come this far to leave without a glimpse inside the house. The drapes in the front windows were drawn. She went down the steps and around to the side of the house. The windows stood about five feet off the ground, too high for her to peek into. Spying an ivy-covered trellis beside a tall window, she kicked off her heels. *Six years of gymnastics should count for something.* One foot caught hold. Almost there.

A heavy hand clamped onto her shoulder.

"May I help you?"

She spun around and almost fell. The man from the lawyer's office held her arm. Jerking away from his grasp, she straightened.

Fear tingled up her spine. "Keep your hands off me. What are you doing following me here?" She reached into her purse and whipped out her cell phone. "I'm going to call the police."

"Maybe I should be the one to call them since I work here." One side of his mouth quirked up. "Why are *you* here?"

"I wanted to see— Why should I believe you? We'll let the police sort this out." She squinted at him, and a sense of déjà vu struck her. She'd said those same words to a younger version of this man with aquamarine eyes in her own backyard several years ago. "You're the. . .pool guy?"

A laugh boomed out of the man. "I haven't been called

that for a long time."

❄

Nick couldn't believe she remembered him. It was a summer he'd tried to forget. His uncle who ran the pool cleaning business had vouched for him, but the girl and her friends had taunted him and made his life miserable for three long months.

Before becoming a Christian, he would have seen this as a chance to get revenge, called the cops, and let her cool off in the county jail. But Jesus' words from the Sermon on the Mount about turning the other cheek captured his mind. "Sorry if I scared you."

She cleared her throat. "I. . .I'm sorry, too. For today and . . .for all the mean things I said to you that summer." She hitched a breath, and he wondered if she would start to cry. "I know I treated you terribly, and I ask your forgiveness."

He blinked. Not what he'd expected to hear.

"I became a Christian three years ago, and I still fail, but I try to follow Jesus' teachings now."

His heart thudded in his ears. "Me, too."

Her lavender blue eyes stared into his. "You what?"

"My boss led me to the Lord last year, so I'm a Christian, too."

"Amazing." She smiled, and a dimple appeared in her right cheek.

"Yes, God is amazing." He scuffed the toe of his boot. His stomach grumbled. "I'm hungry. Would you like to go get a bite to eat?" *Who put those words in my mouth?*

She chewed her lower lip a moment before nodding. "Sure. Maybe you can show me a little of this charming town."

"Okay." *Incredible.* Six years ago he couldn't have imagined this scenario. Miss High-Society going to supper with him—the pool guy who'd admired her from afar.

❄

Thank you, Lord, for changing me. I can't believe I'm going to eat with the pool guy I had a secret crush on. And I don't even know his real name.

Carol followed the truck back into town, retracing the way she'd traveled minutes earlier. He parked in front of a tan brick building with green awnings and hopped out of his truck, and then walked to her car and opened the door.

"Hope you like fried chicken. Big Chic's has the best around."

"I love fried chicken."

They found a table near a front window. A waitress brought by menus and water.

"I'm Nick Powers." He extended a hand. "I know you're Mr. Peterson's daughter, but I don't remember your first name."

She let her hand be swallowed up in his, surprised at its size and warmth. "It's Carol. My parents adopted me right after Christmas, and I'd already been given the name Carol."

"Like a Christmas Carol. Interesting. I didn't know you were adopted."

"Yes, my parents couldn't have any children. I'm their only child." *I don't know why they never adopted again. Did I disappoint them so much?*

"Do you still live in the same house with the pool?"

She detected a glint in his eye. Was he teasing her? "My parents still live there. I share a condo near the Mercer campus in Atlanta with my roommate, Sandi. She's the one who led me to the Lord our freshman year." She sipped some water. "How about you? What have you been up to the last few years?"

"I graduated from Emory a couple years ago and found my dream job here in Monticello."

"Why Monticello?"

"My business degree helps me keep the books straight at the plantation, but I still get to spend most of my time out in God's great outdoors."

Quite impressive. She tucked the information into a corner of her brain while tucking a piece of hair behind her ear.

The waitress arrived at their table. "Hey, Nick. The usual?"

Nick handed the young girl his menu. "Sounds good to me. And a side order of fried okra. How about you, Carol?"

"What's your usual order?"

"Fried chicken, mashed potatoes, gravy, and green beans."

She smiled up at the girl. "I'll take the same."

Nick's ocean-colored eyes searched hers. "What's your major?"

"History and business."

"History was one of my minors. Another reason I like working at the Bellingham Plantation. It's been in the family over a hundred years. It's even on the register of the Georgia Centennial Farms."

While discussing other historical sites in the area, their meals arrived, and the scents from the plate reminded her of her skipped lunch in the hurry to get to Monticello before the lawyer's office closed.

The rugged man across from her held out his hand.

After she placed hers in his, he bowed his head and offered a short prayer.

They both dug in, talking between bites. By the time they had polished off their plates amid the conversation, the sky had darkened.

Nick nodded toward the window. "Guess we won't get to tour the town after all."

She frowned. "I hate to drive unfamiliar roads in the dark. I thought I would find a bed-and-breakfast somewhere."

He grabbed the bill from the table, plopped down a tip, and stood. "I know the perfect place. Follow me."

Chapter 3

Carol awoke and stretched, her hand grazing one of the finials on the four-poster bed. She recognized the wood from her mom's antique furniture—rice-carved mahogany. Glancing around the room, she took in the historical furnishings. The burgundy twill drapes complemented the green, silk taffeta bedspread. Nick had known the perfect place for a history buff. And he'd told her several buildings in this section of town were on the National Register of Historic Places, so she couldn't wait to look around more.

Nick. He'd said he would pick her up after breakfast. What time was it? Had she already missed breakfast? She climbed down the bed step, grateful the owners of the Warren House Bed and Breakfast provided such functional antiques. Otherwise she would have never made it into bed last night. She dressed in jean capris, a pink-and-white-checkered top, and tennis shoes. He'd warned her they would be doing a lot of walking today.

She found her way to the dining room with the huge maple table and sideboard. The buffet was spread with several dishes—a plate of croissants, a jar of homemade fig preserves, and a wide array of fresh fruit. She helped herself to a little of each and set her plate down.

A lovely lady with long blond hair appeared with a silver teapot and several varieties of teas. "Good morning. My name is Judy. How did you sleep?"

"Quite well, thank you. And this food looks scrumptious."

"I'll leave the teas for you to make your own selection. Call if you need anything else."

"Thanks." Carol ate in silence, appreciating the flavors of the food as well as the historical pieces in the room.

She started at a knock on the door. Her hostess answered.

Nick's voice boomed down the hallway. "I'm meeting Carol here. Is she ready?"

Carol rose to meet him by the door. "Let me grab my purse, and we'll go."

He winked. "No hurry. Monticello has been the county seat for over two hundred years, so I don't think it's going anywhere."

Carol took time to brush her teeth and run a comb through her hair before leaving her room. As she descended the staircase she called out, "I'm ready. Where are you taking me?"

"I thought we would do a tour of downtown and then maybe hike around the lake out at Indian Springs State Park. It's only a fifteen-minute drive. And it's one of the oldest state parks in the nation, so it's historical, too."

"Sounds lovely. Especially with my own personal tour guide."

He opened the front door and escorted her out. "How early do you need to head back to Atlanta?"

"I'm staying over tonight. This place has a two-night minimum."

"I didn't know. Hope it's not a problem."

She fell into step beside him. "No, the house is beautiful and very comfortable. But I do have a paper due on Tuesday, so I'll need to get up early tomorrow and head back to Atlanta in time for the late service at my church."

"Too bad you can't stay a third night. This Sunday evening is the last community service of the summer."

"Community service?"

"Yep. Because we have so many churches in the county, they decided to have special services at a different church each Sunday evening of the summer for the whole community. A different preacher speaks each week. My favorite part is the singing. Lots of gospel and spirituals. Kind of like an old camp meeting."

"Wish I could stay. Are there many churches over a hundred years old here?"

"Lots. But that would take longer than a day's tour."

They walked past several homes similar in age to the Warren House or even older. Most showed signs of loving care.

Nick stopped in front of one of the run-down homes. "This is the Malone House, a grand old lady showing her age."

Carol squinted to look at it through hazy eyes. "She could be a beauty if someone took the time and money to fix her up. It would be fun to restore her to her original beauty."

"A noble idea."

They kept walking until Carol stopped at a pale-yellow house with a shingle roof and pointed at an old church with a country gothic bell behind it. "What church is that?"

"Methodist. They no longer hold services here, though." He led the way to a Victorian wrought-iron fence surrounding a cemetery.

Carol stared at the ancient tombstones, some with dates going back to the eighteenth century. "Think of all the history we could learn if these stones could speak."

❄

They picked up a picnic lunch on their way out of town.

Nick drove through the familiar countryside. Entering Indian Springs State Park, he parked under his favorite sugar maple.

After helping Carol out of the truck, he spread a blanket under the shade and then stared up at the top of the tree forty or more feet above the ground. This beauty would soon be ablaze with color. The beauty accompanying him already held his attention with her becoming outfit. The long-ago, ill-fated attraction he'd felt toward her resurfaced.

"Can I help?" Carol's voice called him out of his thoughts.

"Sure. Get the basket from the back of the truck while I find some rocks to hold down the blanket corners."

He set the rocks in place and then propped himself up on his elbows and watched as Carol laid out their food.

A chickadee sang from high up in the tree. Soft breezes kept the day from being a scorcher.

Carol seated herself across from him.

He bowed his head and asked God's blessing on the food.

They ate in a peaceable silence for a few minutes. He loved the quiet and enjoyed sharing silence with someone else.

A squirrel scolded them from a branch.

"I guess the poor fellow doesn't enjoy silence like we do." Carol grinned.

"He doesn't know what he's missing. Beautiful silence and a lovely view." And he didn't mean the tree and its surrounding countryside. "Ready for a walk?"

"The perfect thing to do after eating."

Nick stood and then helped her to her feet. He drew in a deep breath of the country air. This had been a perfect day in every way—weather, sights, and the company.

They followed the path to the lake.

Walking around Chief McIntosh Lake had been one of his favorite jaunts ever since he discovered it when he moved to Jasper County. Sharing it with Carol made it even more special.

He pointed. "See that turtle sunning himself on a rock?"

"Oooh. He's a big one."

"Probably over a hundred years old."

"Really? Did you also have a minor in biology?"

He scuffed his boot then looked up. "Matter of fact, I did. I like anything to do with the outdoors."

Her eyes smiled at him. "I can tell."

Time to walk a little faster. What was he doing here with this girl who made his heart beat faster than a poppin' John tractor in high gear? She was so far out of his league he needed to have his head examined for craters.

"Nick?"

"Huh? Sorry." He looked up again but made sure he didn't stare at her eyes.

"Look at those ducks over there. A mama and four little ducklings. It reminds me. . ."

"Reminds you of what?"

"I told you I was an only child."

He nodded.

"I am in my adoptive family. But I recently found out I have three sisters. We're all identical quadruplets adopted to different families. That's why I'm here—why I went out to the Bellingham Plantation."

"I don't understand. What does the plantation have to do with you being a quad?"

"I don't know all the details, but I have to meet there on Christmas morning with the three sisters I didn't know I had. Then the next day we'll meet with Mr. Brockman about the will and the house and land."

Nick's gut felt like he'd been sucker-punched. Is this what Mr. Brockman was talking about? Could Carol be one of the new owners of the plantation? He turned away toward the lake.

Carol's warm hand touched his arm. "Nick? Is something wrong?"

"No, but I just thought of someplace I have to go tonight. We'd better leave right now." *The sooner I talk with Mrs. Bellingham, the better.*

Chapter 4

Nick walked Carol to the door of the B and B. "Sorry I have to run. I enjoyed our time together."

"Me, too." Her beautiful eyes filled with unspoken questions. She disappeared inside and closed the door. Closed the connection between them.

Nick forced himself to stay under the speed limit as he drove to the plantation. Although he'd hoped to spend the evening with Carol, those plans had come to a complete stop when he realized she might be related to Mrs. Bellingham. Mr. Brockman had suggested he speak to his employer. Nick wished he'd done so before he'd spent the day with Carol.

The sight of a light in the parlor set his pulse to galloping. He needed to question Mrs. Bellingham, but how to approach this subject? Raising his hand, he knocked.

His boss opened the front door, meaning Juanita had gone home. "Why, Nick. What a pleasant surprise." She stepped back. "Come in. Could I offer you something to drink?"

"No ma'am. I don't want to interrupt your evening."

"It's not an interruption but a delight to see you." She preceded him into the parlor and seated herself.

Nick sat across from her on the sturdiest chair he could find. He crossed one foot across the other knee and then put it back on the floor.

Mrs. Bellingham's eyes studied him. How had he never noted their color before—the same as a periwinkle. The same as Carol's. "Is there a problem, Nick?"

"I'm not sure." He swallowed. "I guess the only way to find out is to tell you what I know."

She nodded. "Go on, please."

"I met with Mr. Brockman yesterday. He wanted me to know about a possible change in my employment in the new year."

"Yes. I told him it was only right you should know things might be changing soon."

"In his office and later on here at the plantation I met a young lady named Carol."

Mrs. B placed a delicate hand across her pale throat. "Carol? Here?"

"Yes, ma'am. She drove down from Atlanta to ask Mr. Brockman some questions after she received a letter. He didn't tell her or me anything, but he did suggest I talk with you."

The woman stood and began to pace. "What did you tell Carol?"

"Nothing, except I manage the plantation. I didn't realize there was any connection until she mentioned she'd recently found out she was one of a set of identical quads and would be meeting her sisters at Bellingham Plantation on December twenty-fifth. Since Mr. Brockman had already told me the new owners would be here, I put two and two together and came up with four, literally."

"Yes, my four granddaughters. I can't believe I'll finally get to see them again." She sat again, her face still pale.

"I spent some time with Carol today and had planned to see her again this evening, but thought I'd better talk with you first. Do you want me to not see her again?" His heart flopped like a fish out of water at the disturbing possibility.

After several long moments, Mrs. B smiled at him. "I would love for you to continue to see my granddaughter. . .if you can promise me you won't reveal anything about me or the farm."

"Of course, I promise."

His genteel boss surprised him with a wink. "In fact, I can't think of anyone I'd rather her spend time with. But you must keep her away from the farm and anywhere you might run into me."

"Like church on Sundays?"

"Exactly."

"Will do." He stood. "I should tell you that Carol and I first met six years ago when I helped my uncle clean the pool at their house."

"Did you all date then?"

I wish. "No way. We clashed big-time, but we both apologized yesterday. I told her I was a Christian now, and she said she was, too."

A smile bigger than the sky lit up the woman's face. "Ah. One of my prayers already answered." She lifted her head to the heavens. "Thank you, Lord."

Nick's throat swelled with emotion. "I'll see myself out."

❄

Carol had spent the evening curled up with a book in the sitting room, although her mind kept wandering to a certain tall, dark-haired farm manager. She stood and stretched and then headed to the stairway when a knock sounded at the door. Opening it, she gasped. "I. . .I didn't expect to see you."

"May I come in for a minute?"

She waved a hand toward the hall and stepped back.

"I remembered you said you would be leaving early

tomorrow, so I wanted to stop by and apologize again for leaving so suddenly today. And I wanted to exchange contact information and. . .maybe come up to Atlanta to see you some weekend?"

A thrill swept up and down her body. She realized her mouth stood agape and snapped it shut and then opened it to answer him. "Of course, let me get some paper and a pen."

He whipped out his cell phone. "I can store them in here."

She rattled off the information, her gaze never leaving him as he punched in the numbers and letters.

He looked at her, his eyes telegraphing. . .what? Hope? "I'll be in touch, Carol. I promise." He walked to the door and opened it. "Bye now."

"Good-bye," she whispered, hoping he heard. Hoping he called. Hoping he kept his promise.

Chapter 5

The drive back to Atlanta on Sunday morning took a little over an hour. Carol arrived at church in plenty of time to seek out a friend before the late service began. Catching sight of Sandi's mop of blond curls, Carol wove her way across the crowded lobby.

She touched her roommate on the arm. "Hey, girlfriend. Did you stay out of trouble while I was gone?"

Sandi twirled, her curls brushing Carol's shoulder. "Whoa! What's that glow I see on your face? Your eyes are shining brighter than Rudolph's nose. That lawyer you went to see must have been young and cute."

Carol shook her head. "No, definitely not the lawyer."

Her friend squinted. "So who else did you meet in. . . what's the name of the town?"

"Monticello." Carol linked arms with her best friend and confidante. "Come on. The music has already started. I'll tell you all about it over lunch." Right now she had many reasons to thank God.

❋

Carol and Sandi parked their cars side-by-side in the Mexican restaurant's parking lot.

Sandi jumped out of her car, pulled open the passenger door on Carol's vehicle, and then plopped down. "I can't wait another minute. Spill the refried beans."

"Remember the pool guy I told you about that my high school friends and I tormented one summer?"

"Yeah. The one you had a secret crush on?"

"Right. I got the chance to apologize to him. And. . ."

"And what?"

"He took me out to dinner, and the next day we went for a walk and a picnic. Then last night he asked for my number to call about coming to Atlanta to visit."

Her friend's eyebrows disappeared under her bangs. "All this in one weekend? Besides, I thought you clashed with the guy."

"That was before you introduced me to the Lord. He told me he became a Christian about a year ago, too."

"Wow."

Carol's phone played a minuet. An unknown number. She looked at Sandi.

"So answer it already."

"Hello?"

"Carol. This is Nick. I just left church and thought you might be out by now, too. I wanted to make sure you got home okay."

The deep timbre of his voice echoed in her ear. "Yes, I made it fine, and we just got out of church, too."

"You're with someone. I'll call you later now I know you're all right. Bye."

She didn't want to hang up. "Thanks for calling." What if he thought she was out with a guy? She hadn't had time to tell him she was with her roommate.

As soon as Carol pushed the OFF button, Sandi shrieked. "That was him, wasn't it?"

Carol nodded, willing her heart to settle down. "Let's go eat. I'm starving. I'll catch you up on the details over lunch."

❄

Nick stuck the phone in his pocket and remained in his

car, deflated at the brevity of their conversation. How long should he wait to call again to make plans for this weekend? Six more days until he could see her again. If she didn't have plans. Which a pretty girl like Carol probably did. She may have even been with a guy when he called. Like one of those rich guys who'd hung around her pool.

A tap on his window pulled him back to the present. His friend Scott moved his fisted hand in a circle.

Nick turned on the key to let his window down. "Hi, Scott. How's it going?"

"I'm fine, but you looked a trillion miles away."

More like seventy. "Not that far. Just doing some figuring in my head."

"Want to have some lunch?"

"Sure. Where do you want to go?"

"How about the new barbeque place in Jasper? They have an all-you-can-eat buffet on Sundays."

"Sounds good. Hop in." At least it would pass the time and keep his mind off Carol.

Scott jogged around the car and settled himself in. "I saw you in Big Chic's the other evening as I walked by. Who was the cute brunette? Didn't look like anyone from around here."

God, help me to be truthful without revealing anything I shouldn't. "A girl from Atlanta. She's a history major, and I showed her some of the historic sites in Monticello."

"How did you meet her?"

"About six years ago when I worked in Atlanta for my uncle. I cleaned her family's pool."

Scott whistled. "Little rich kid, huh?"

"I guess, but she's a Christian now and so different."

"You sound like a goner, man. Is there anything you don't like about this girl?"

Nick shook his head. "Can't think of any except she's in Atlanta, and I'm here."

"So what are you gonna do about it?"

"Call her soon." *Tonight if I can force myself to wait that long.*

❄

"Hello?" A vibrant alto voice answered.

It didn't sound like Carol, but he was certain he'd hit the correct speed-dial number. "This is Nick. Is this Carol?"

A giggle escaped across the line. "No. This is her roommate, Sandi. She's in the shower, but I'm sure she'll call you right back."

"Okay. Thanks."

Nick paced his small apartment in the plantation guesthouse. Would this still be his home come January? If not, what would he do? Where would he go? He knew he didn't want to leave Monticello.

His phone rang, and he snatched it up. "Hi, Nick here."

"Hi, Nick. Glad you called."

Me, too. "Do you have time to talk?"

"Sure. I'm settling in for the night. I need to work some more on the paper I told you about, but it can wait awhile."

"Good. Tell me about your trip home." He listened to the details of her drive, trying to garner the courage to ask what he'd really called for.

". . .and then I went to church and lunch with my roommate, Sandi—the one you talked with on the phone."

Pleasure filled his gut at knowing it had been her roommate she'd eaten with and not some other guy. "She

116

seemed nice. I hope to meet her sometime. . .if it's okay to come to Atlanta to visit you."

"Great."

"How about this next weekend? I can be there Saturday by two, and we could go to the aquarium and then maybe grab some supper."

"Sounds wonderful."

He wished he could think of something else to say to keep her on the line, to keep hearing her voice. "Okay. See you Saturday." *How am I going to keep from going stir crazy for five and a half days?*

Chapter 6

Nick tapped his fingers on the steering wheel to the beat of a David Crowder Band CD. A few more minutes and he would see Carol again after the longest week of his life. He soon parked in the drive of a red brick condo with white shutters and trim. Pretty fancy digs for two college students.

He walked up the drive, eager to see her, yet nervous. Could today be as special as last Saturday? As he lifted his hand to ring the bell, the door opened. There stood the girl he'd gone to bed thinking about all week. But she looked even better than in his dreams.

"You're right on time. Come in, and I'll introduce you to Sandi. She's dying to meet you."

A tall blond with curls springing out in all directions came in the room. "Not literally, of course, but I have been looking forward to seeing the guy who has kept my roommate on the phone late every night this week."

Nick grinned. "Guilty as charged."

Sandi waved as she grabbed her satchel and headed for the front door. "Don't get eaten by any sharks or swallowed by a whale."

Nick put his arm around Carol, and warmth filled him. "Don't worry. I'll protect her."

"I bet you will." Sandi winked at them as she left.

Red filled Carol's cheeks and she stepped away from him.

Nick's arms felt empty and cold.

"Sorry. I love my roommate, but she can be a little over the top sometimes." Carol grabbed a brown purse.

Nick followed her lead and opened the front door. He wondered how she felt about riding around Atlanta in a truck. A farm truck, no less, although he'd spent most of the morning giving it a good cleaning and wax job.

He shouldn't have worried. Carol seemed as comfortable in his truck as in her own pink Audi. She hummed along with the CD, and they made small talk all the way to the aquarium.

In the parking lot she touched his arm. "I have to admit I've only been here once, on a high school field trip."

"Then you're in for a treat. The number of exhibits has grown over the last few years. I love to come any chance I get."

He purchased their tickets and then motioned for her to precede him. "I thought we'd start at the Ocean Voyager and meet some manta rays. They're some of my favorites."

They entered the tunnel and were enveloped by the colorful fish and beautiful blue water. Carol gasped. "Wow. I feel like I'm scuba diving. . .in dry clothes."

"You've gone scuba diving?"

"Several times."

Scuba diving topped his bucket list of things to do. "Where have you gone?"

"Mexico and Hawaii. But Australia is my favorite place to dive."

You're way out of your league, man. Like twenty thousand leagues under the sea.

Carol continued to turn her head from side to side and up above. A hammerhead shark butted the acrylic wall next to her, and she squealed and jumped back into Nick.

He steadied her and took her hand in his. "Don't worry. Remember I promised Sandi I would protect you."

Her lavender eyes locked with his. "Okay." She blew out a puff of air. "I try to avoid sharks when I dive."

"Smart girl." Giving her hand a squeeze, he stepped forward. With his free hand he pointed. "Look. There go two of the rays. This is the only aquarium in America that has mantas."

They reached the end of the acrylic tube. "So you want to go back through it again, or do you want to look through the viewing window?" He led her to the huge transparent panel.

Her head tilted back until her short frame almost did a back bend. "How big is this thing?"

He led her farther away to make it easier to see the whole window. "Over twenty feet tall by sixty wide. And it's two feet thick."

"I'm impressed. I could stay here all day."

"But then you would miss all the other exhibits." He tugged her hand. "Come on. I want you to see the River Scout."

❄

Carol followed him to a sign that read "RIVER SCOUT, FRESHWATER MYSTERIES."

Nick squeezed her hand. Funny how it felt so good, so protective, making her aware of his presence.

He nodded toward the sign. "Ready to take a river walk like you've never seen before?"

"If you're the guide."

He winked at her. "You got it."

They entered the exhibit and were greeted by three otters. One of them put a small paw to his mouth.

"Hear no evil, see no evil, speak no evil."

The other two otters held a scratching contest. "Or scratch no evil," Nick ad-libbed.

Carol laughed, free from her usual worries about studies or projects or, since last weekend, her long-lost sisters. "I haven't had this much fun in a long time." *Since the day we enjoyed our picnic.*

"Me either." Nick closed his hand over hers again. "Here comes the interesting part."

They walked down a ramp until they could look up and see a river flowing above them.

Carol sucked in a breath. "Amazing."

Nick's gaze remained on her. "Yes, it is."

She forced herself to pull her eyes away from his. "What river is this?"

"It's a simulation of all North American rivers, from the Mississippi to our own Chattahoochee." He pointed to a small gray fish. "There's a crappie. Good eating."

A larger flat-nosed fish appeared. "What's that one?"

"Bluegill. Another good one to fry."

She giggled. "Are you getting hungry?"

"Come to think of it, some fried fish does sound tasty. But there's nothing as good as the ones you catch yourself. Do you like to go fishing?"

"I don't know. I've never been."

His eyes grew double in size. "Are you kidding me? I thought all Georgian girls had wetted a line in a pond or stream somewhere."

"Not this one."

"We'll have to remedy that. Soon."

They walked on until they came to some alligators, their green eyes bulging out of their olive-and-black scaly heads. She shuddered. "Only if you promise no alligators."

"I promise."

They meandered their way through the exhibits of river creatures from other countries. In the South African section, she laughed at a dark-brown fish with a protrusion resembling a hose. "What's this one called?"

"What animal does it remind you of?"

She squinted and thought. "A small elephant."

"Bingo. It's an elephant nose fish."

"I think I'll pass on eating that one."

"Me, too, but it's near closing time, so how about we go somewhere to eat and come back to see the rest of the aquarium another day?"

"Okay. What do you have in mind?"

"How about someplace historical?"

"A historical restaurant in Atlanta? Do tell."

"Yep. Trust me."

I am beginning to trust this guy.

Chapter 7

Nick pulled out of the parking garage and headed toward the Virginia Highlands area of Atlanta. He knew she'd love all the older architecture.

Carol glanced around. "Are you going to tell me where we're going? We're getting close to Underground Atlanta, and it has a lot of historic buildings."

"Nope, but why don't you fill me in on some of the history of the place while we drive?"

"Okay. You know that much of Atlanta was burned to the ground during the Civil War, so all of the buildings down there are postwar era. The Georgia Railroad Depot was built in 1869 to replace the one destroyed by Sherman and his troops. When viaducts were built to raise the street level for automobiles, the bottom floor of each building became storage and lay forgotten until the 1960s, when two Georgia Tech grads discovered them. Underground Atlanta opened in 1969."

"I might have enjoyed history more if I had a teacher like you. Do you plan to teach after you graduate?"

"No, I don't have an education degree, but I would like to share history with the public in some sort of historic place, maybe be a tour guide or a docent for an old home or museum."

She doesn't have a clue she'll soon be inheriting an old home. "Sounds like a good plan. Tell me some more."

"Underground Atlanta has changed over the years. Now you mostly see some street people, tourists, and college students. I haven't come down here for several years."

"I haven't been here since I moved to Monticello and became a Christian, but I'm afraid I was one of the college students who partied here while going to Emory."

Spotting a parking place on the street, he pulled into it. They'd have less than a block to walk. He grabbed a sports jacket out of the backseat.

Carol looked around at her surroundings as he helped her from the truck. "We're in the Virginia Highland area. Almost all the restaurants around here are in historic buildings. You do know your way around Atlanta."

Not that he'd eaten in this area except for the one time he had an interview with an agriculture supply company. He'd been happy when he'd turned that job down for the one at Bellingham Plantation.

They entered a century-old brick building and were soon seated at a table lit by candlelight. Soft jazz played in the background.

A waiter brought menus and filled their water glasses. "Can I get madam something else to drink?"

"Do you have Georgia peach tea? The nonalcoholic kind?"

The man nodded and bowed. "Of course."

"I'll have a glass of that, please." She glanced at Nick. "I love the peach sweet tea."

I like the sweet Georgia peach sitting across from me, too.

After perusing the menus, Nick decided on the pork tenderloin. Carol chose grilled chicken.

Nick asked a blessing before they began to eat. They ate and talked and ate some more.

Carol placed her napkin over her plate. "I'm stuffed. And

the chicken is good, but not as good as Big Chic's."

A girl after my own heart. Nick finished up his meal. "Do you have time to walk around a little before I take you home?"

"Sure. I could use a walk after all those calories."

They strolled down the street, hand in hand. It seemed so natural to be doing this with Carol.

Some boisterous guys came out of one of the sports bars as they passed. One of them knocked into Carol.

The guy looked at her and then at Nick. He blinked. "Nickeroo. Is that you, buddy? Ain't seen you in a long time."

"It's me, Dave. And you owe this lady an apology." Nick's voice sounded harder than iron spikes, but he didn't care.

"Sorry, pretty lady." Dave studied Carol from her head to her toes and back up again.

Nick's blood boiled with righteous anger. *If Dave touches her I'll. . .*

He glanced at Carol. Her hands were balled at her side, her face drained of all color. He took her by the elbow. She stiffened.

"Let's go, Carol."

Dave, as usual, managed to get in the last word. "Come back and join us in some brewskis, Nick. You never quit this early before."

Nick increased his pressure on her arm and kept walking.

❄

Carol allowed Nick to lead her to his truck, not wanting anything to impede their departure. She sat as close to the door on her side as possible. *How could I let myself fall for his sweet-talking? How could I let myself be attracted to someone who could have put Bill in his wheelchair?*

Bill, her closest relative next to her parents. She saw her cousin lying in his hospital bed for days in a coma. Now paralyzed in his wheelchair. He would never walk again due to a drunk driver. A drunk like the one who'd bumped into her tonight. A drunk like Nick had once been. Maybe still was. She knew so little about him and didn't care to know any more.

Nick said something, but she didn't respond.

He spoke again, and she tried to shut out his voice but couldn't. "I'm so sorry, Carol. I haven't been drinking with that bunch since I became a Christian. I phoned the guys a few times just to stay in touch. I'd hoped to be able to witness to them, let them see what a difference Christ had made in my life."

She didn't want to respond but needed for him to hush. "Please, I have a terrible headache. I need quiet."

"Okay, but I'm truly sorry."

She almost wished she could believe him. Wished they could have built a relationship. Wished she could live miles away from Atlanta in a town like Monticello.

❄

Nick drove home in silence, wondering what he could have done differently. Wondering how he could explain it in a way she would understand. If she would ever talk to him again.

He phoned on Sunday night, and Sandi said Carol was in bed with a headache. Same thing on Monday evening. On Tuesday Sandi told him Carol had asked her to tell him not to call anymore.

Nick did the only things he knew to do. Prayed. And worked from sunup to sundown. Worked until he was so tired he fell asleep as soon as his feet left the floor. Then awoke and did it all again. For the rest of the week. He couldn't wait for Saturday when he could drive to Atlanta again. When he could talk to her in person. When he could see her beautiful eyes of lavender blue.

A song his mother had sung to him as a child ran through his mind. It was the song he'd been humming since the day of the picnic.

> *Lavender's blue, dilly dally, lavender's green,*
> *When I am king, dilly, dally, you shall be queen.*
> *Who told you so, dilly, dally, who told you so?*
> *'Twas my own heart, dilly, dally, that told me so.*

His heart was telling him he wanted Carol to be his queen. Would she ever want him to be her king?

Chapter 8

On Saturday afternoon Carol opened the front door to find Nick staring back at her. All six feet of him. Nick. The one she'd thought of every night in spite of her resolve not to see or speak to him again.

"May I come in?" His eyes seemed darker, stormy—more green than blue today.

"I. . .we really don't have anything to say."

"Maybe you don't, but I do. I need a chance to explain."

She grabbed her cell phone off the table. "Sandi is having her study group meet here in a few minutes, so let's go for a walk."

"Good. I always think best in fresh air."

When she reached the corner she decided to head to the park. Nick matched her pace but didn't speak until they reached the green area.

He pointed to a bench by a maple tree. "Can we sit there in the shade?"

She didn't answer but crossed over and sat down.

He seated himself on the other end of the bench. "I know our encounter with my old friends upset you, and rightly so. But I'm not the same guy who used to run with them. I haven't had a drop of liquor since I became a Christian. I know God has forgiven me. Why can't you?"

"Okay. I forgive you, but I still can't stand the thought of da. . .of being with someone who has had a drinking problem. What if you go back to your old habits?"

Two young women jogged by in skimpy shorts and tank

tops. The taller one stopped and bent over, hands on her knees. "Carol Peterson, is that you?"

"Hi, Rachelle."

"Do you live around here?"

"Sandi Monk and I live in one of the condos on the other side of the park."

"Sandi? Your Miss Holier-Than-Thou roommate from the dorm? Remember how we all used to make fun of her and her down-to-her-knees skirts and up-to-her-neck blouses? I used to laugh until I cried at the parodies you would do of her clothes and—"

Carol stood. "Sandi is the dearest and truest friend I've ever had, so—"

"La-dee-dah. Any friend of Sandi's is so not a friend of mine. Call me if you come to your senses." Rachelle jogged after the other girl.

Carol watched her go, knowing what she and Rachelle had shared hadn't been a true friendship at all—just companions in ugliness and put-downs. She plopped down on the bench. "I'm sorry you had to hear all that, Nick. You of all people know I used to be like her, but I'm not anymore."

"I know." He took her hand in his. "And I'm not the person I used to be back then, either. Can you give me a chance to prove it to you?"

Shame flooded her. "I wish I could, but every time I see someone drinking it reminds me of my cousin Bill. He was paralyzed by a drunk driver his senior year of high school. He'll never walk again."

"I'm so sorry." He squeezed her hand. "Could we go visit Bill? I'd love to meet him."

She gazed into his eyes, recognizing the sincerity shining

there. Knowing he had changed as much as she had. "I know he'd love to meet you, too. I'll call him on the way back to your truck."

❄

Humming "Take Me Out to the Ball Game," Nick drove back to Monticello late that evening. He and Bill had hit it off from the start. Noticing Bill's Braves cap, Nick suggested a trip to Turner Field for the evening game. A smile big enough to melt all the ice cream at the ballpark covered Bill's face.

Nick didn't know who had enjoyed the evening more— him, Bill, or history-buff-turned-sports-fiend Carol. She'd whooped and hollered and whistled and eaten more hot dogs and popcorn than anyone else. He'd take her to all the ballgames he could this fall. Maybe even the play-offs if the Braves made it that far.

Thank you, Lord, for second chances with you and with Carol.

This day had ended so much better than it began. He could hardly wait for Carol to come to Monticello next weekend for the fall festival at the elementary school. He'd have to remember to tell Mrs. Bellingham to stay clear of the school that evening, and he'd have to take Carol to church somewhere else on Sunday morning.

Could he keep two of the most important people in his life apart from each other for the next three months?

❄

Friday evening Carol put the car on cruise as soon as she got on I-20, afraid she would go way over the speed limit if she didn't. She hadn't been to a fall festival since her own elementary years. Cotton candy and games and a cakewalk.

But she had to admit the person she would be attending with was the real draw.

Warmth filled her heart as she drove through the center of Monticello. Big Chic's windows and green awnings winked at her like an old friend. An older man sitting on a bench across from the courthouse waved as she drove past. She returned the wave. Why couldn't she have been adopted into a family who lived here? A friendly place with friendly people.

After parking next to the old barn in back of the Warren House Bed and Breakfast, she grabbed her overnight bag from the backseat. She hoped she'd get the room she'd requested. The one with the high four-poster bed and the little bed step.

Closing the door to her room and depositing her bag on the floor, she drew a deep breath and allowed all the worries of the past week to melt away. Banishing thoughts of term papers and tests, she concentrated on spending the next two days with Nick.

God had certainly worked big changes in both their hearts the past few years. She was no longer the selfish rich kid who went along with her snobbish crowd.

Nick had changed from a fraternity guy with a drinking problem into a hardworking farm manager. And he had the muscles and physique to prove his work ethic. Plus the dreamiest eyes she'd ever seen.

Ring. Ring.

She scampered down the steps.

Opening the door revealed the guy of her daydreams. "Hi, come on in."

He entered, hands behind his back.

"What are you hiding, Nick Powers?"

"Nothing." He handed her two boxes of popcorn and then drew two bottles of pop out of his jeans back pockets. Next, a DVD case out of his jacket.

"What movie did you bring?"

"*Facing the Giants*. Have you seen it?"

"Yes, but it's one of those rare ones good enough to watch again."

"I hoped you would think so. Did you know it was produced by a small church a couple hours south of here in Albany, Georgia?"

"Yes, our singles' group at church watched it a couple months ago. Very inspiring."

"I agree. Oh, I almost forgot." He pulled two chocolate bars from his shirt pocket. "Now we can get started."

Carol laughed. "Mr. Prepared has thought of everything."

❄

As Carol waited for Nick to pick her up on Saturday afternoon, her mind drifted back to the previous evening. Nick had certainly thought of everything. Everything except kissing her good night. Would he tonight? Did he not want to kiss her as much as she wanted to be kissed by him?

The doorbell rang. She loved the sound of the old-fashioned bell. She grabbed her purse and opened the door. "I'm ready."

"Are you hungry for chili and peanut butter crackers?"

"It sounds delicious, and I am so ready to be a kid again." *Or maybe to savor a piece of the childhood I missed.* "I want to toss the beanbags and tour the haunted house and maybe even win a goldfish."

Nick shook his head. "A goldfish?"

"A girl can dream, can't she?"

"Let's go. I wouldn't want to keep a girl from her dreams."

The evening played out like a movie. They played several games, ate the best chili she'd ever had, and then played some more. Nick kept buying tickets by the roll, and she kept spending them.

A child-sized basketball goal came into view. Nick pointed. "I think I'll try to win a prize at that one."

He shot the first ball and made it; then the next two also went straight in.

Carol placed her hand over her heart. "Nothing but net!"

The parent running the game stepped forward. "You got all three, so you can have your choice of a grand prize—a live goldfish or a ring for your girl."

"He wants the ring," Carol blurted out, surprising herself and, by the expression on his face, also surprising Nick.

The guy deposited a faux pearl ring in Nick's palm. "The lovely lady knows best."

Nick turned to Carol. Taking her left hand, he slid it on her ring finger, crimping it a little where the two pieces of metal met in the back. "For my lovely lady."

Carol didn't think the night could get any better until Nick walked her to the front door of the bed-and-breakfast.

Taking her hands in his, he twirled the ring around her finger. "I've never had this much fun at a fall festival before."

She studied the deep pools of his eyes. "Me either."

"And I've never given a girl a ring before."

Silence. Except for the pounding of her heart on her eardrums. He leaned toward her. His breath caressed her ear, her nose. Her eyes drifted shut. His soft, warm lips touched hers for a millisecond and then drew back. "Good night, Carol."

Chapter 9

Nick traveled the now-familiar road between Monticello and Atlanta—the same path he'd driven the past five weekends. He and Carol had enjoyed walking all over Atlanta in the beautiful fall weather. They had toured more historic sites and taken Bill to another Braves game. Even gone fishing. And spent countless hours with his aunt and uncle and cousins. They had all accepted Carol as part of their family.

His phone played "Georgia on My Mind." The ringtone he'd programmed in for Carol—the Georgia peach who constantly occupied his mind. "Hello."

"Hi, Nick. I'm still at the library doing research. Can you pick me up, and we'll go to Aunt Molly's from here?"

"It should take me twenty to thirty minutes to get there."

"Okay. I'll meet you in front of the university bookstore in half an hour."

He kept his eyes on the growing traffic, glad he didn't have to drive through this madhouse every day. His stomach lurched at the reminder of the conversation he'd had with one of his college professors, who thought he could help him procure an assistant's position if he wanted to come back to work on his master's degree.

A few months ago he would have laughed at the guy. But now, with the uncertainty of his job, and not knowing if Carol would find work in this area or somewhere else, he knew he had to look at some of the possibilities. And he needed to find out what Carol planned to do. What he planned to do.

The traffic thinned as he got through the downtown section. Pulling into University Circle in front of the Mercer campus, he thought of the many times he'd passed this place when he'd attended Emory. And how much his life had changed since then.

He pulled up to the curb outside the bookstore and let down his window. "Going my way?"

Carol flashed her gazillion-watt smile as she slid into the car. "Sure. Especially if you're on the way to Aunt Molly and Uncle Rick's house."

"Now they're your aunt and uncle, huh?" *If we married, they would be her aunt and uncle for real.* Now where had that thought originated?

"Yep. They told me to call them that when I picked up Aunt Molly for a book club meeting on Wednesday."

"So you and Aunt Molls have a lot in common?"

"She knows more about Atlanta and its history than I could ever hope to."

Smart girl and gorgeous to boot.

Carol turned on his CD player and hummed along to a Toby Mac song. They drove in silence, punctuated by her singing the chorus. Every time. If only she could carry a tune. Her one flaw.

As he parked the truck in front of Uncle Rick's house, his twin teen cousins ran out.

Kati opened Carol's door.

Kaci reached in and pulled Carol out. "What took you all so long? We've got dates, and we need your help deciding what to wear."

The three of them hurried into the house, leaving Nick

at the curb alone.

His uncle stepped out of the garage. "Feeling like a kid waiting to be picked for the team?"

"Something like that. I remember when they used to greet me and drag me into the house."

Uncle Rick rubbed his chin. "Me, too. But at least you know they approve of your choice in girlfriends. As do your aunt and I. You've both changed a lot since that summer you helped me work on her pool." He patted Nick on the shoulder. "We'll be outnumbered, but let's go see what the girls are up to."

"Joe and Jay not around?"

"Nope, they have dates, too. Soon Molly and I will be some of those empty-nesters." He elbowed Nick. "Until you and the rest of 'em make us grandparents."

Nick didn't know what to say, so he continued on their walk to the house.

Aunt Molly stood at the stove, spoon in hand, her ample form covered by her perpetual white apron. "Come on over here, and give me some sugar, Nicky."

She was the only one who could get away with calling him the name she'd used ever since he came to live with them at the age of ten when his own parents died in a car accident. Nick planted a big smooch on her cheek. "How's my girl?"

His aunt raised an eyebrow and the wooden spoon. "Which one do you mean?"

"You, of course."

She grinned and lowered the spoon back into the pot. "Right answer. I'm doing fine now you and Carol are here. This old woman is too worn out to help teens get all gussied up for a date."

"You'll never be old, Aunt Molls. You're like a fine antique—more valuable every day."

"Maybe so, but it was easier raising the boys in my younger days than these two girls."

The thundering on the steps told of the approach of the twins. Carol followed them down at a more sedate pace.

He gave her a hug while glancing at his cousins. "Looks like you did a pretty good job with them. Considering what you had to start with."

Kaci whipped a tube of lipstick out of her purse. "Maybe Carol would like to see what you look like with makeup on."

"Oh no. You only succeeded the first time because I was sound asleep on the couch. And you had a passel of other girls to help." He looked to his aunt. "Why didn't you warn me what went on at girls' slumber parties?"

"We girls stick together. Right, Carol?"

"Right. Here, let me stir the soup for a while, and you rest your feet." Carol took the spoon and nudged his aunt in the direction of the kitchen table.

The girls' nervous dates came in to meet their parents. After they'd left, Nick glanced at his uncle. "You always did keep all of us kids scared of you both."

Uncle Rick raised his eyebrows a couple of times, Groucho Marx-style. "It worked, didn't it?"

"Sure did. I wouldn't be a college graduate today if you two hadn't made me go back that first semester when I wanted to chuck it all."

"Nope. You'd probably still be cleaning pools." He winked at Carol. "But you can meet some pretty nice people doing that."

Carol laughed. "Anybody ready for some soup? The aroma is making my stomach talk to me."

Nick retrieved four bowls from the white Hoosier cabinet that had graced his aunt's kitchen as long as he could remember. "I'm ready." He handed the bowls to Carol and then added some spoons, napkins, and crackers to the table.

His uncle poured four glasses of iced tea from a pitcher; then they all sat down and linked hands. Uncle Rick's familiar voice intoned, "Bless these gifts to the nourishment of our bodies and our bodies to Your service. Through Christ our Lord."

They all joined in on the "Amen."

For a few moments the only sound was the clanking of spoons against bowls.

Carol wiped her mouth with a napkin. "This vegetable soup is the best I ever tasted. May I have the recipe?"

"I could tell you what's in it tonight, but I never make it the same twice. It's just whatever is in the fridge or freezer with whatever kind of meat I have on hand."

"Maybe I can help you make it next time and learn how."

"We'll do that. But first we'd better be making some plans for Thanksgiving. It'll be here in a couple weeks."

Nick rubbed his middle. "Thanksgiving. Words to thrill a man's stomach."

Uncle Rick looked at Carol. "We want you to celebrate Thanksgiving with us, so check with your parents, and see when you can work us in your schedule. We'll plan our meal around yours."

Carol's eyes glistened with tears. "That's so sweet, but no need to work around it. They probably won't be back from their trip by then. We don't usually make a fuss over

Thanksgiving." Her gaze fell to her lap.

Aunt Molly stood and uncovered the cake box, revealing Nick's favorite—German chocolate. "Anybody got room for some cake?"

"I do, and I'll eat anyone else's share, too. You do have vanilla ice cream, don't you?"

❄

Carol dropped onto the couch in the living room of the condo. Today had been tiring, but special. Like all her days spent with Nick. Very special.

She glanced at the flickering red light on her answering machine and then leaned over to push the button.

"Carol, it's Mother. Your father and I wanted you to know we'll be home for a couple weeks the end of November before we leave for our Christmas cruise. We've told Thelma to air out the house and plan to cook a big turkey dinner on Thanksgiving Day. See you then—at seven sharp." The silence at the end of the message burned into her brain. A short message and then silence. For days or weeks. Typical communication from her parents.

She speed-dialed Nick.

"Already miss me?" His chuckle sent goose bumps up and down her arms.

I do. "Yes, but I'm also calling to tell you we'll have to do lunch at Aunt Molly and Uncle Rick's on Thanksgiving. My parents left a message while I was out. They're going to be home that week and want me there at seven." *Sharp.* "And I want you to go with me."

"Are you sure?"

"Yes. We can go straight from Aunt Molly's house to my parents'."

"Want to make any other plans for the rest of the weekend?"

"Better see how this goes first." The last few times she'd seen her parents had ended in disaster.

Chapter 10

Carol pulled on her dress jeans and topped them with a white shirt and a bright-red blazer. She grabbed a long black skirt on a hanger to change into for dinner. Her mother would think it improper to wear jeans to dinner anywhere. But Aunt Molly wouldn't care.

Nick's special knock of two shorts and three longs greeted her ears. She liked to imagine he was thinking, "Car–ol, I love you."

Running down the stairs, she flung open the door and hugged him, skirt and all.

He grinned. "Can I knock and come in again?"

She pulled him into the living room. "No, but you'll get another hug as soon as I empty my arms." She dropped the skirt on the couch and made good on her promise.

Drawing her closer, he added a kiss. And another kiss.

Hating to stop but knowing they'd better, Carol released her hold.

Nick, always the gentleman, followed her lead. "Anything I can carry?"

"Two pies in the white container on the counter."

"Yum. What kind?"

"One's a pumpkin, and the other is a recipe Sandi and I came up with. We love chocolate chip cookies and pecan pie, so combined them into chocolate chip pecan pie."

"Can I have a piece now?"

"No, but you can grab the whipped topping out of the refrigerator."

"Got it. Ready to go?"

"Uh-huh." She held the door for him, grabbed her skirt and purse, and followed him to the truck.

As he pulled the truck into drive, he turned to her. "Oh, I forgot to tell you."

"What?" She held her breath. Was he going to cancel going with her later? How many times had her parents disappointed her when they had something "more important" to do?

He shot her a sideways not-a-care-in-the-world smile. "Happy Thanksgiving."

She blew out her breath. "Happy Thanksgiving to you, too."

Fiddling with the radio, she finally found a station without Christmas music. "I love Christmas songs, but I want to at least wait until tomorrow to start."

"I agree."

Nick drummed out the rhythm on his steering wheel. They made a good duet. A good couple.

When they parked in front of Aunt Molly's house, the twins came running to greet them.

Kaci opened her door. "We're so glad you're here, Carol."

"Happy Thanksgiving." Kati shut the door and looped elbows with Carol.

She looked over her shoulder. Nick had her skirt folded over one arm and the food stacked in the other. He looked like a snow lady with a black skirt and a white toboggan on top. "Need some help?"

His reply was swallowed up in the noise once she entered the kitchen. "Happy Thanksgiving, Aunt Molly, Uncle Rick. Where are Jay and Joe?"

"Gone to get their dates. Don't know where we're gonna put all of you young'uns." Uncle Rick shook his head.

Aunt Molly swatted at him with her dish towel. "You hush now. You know you've been looking forward to this day all week."

Jay and Joe followed Nick into the room, each of them holding hands with a pretty girl.

Jay pulled his date closer. "This here is Winnie."

"And this is Sharon." Joe beamed at the girl.

Nick patted his cousins on the back. "Hi, Sharon and Winnie. I'm Nick, and this is Carol." He grabbed her hand.

"And I'm hungry," Uncle Rick bellowed, causing a round of laughter.

"Then everyone grab a dish and carry it into the dining room. The girls already set the table."

Carol grabbed some cranberry sauce and followed the procession, thinking how this meal differed from the one later at her parents' house.

"Woo-wee." Jay elbowed Joe. "I don't know which is prettier, our girls or this spread."

Joe glanced at Sharon. "No competition. The girls win hands down, but that doesn't mean I'm gonna pass up this food." He surprised Carol by holding out his date's chair before seating himself.

Jay seated Winnie, and Nick held out Carol's chair. As did Uncle Rick for Aunt Molly. *Now I know where Nick gets his gracious manners.*

Uncle Rick cleared his throat. "Our Thanksgiving tradition is to hold hands and go around the table and each person pray one thing they're thankful for. If you don't want to say it out loud, just squeeze the next person's hand. I'll start, and Nick here on my left can finish."

They bowed their heads.

Uncle Rick's voice softened. "Thank You, God, for my wonderful wife and this crowded table You've blessed us with."

Kaci continued. "Thank You for my twin that I love even when she wears my clothes like she's doing today."

Kati followed with "Thank You that Kaci and I are the same size."

Jay coughed. "Thank You for all these beautiful women around our table."

Winnie must have passed because the next voice was Aunt Molly's. "Thank You, Lord, for each precious soul around our table."

"Thank You for this food and all the good cooks in our family, even my sisters." Joe's voice cracked.

Carol felt a squeeze on her hand from Sharon, so she added her thanks. "Thank You, Lord, for letting me be a part of this big, happy family."

"Thank You, Lord, for all Your blessings. For family and food and special friends." Nick squeezed her hand as they all said, "Amen."

Nick is a special friend, but does he see me in any other way?

❄

Carol closed her eyes and leaned against the headrest as Nick drove across town to her parents' house. How different the atmosphere in the smaller house had been—warm and noisy and boisterous. All the things she'd missed growing up. A true home.

She must have dozed off because she startled when Nick stopped the truck. As she opened her eyes, she realized they sat in front of her parents' home.

Stretching, she gazed at him. "Sorry. I'm not very good company today."

"I've heard eating too much turkey makes a person sleepy." He grinned.

She punched his shoulder. "You think I ate too much turkey, huh?"

"No, but I wanted to make sure you were wide awake before we see your folks. Are you ready?"

Carol blew out a breath. "As long as you're with me. Let's go."

He walked around and helped her out of the truck. "May I escort you, my lady?"

Ensconcing her arm inside his, she felt his warmth, his strength. "Yes, indeed."

A maid in a black-and-white uniform opened the door. "Hello, Miss Carol." Her dark eyes traveled from Carol's face to Nick's and then back down again.

"Hello, Thelma."

A twinkle gleamed in the older woman's eye. "Your parents are in the drawing room. They're expecting you."

Carol led the way but didn't release Nick's arm. Her father stood in front of the fireplace, his back to them. Her mother sat erect in a wing chair.

She arose and walked to meet them and then kissed Carol on both cheeks, and Carol returned the gesture. "You should have told us you were bringing a guest, my dear." Her mother's smile didn't match her chilly voice.

"I didn't get a chance since you left a message. Mother, this is Nick Powers." She turned toward him. "Nick, my mother, Paige Peterson." Her mother gave a short nod.

Her father approached them, his eyes appraising Nick. "I didn't know we were expecting guests. Although I must say, you look familiar. Do you belong to the country club?"

Carol burned inside at the rudeness her parents were showing. "Father, this is Nick Powers. Nick, my father, Walter Peterson."

Nick extended a hand, but her father ignored it while continuing to study him.

"I know I've seen you before. Have we met?"

Nick nodded. "Yes sir. In your backyard several summers ago. I was assisting my uncle in cleaning your pool."

Her father's eyes pierced Carol with a glance.

Her mother grabbed her by the arm and pulled her into the hall, leaving the door ajar. "Carol Peterson, how dare you."

❄

Nick studied the man in front of him, but his ears focused on Carol and the tongue-lashing he couldn't help but hear.

The older woman's voice rose with each word. "A pool cleaner? How could you do this to us after all we've done for you, all we've given you?"

"Mother, I appreciate all you've done, but you've never given me what I really wanted, dearly needed—a close family and"—Carol's voice choked—"love."

"You're an ungrateful daughter. You've always been a disappointment, and—don't you run away from me, young lady."

Nick bolted from the room and followed Carol out the front door. He reached her as she dropped to a bench under an oak tree in the side yard.

Embracing her, he let her cry on his shoulder for a long

while. He stroked her silky hair and whispered, "I love you," wondering if she could hear the words above her sobs.

Finally reduced to sniffling, Carol reached into her purse and pulled out a tissue. "Pretty bad scene. I hate the rude way they treated you."

"Treated me? I don't care how they treat me, but your mother had no right to speak to you that way. Has it always been like this?"

"No. I can remember thinking I was happy as a child because the other kids told me how lucky I was to have such rich parents who bought me every new toy on the market. But as I grew older and visited other homes where the kids received more love than gifts, I realized what I was missing. Then, when I became a Christian, I truly felt that love inside for the first time. When I tried to explain it to my parents, they became defensive. That was the first time my mom called me ungrateful."

He wanted to take her back into his arms and stroke her hair and drive all those harmful words from her thoughts. Instead, he decided listening would be the best gift he could give her right now.

Bending over, she grabbed two acorns. "I used to sit on this bench and pick up acorns and name them." She studied her hands. "The larger one could be the grandpa acorn, and this little one his granddaughter. I would make them act out taking walks together and him reading stories to her. . . and all the other things my parents never did with me."

"Very creative."

"You always seem to say the right thing."

"We aim to please, ma'am." He winked.

She laughed. "So, what do we do now?"

He stood and pulled her up. "If you're hungry we can stop somewhere and get something to eat."

"I just want to get out of here."

He pointed to the truck. "Your chariot awaits. Where shall we go? Back to the Powers clan? Your condo? Monticello?"

"I'll take door number three, please."

"Monticello, here we come."

Chapter 11

Carol awoke in the now-familiar bed at the Warren House and glanced at her watch. Ten o'clock? She searched for the step with her toes and then climbed out of bed.

Throwing on what she'd worn last night, she scampered down the stairs to the dining room, thankful to find she hadn't missed breakfast. She'd had a craving for fig preserves since the last time she'd stayed here.

She smeared some on a croissant. Mmmm good.

The teapot with its cozy still held hot water, so she steeped some raspberry tea and savored it with another croissant and preserves. *Guess I'm entitled since we skipped dinner last night.* She hadn't wanted to eat after the scene with her parents.

It had been after eleven by the time they'd stopped by her condo to pack a few things and then driven to Monticello. Nick had said he would try to meet her for lunch today.

Emerging from the shower wrapped in a towel, she padded across the room to answer her cell, which was playing "William Tell's Overture" by Rossini. She'd chosen that ring-tone for Nick because he was a lone-ranger, one of the few good guys she knew.

"Good morning. Did you get your beauty sleep?"

"Sure did. You'll have to wear your shades when you pick me up."

His laughter traveled through the phone, warming her heart and making her realize how much she missed him.

149

"That's why I'm calling. I won't be able to make it for lunch. A neighbor has some horses out, and it might take a couple hours. I'll call you when I head into town, but until then, why don't you walk around a bit? It's already seventy. Might be our last day of Indian Summer."

"Sounds like a plan. See you later."

She slipped on her well-loved jean capris and an elbow-length orange blouse and then slid her feet into comfy leather walking sandals. Placing her phone in her purse, she jogged down the steps, ready to see more of her favorite town. If memory served her correctly, it was only a couple blocks' walk to the downtown area.

The temperature was perfect, not too hot or chilly. She turned right, as she had with Nick. Stopping in front of the Malone House, she whispered a promise of future help to the "grand old lady showing her age." She passed the Methodist parsonage and cemetery, amazed again at the history contained in this town.

Continuing on her way, Carol passed a dentist office and an auto-parts store. A few more steps and she reached the historic town square. She crossed to the center to study the Confederate monument again. One of the saddest times in our country's history for both sides.

Walking past the Trading Post, she remembered meeting the young-at-heart Mrs. Luke, who still ran the store at ninety-five. She entered Perry & Plummer Antiques. Maybe she could find something rare for her mother. In spite of what they thought, she did appreciate all her parents had done for her.

A distinguished-looking gentleman approached. "May I help you?"

"I hope so. I'd like to find a Christmas gift for my mother, who is one of those people who have everything."

"I see. Does she like antiques?"

"She likes anything rare enough that one of her friends doesn't have the same thing."

"Aha. Let me show you around." He extended a hand. "My name is Rod Perry."

"Oh! The Mr. Perry who owns the Warren House?"

He nodded.

She shook his waiting hand. "I'm Carol Peterson. This is my third stay at your bed-and-breakfast, and I love it. Especially the fig preserves."

The man chuckled. "I do, too. Now let's find something for your mother."

Carol left the store after purchasing an antique Sheffield talcum shaker, which Mr. Perry promised to hand deliver. She stepped out into the warm fall air.

A pang of thirst hit her. Eyeing a sign for a teashop, she walked up the bricked path and entered the door, a bell announcing her presence.

A voice from behind a door answered the ring. "Be with you in a minute."

Carol glanced around the shop. Only four tables with a couple chairs at each. How did such a small place stay in business?"

A tall, slender woman emerged from the back, wiping her hands on a clean apron edged in lace. "Hi, would you like a cup of tea?"

"Sounds lovely. And a glass of water, please."

"What flavor tea would you prefer?" The woman pointed to a colorfully decorated sign on the wall.

Carol scanned it and made a choice. "Blackberry spice, please."

"One of my favorites. You have your choice of seats, so make yourself at home. My name is Phyllis, so just holler if you need anything."

Carol sat down and glanced around the shop some more. She saw a sandwich menu but didn't want to order anything so filling in case Nick called soon.

Phyllis approached carrying a tall glass of ice water and a sheet of pink paper. "Here you go. And here's a menu in case you want anything else."

"Thanks. I'm parched after my walk around town." She took a long draw of the cool water.

Phyllis pulled out a chair and sat across from her. "I've got your water on to boil, so we have a few minutes. What brings you to Monticello?"

A long story. One that would take more than a few minutes. "I'm staying at the Warren House and visiting a friend. He had to help round up some horses this morning, so I had time to explore on my own."

"And what do you think of our little town?"

"I love it and would move here in a heartbeat." *I wish I'd been born here.*

Phyllis draped a strand of long black hair behind an ear. "It is a nice place to grow up and to raise kids. Do you have any?"

"No. I'm not married."

"I'm not married anymore, but I wouldn't trade my two kids for anything." She fished in her pocket and pulled out two small school photos. "That's Yvonne, she's in kindergarten, and Connie's in second grade."

Carol's heart melted at the joy and promise she saw in the two dark-haired cuties' faces. The youngest sported a toothless gap in the middle of her mouth. "They're beautiful. And so full of life."

"True. God has really blessed me."

A whistle went off. Phyllis arose. "The teapot's singing. I'll be right back."

Carol studied the menu and noticed some fig preserve scones. Yummy.

Phyllis carried a steaming teapot muffled in a flowery cozy. She set it on the table. "Anything else?"

"I'd love to try your fig scones if you have any left and maybe a touch of preserves to spread on them."

The waitress smiled, erasing some of the tired lines from her face. "I'll go check."

I wonder what her story is. Wish I could know her better. Maybe help out in some way.

Another customer entered the belled door as Phyllis came back with two scones and a small pot of preserves.

"Thanks." Carol smiled.

"Thank you." Phyllis scurried off to wait on the gentleman. By the time his order of four sandwiches was completed, Carol had finished. She laid a twenty on the table. "Thanks, Phyllis. I plan to stop by again sometime."

The waitress waved. "I'll look forward to it."

Carol stepped out on the street, her heart happy at making another friend in Monticello but sad because of the weariness she'd seen in the waitress's eyes and body.

Refreshed, she visited the Chamber of Commerce building, which had been closed on her last visit. She learned it was housed in the renovated Benton Mercantile store built in 1903. Monticello was a place filled with history. A place after her own heart.

As she left the building, her eyes gravitated to the sign on the side of Big Chic's. Remembering her banter with Nick about the sign, she walked to get a second look. Her phone rang. *Duh ,duh, dum, duh ,duh, dum. . .*

"Where are you?"

"Admiring the Bear-Lax sign outside Big Chic's."

"Great. Stay right there, and I'll see you in a minute."

❄

Nick admired the view of Carol admiring the sign as he walked up the sidewalk. He placed a hand on her shoulder. "So you like one of Monticello's famous tourist attractions?"

"Yes. It's part of the charm of this place."

"Want to eat at Big Chic's again?"

"I thought you'd never ask."

They entered, and when the waitress approached, Nick looked at Carol. "Want anything different?" When she shook her head no, he turned to the waitress and ordered, "Two of my usuals, please."

Carol's eyes never left his, sending a warm sensation through him. She studied him. "You don't look any worse for wear."

"I did take time to clean up a little when we got done. How was your day?"

"A wonderful Indian Summer walk as you suggested."

They ate around bits of conversation. She told him more about what she'd seen and about the young mother she'd met. "I wish I knew how to help her."

"Have you heard the song 'The Twelve Days of Christmas'?"

"Sure, do you want me to sing it for you?"

He held out his hands like two stop signs. "No, that's all right."

She chuckled. "I know I can't carry a tune in a net. I guess that's why my parents made sure I took piano lessons for twelve years."

Something else she doesn't know she shares with her grandmother. "I was thinking about a tradition Aunt Molly and Uncle Rick started years ago—choosing a person in need and giving them a gift the twelve days leading up to Christmas. Sometimes they meet their physical needs, and sometimes emotional, or spiritual, or all three."

"What a great tradition."

"Would you like to do something similar for Phyllis and her kids?"

"I'd love to. Where do we start?"

"First, we need to make a list of possible items to give each day. Then we have to figure out how to surprise them. When do you get out of school?"

"December thirteenth."

"So you could be here on the fourteenth to help deliver the first gift?"

"I think so, but it might be hard for me to stay here for all twelve days."

He wished she could stay with her grandmother, but since he'd promised Mrs. Bellingham not to tell, that wouldn't work. "I don't think it will be a problem. Some of the things we can have delivered by the florist, the grocery, or a friend. In fact, let's go talk to my friend who is a minister. I'm sure he'll know how to help."

Chapter 12

C arol drove back to Atlanta on Sunday morning, her heart much lighter than when she'd traveled this same road a couple days earlier.

As she sat in church, a skit about giving being the reason for the season brought joy to her heart as a confirmation that she was doing the best thing. Instead of feeling sorry for herself, she would choose to make someone else's Christmas brighter, which also lifted her own spirits. A win-win situation.

On the way home from church, she and Sandi decided to pick up Chinese. Carol couldn't wait to tell Sandi their plans.

Sandi set out plates and napkins. "Spill the beans or rice or whatever. I can see in your eyes something's up."

"Yes, and I need your help." Carol opened her chopsticks and attempted to pick up a piece of General Tso's chicken and place it in her mouth. "Nick and I have adopted a family in Monticello. We're going to take or send them a gift each of the twelve days leading up to Christmas."

"A super idea. How can I help?"

"We want each day's gift to somehow go along with the song. Like on the first day instead of taking a partridge in a pear tree, we plan to take a Christmas tree with a bird's nest in it for good luck. The second day, we're going to leave two live turtles in bowls for the two children. The third day, three frozen turkeys so they'll have one for Christmas and two to stretch their groceries in the new year."

Sandi bounced up and down on the couch. "I love it! What's for the fourth day?"

"Four poinsettias."

"And the fifth?"

"We're stumped there. Can you think of anything kids would like with golden rings?"

Sandi's face scrunched up. "Not really. What else do you have planned?"

"The only other one we're sure of is to deliver twelve gifts on Christmas morning."

Her roommate hugged her so tight she could barely breathe. "This is going to be the best Christmas ever!"

The best Christmas ever. How true. And in all this excitement she'd almost forgotten—on Christmas morning she would meet her three birth sisters. What could be better?

❄

Nick counted the buzzes as he waited for Carol to answer her phone. . .three. . .four. . . . *Pick up, Carol. This is too important to leave in a message.*

She answered on the fifth buzz. "How's my Christmas elf today?"

"I think I've got the gift for day five figured out. How about one of those backyard play-gyms with five rings for the girls to exercise on? Plus the slide and swings to go with it."

"Perfect. Unless you think it's over our budget. I know you said you wanted to pay half of everything, but if it's a problem—"

"No problem. I only have my aunt and uncle and four cousins to buy for." And a certain lovely lady. "Besides, buying for kids is much more fun."

"Any other ideas?"

"How about three jackets and three pillows for day six—all filled with goose down, of course."

"You must be wearing your creative hat today. Oh, oh—"

"Did you hurt yourself?"

"No, silly. Your idea sparked one in me for day eight. How about eight milk products—cheese, ice cream, yogurt—anything that contains milk. Think that would work?"

"Yep. As long as we include milk chocolate."

"I love the way you think."

That was the closest she had come to saying she loved him. Of course, he hadn't said it aloud either, except that night in her parents' yard. Which he doubted she even heard. "Only seven, nine, ten, and eleven to go."

"Piece of cake."

"You want to give them that many pieces of cake? Now who's being silly?"

"Ha-ha. How about on the eleventh day we send eleven other grocery items to go with the turkey—potatoes, stuffing mix, and more. I'm sure we can figure out the rest."

"Yep. Working together we can do anything."

"We do make a good team."

I'd like to make us a permanent team.

❄

The morning of December fourteenth, Carol packed up most of her belongings to take to her parents' home until she found a job after the holidays.

Sandi bounced down the steps, dropping her load of shoeboxes. "I thought of an idea for day ten."

"Shoot."

"How about ten ten-dollar bills? So the mother can get whatever she needs for her or the kids."

"I love it, and I bet Nick will, too. I can't wait to tell him tonight." *And I can't wait to see him tonight.* The past two weeks had been the longest they'd been apart. She'd had several projects to finish, so they'd settled for burning up the phone lines instead. This short separation had shown her how much she would miss him when she got a job and perhaps had to move to another area of the country.

He'd felt bad about not being there to help her move, but she'd assured him she was only hauling personal items like clothing. Just enough to make a space for Sandi's new roomie.

Carol pulled Sandi into a hug. "I'm going to miss you like a sister. And even though I'll soon meet my birth sisters, no one can ever take your special place in my life. You led me to Jesus, so we are sisters in the most important way."

Sandi's eyes glistened. "Yep. Sisters forever and eternity."

Carol soon had her car packed to the ceiling.

After an uneventful trip, she pulled into the circular drive in front of her parents' house, a pang of regret sweeping over her—regret for what had never been.

Walking into the empty house, she tripped over a box. Stooping to pick it up, she saw a card lying beside it.

Her heart hammered in her chest. She steeled herself to open the card. What if her parents said more hurtful words? What if they wanted nothing to do with her? Ever again?

Unfolding the sheet of parchment paper released her mother's signature scent, the perfume she'd worn as long as Carol could remember, evoking remembrances of happier days. Days when she'd pleased her parents, made them proud of her.

She dropped her gaze to the lovely script on the cream colored page.

Our dearest Carol,

Your father and I want you to know how sorry we are for the scene we caused on Thanksgiving. We never gave you and your young man a chance. We want you to bring him back as soon as we return in January, and we promise it will be different then. We thought of canceling our trip but didn't want to infringe on your meeting with your biological siblings. They are welcome in our home anytime, even to live here if you want.

You have always been the bright spot in our lives, even when we didn't know how to show it. Growing up as only children ourselves, we never learned how to interact with other children, even our own precious daughter. We have been doing some soul searching and hope you can find it in your heart to forgive us and give us a second chance. And we hope you love your gift, which is the best thing we thought we could give you to make you happy.

Love always, your parents

Tears streamed down Carol's face and onto the letter, causing the ink to blur. She blotted it with a fingertip, not wanting to erase any of the loving words from her mother.

Sitting on the bottom step, she sent up a prayer of thanks to her heavenly Father for placing her in this particular family and working all things for good.

She picked up the gift and studied it. Wrapped in beautiful red foil paper with an exquisite silver bow, it weighed hardly anything. Another piece of expensive jewelry like she'd received on countless birthdays and Christmases? But why had they thought this gift would make her happy?

Unwrapping the paper, she opened the lid on the box to find another single sheet of the vellum stationery. The same scent tickled her imagination. She unfolded it with gentle hands. A border had been drawn around the outside edge, making it look like a gift certificate of some sort.

> *This certificate entitles the bearer to invite her parents to church again as she did so long ago. This certificate also promises that said parents will accept the invitation each and every time it is extended. And said parents will love the bearer until the day they die.*

In the corner in tiny script she read, expiration date—never.

Carol had thought this Christmas couldn't get any better than the happiness of helping the young mom and her family and meeting her own sisters. But this gift from her parents filled her with even greater joy, a joy that could last for all eternity.

For the first time ever she looked forward to a joyous Christmas. And a big part of her joy was Nick Powers, the man she would see in a few short hours when they did their first Christmas delivery.

Chapter 13

Carol parked by the old barn again, eager to meet up with Nick that evening. He'd shared her joy when she phoned him about her parents and their letter and gift. And he said he would be praying for them, which melted her heart.

He also relayed that he'd cut and mounted the Christmas tree on a stand. She loved when he added that he'd hunted for over an hour to find one with a bird's nest in it. Not that she believed in luck but because she wanted their gifts to match the song.

Unpacking her suitcase since she planned to stay for three days this time, she found her Bible and searched the concordance for verses about gifts to include with each day's surprise. For tonight she chose James 1:17. Perfect. They wanted this young family to know who was the true Giver.

She dressed warmly against the colder temperatures, covering herself in black to keep from being seen. Her heart beat faster than the twelve drummers drumming. Was it the anticipation of their surprise or the excitement of seeing Nick and spending time again with him?

Nick arrived at seven. Also dressed in black down to his ski mask and gloves, he pulled another ski mask from his pocket. "I love the golden streaks in your hair, but we need to cover it tonight."

"Thanks." He'd used the word *love* again. This time about her hair. Would he ever say he loved her? She took the mask and pulled it over her hair, only leaving her eyes, nose, and mouth uncovered.

When she turned to face him, he kissed her on the tip of her nose. "You sure make a cute burglar."

"I guess that's better than a cat burglar."

"I'm allergic to cats, so I'm glad you're not one."

"Me, too." She had a lot to learn about this man, but she already knew the important things like his love for God and others.

He helped her into the truck.

"Thanks." She looked at the tree, which filled up most of the truck bed. "It's beautiful, so full and green."

Nick hummed and then began to sing, "Lavender's blue, dilly dally. Lavender's green." His eyes locked on hers. "I've been humming that song ever since we met again this fall. I see your lovely lavender blue eyes every night when I go to sleep and when I awake in the morning." He moved closer to her. "But tonight, in the dark, your eyes look lavender green."

"Maybe it's the reflection from the tree." *Me and my wise mouth. Right when he might have kissed me.*

He scooted back to his side and started up the truck. "Maybe."

The young mom's home was only a few blocks from the Warren House. They drove the dark streets in silence. Nick shut off the engine and coasted to a stop two doors down in his minister friend's drive.

"Stay warm inside until I get it untied." He hopped out of the truck and spent a couple minutes unloading the tree and then brought it around to her door. He tapped on the door—two shorts and three longs.

She slid out beside him. "Can I help?"

"I've got the heavy end. You get the top of the tree."

"Okay." The light-brown bird nest near the top glowed in the moonlight. She wished she could be inside when the children noticed it.

They quietly situated the tree on the small front porch. Nick motioned her to go on and hide behind the neighbor's bushes. As she did, she heard the sound of a doorbell and then felt two strong arms around her as he slid into place beside her.

The front door opened. A child's high-pitched voice hollered out, "Mom, come look what's on our porch."

Another child began to clap. "It's a Cwismas tree, a Cwismas tree."

Phyllis stood on the porch, her arms around each child protectively.

The older girl pointed up. "Look, Mom, a card."

The young mother picked off the note and read, "Every good and perfect gift is from above, coming down from the Father of the heavenly lights." Her gaze searched the yard, and Carol could see the woman's tears glistening. "God sent us this gift through His helpers."

"Like Santa's elves?" asked the younger child.

"Only better." Phyllis motioned to the taller girl. "Connie, if you get hold of the treetop and pull, I think I can get the rest of the tree inside."

The shorter child began to jump up and down. "Can we decowate it tonight? Pwease?"

"Yes, honey. God has given us this tree, and we will decorate it to be the prettiest one on the block. I'll even pop some popcorn and teach you. . ." The mom's words faded as the door closed on the happy family.

Carol lifted one gloved hand to wipe at the moisture in

her own eyes. Surprised to find her other hand warmly held in Nick's, she wondered when and how it had gotten there. Although he might not know it, he also held her heart. She loved him.

※

Nick loved the wonder on the faces of the two young girls and the joy and pleasure he read on Carol's face. *I love Carol Peterson. Now what am I going to do about it?*

I told her once—why can't I tell her again? Do I not think I'm good enough for her? When they were teens that had certainly been part of the problem. He knew one thing for sure. He had a lot of praying to do tonight.

As he prayed in bed that evening, God's Spirit convicted him of having the same skewed thinking Carol's parents possessed. They thought he wasn't good enough for their daughter. He'd believed that, too, as a teen. That had been one of the reasons he'd pushed himself so hard in college and afterward, to prove to them, to the world, that Nick Powers was important, that he had what it took to succeed.

He realized he had another sin to confess. Pride. Pride in what he'd done, instead of what God had done in his life. God had led him to the Bellingham Plantation, had led him to Mrs. B, so she could tell him the story of Jesus, had led him and Carol back together when they were both ready for a relationship. One built on Christ and His principles.

He confessed his sins, asked for forgiveness, and fell into a deep sleep.

When the alarm went off at five thirty, he hopped out of bed and headed to the shower. He couldn't wait to see Carol again, to see the children's reactions to the turtles, to live life to the fullest every moment of every day.

❄

Nick headed out the door, carrying two turtles and two bowls.

A bundle of black met him when he stopped at the Warren House. One black arm revealed a hooked thumb. She mouthed, "I'm freezing."

He slid across to open her door. "What are you doing out here?"

"I was too excited to sleep. I can't wait to tell you the verse for today. It came to me while I was trying to go to sleep last night."

"And?"

"You're going to love it. It's from Genesis, chapter seven. 'Pairs of all creatures that have the breath of life in them... entered the ark.' But I crossed out ark and wrote bowls."

He chuckled. "You're right. I do love it. And the kids will, too. I'm sure they know the story of Noah and the ark."

They followed the same procedure as the evening before—donning gloves and ski masks and then placing the bowls with turtles on the stoop, ringing the doorbell, and scrambling for the bushes.

This time all three of the family members answered the door. No one saw anything until the youngest glanced down. "Look, Mommy. Jesus' helpers have been here again."

The older girl lifted up a turtle in a bowl. "Can I have this one?"

"And I want this one." The younger one looked up at her mother. "This is like the counting books my teacher reads us at school. First we got one Cwismas tree, now we got two turtles. I wonder what we'll get free of tomorrow?"

"Let's not expect anything, so we can be surprised." The mom read the note and verse and smiled. "Let's get the two turtles and you two girls in where it's warm, and I'll share another Bible verse with you."

Nick and Carol remained in the bushes for a few more minutes, until the pinkish-gray light of a winter's dawn began to streak the sky. She started to rise, but he pulled her back down. Her eyes were aglow with the excitement of helping others, making him love her more than ever.

He looked deep into those eyes he loved so much. This wasn't the time or place, but he couldn't hide his feelings any longer. "Carol, I didn't plan to do this here, but I can't wait another minute to tell you. I love you. I have for a long time, and I hope you love me, too."

Her gloved hands cupped his cheeks. "Oh, Nick, I love you, too. I mean really love you, not just the attraction we shared as teenagers." She winked. "Although that is part of it, too."

He laughed. "That's good to hear." He leaned forward and kissed her lips, or at least as much of them as he could through two ski masks. "Let's go somewhere we can take off these masks."

"We'd better hurry. It's almost daylight." She stood. "Race you."

They ran to his truck, each touching the hood at the same time.

Carol raced to open her own door. "We've got to make a quick getaway. The neighbors are starting to leave for work."

"Where do you want to go for breakfast, my partner-in-Christmas-crime?"

"I asked Judy if it would be all right if you joined me for breakfast at the B and B. She said it would be fine. And I bet you'll love the croissants and fig preserves."

"Sounds good." *I'll love anyplace with you.*

Chapter 14

With sadness mixed with anticipation, Carol packed her car to travel back to Atlanta for a few days. Although she hated to leave Nick and hated to miss the excitement of seeing the family with their presents each morning, she knew she had to go. She needed to do some shopping for Nick and his family and Sandi. And the family in Monticello. Plus her three sisters. Whom she would meet in nine more days.

Thank You, God, for all the friends and family You've blessed me with. More than I could have ever imagined.

That reminded her of another of her favorite verses. She'd had so much fun searching for the right verse for each day's gift. They had watched as the grocer delivered three frozen turkeys the day before and heard the youngest girl call out, "I knew it would be free things!"

Today the florist would deliver four poinsettias. And tomorrow Nick and some of the other church members would build the girls their own jungle gym in their backyard, complete with a tower, swings, a slide, and five rings to hang from.

She knew Nick and his buddies would handle the remaining gifts until she returned for the last three days leading up to Christmas. How she looked forward to being in Monticello. And to meeting her sisters on the twenty-fifth. Her birthday. Their birthday. She planned to get them each two gifts. She hadn't liked it when someone only gave her a combination Christmas/birthday gift, so she wouldn't do that to them.

There was a lot to do in the next six days. Good thing she'd decided to wait until after the holidays to search for a job.

❄

Nick and his friends stowed the last pieces of scrap lumber in their trucks as the school bus rumbled down the street, stopping a block away. "Saddle up, everyone. Thanks for all the help."

After the other guys departed, Nick rolled down his window and slid down in the seat with his cowboy hat over his head.

The two girls skipped past him.

Their mom, who had been told by the minister about the surprise, met them in front of the house. "I need you all to come with me to the backyard before we go in."

Hands joined, the three walked around the house.

Nick could tell the instant they saw the playhouse/gym because their hands fell, and they stared at their mom like they were dreaming.

"It's Cinderella's castle."

"Or maybe Rapunzel's." The older girl pointed. "Look, Yvonne, count how many rings to swing on."

"Five, five, five." Yvonne jumped up and down. "I knew it would be five." She took her sister's hand. "Let's go play."

"Okay, Mom?"

"Okay. I'll make some hot chocolate to warm you up when you come in later."

"With marshmallows?"

"Of course."

The mom waved to Nick and then entered the house.

He drove off, thinking of how much he needed to do before Carol came back in five days, and of how much he would miss her until then. He hoped they would never have to be apart again after this Christmas.

❄

Nick crossed days six, seven, eight, and nine off his list. He had the ten crisp, new ten-dollar bills in a Christmas card in his pocket ready to deliver tomorrow morning. They would have eleven food items delivered by the grocer on the eleventh day, and Carol had shopped for and wrapped twelve gifts to deliver on Christmas morning, four apiece. She'd said she could judge their sizes after seeing the family several times.

Now, all he needed to do was go to the post office to pick up the gift he'd ordered online for Carol.

He'd given Mrs. B her gift yesterday, although the sweet older lady had insisted his keeping her secret was the best gift he could have given her. Until he told her what he had planned for Carol on Christmas. Then she'd insisted that gift was the best. And insisted he take one of the family heirlooms since Carol was part of her family.

Driving past the Warren House, he noticed Carol's car parked in the back. He stopped and rang the bell.

She opened the door, a harried look on her face.

"What a nice surprise to see you in town so early."

"Uh, this is a surprise. I didn't expect you until seven."

Her words caused him to pause. "Okay. Should I leave and come back at seven?" What was going on here?

She grabbed him by the arm and pulled him inside. "Of course not." She kissed him, the first time she'd ever initiated a kiss.

The kiss rocked his boat and truck and tractor, and he drew her closer, never wanting to let go.

She slid down from her tiptoes, breaking contact.

"I'd be happy to leave and come back several times if that's the reception I'm going to get."

She swatted him with a potholder. "You'd better be good, or you might not get the supper I'm preparing for you."

"Supper? I thought I'd take you out to Big Chic's."

"I love Big Chic's, but I had something more private in mind."

He sniffed the air. "Do I smell something burning?"

"Oh no." Carol ran to the kitchen.

Following her, he noticed the dining room set with china and fresh flowers. The kitchen counters were covered with pots and pans of all sizes. "Looks pretty fancy. Is all this for me and you?"

She nodded, a tear trickling down her cheek. "All except the strawberry glaze for the cheesecake, which I just burned."

He wiped her tear with his thumb. "I like plain cheesecake better anyway."

She leaned against him, and he got a whiff of the citrus-scented shampoo he loved. "You're a pretty bad liar."

"I'd rather be a bad liar than a good liar."

The corners of her mouth tweaked up into a smile. "You're too distracting. If you want anything to eat, you'd better get out of here and come back at seven as planned."

He began to back out of the kitchen, not wanting to lose sight of her. "I shall return."

❈

On the morning of the twenty-third, Carol waited on the curb for Nick. The candlelight dinner had exceeded her expectations. Even the cheesecake—which Nick kept insisting was the best ever.

When he pulled up, she let herself in and buckled up. "Hungry?"

"I couldn't eat a bite after our feast last night. A feast for my stomach, my soul, and my eyes." He wiggled his eyebrows at her.

She swatted at him with her ski mask. "I bet you say that to charm all the girls."

"Nope. Just you."

He parked down the street, and they deposited the Christmas card with the cash on the porch and ran to their usual hiding place.

The whole family appeared again. When the younger child saw the envelope, her lower lip drooped. "I thought it would be ten somethings today."

Opening the card, the older girl handed it to her mom. A bill fell to the ground.

The younger child scooped it up and shouted, "It's a ten-dollar bill."

Phyllis folded back the card and counted the money. "It's ten ten-dollar bills."

"Ten times ten is one hundred, right?" the older girl asked. "So does that mean we have one hundred dollars?" Her eyes grew as big as the poinsettia blooms.

"Yes, it does, and I'll tell you what we're going to do with it. We're going to put one of the bills in church on Sunday, give one away to someone else who needs it, and use the rest to pay our gas bill."

"Aw. You mean we don't get to keep any of it?" The lower lip came out again.

Her mom stooped down to the little girl's level. "We should be thankful for money to keep our heat on this winter. And enough to put in church and to share."

"Like the people who are doing this share with us?"

Her mom nodded.

"Okay, then I want to share our money and be like them, 'cause they make me happy. Now we get to make other people happy. Right?"

"Right." She placed her arms around her daughters. "I am so proud of you both. Let's go on in and decide who needs ten dollars more than us."

Chapter 15

Nick couldn't believe Christmas Day had finally arrived. He stopped in front of the B and B and rang the now-familiar bell.

Carol opened the door, a package spilling out of her arms.

Judging from the gaily wrapped boxes, Carol had been in her element shopping for Phyllis and her girls. "Did you leave anything for the other customers?"

"A few things. Did you get the bikes?"

"Yep. They're already loaded." He started picking up boxes to carry out. "Who is that other sack of presents for?"

She winked. "One might be for you, and the rest are for my sisters."

"I thought you only had three sisters."

"I do, but they have to receive two each—one for Christmas and one for our birthday."

Thanks to Mrs. B, he had two gifts for Carol. "Speaking of birthdays, happy birthday to the sweetest girl of all. And I do have two gifts for you, too, but they're wrapped together. Do you want them now or after we deliver these presents?"

"Later. I can't wait to see the kids' expressions when they see their bikes and all the other gifts."

"Me either." *And I can't wait to watch you open yours.*

After a couple trips, the truck was loaded, and they drove the familiar blocks.

Each gathered up an armful of boxes then approached the house. As they set down the presents, they noticed a plate of decorated Christmas cookies with a note.

Carol read the note and began to cry. Nick slid it out of her hands, hoping and praying nothing was wrong. It read:

> *Dear Jesus' helpers, we so much appreciate all your gifts, so we wanted to share some of our Christmas cookies with you—cookies made with the flour, butter, sugar, and eggs you provided. We also wanted to share our mom's favorite Bible verse about the greatest gift of all. "Thanks be to God for his indescribable gift" (2 Corinthians 9:15).*
>
> *Love, Phyllis, Yvonne, and Connie*

Nick swiped at his own eyes and then lifted the plate of cookies and took Carol by the hand to go back for the bicycles. When they reached the truck, he whispered, "What's wrong?"

She sniffled. "Nothing. Did you read the verse?"

"Yes, it's one of my favorites, but why are you crying?"

She lifted the card she'd taped to one of the bicycles.

He read it and then looked at her, amazed. Carol had chosen the same verse. "A God-incidence?"

"Definitely. Only He could have so perfectly orchestrated everything."

They rolled the bikes to the edge of the porch. Carol waved Nick to go first, so he hid in the bushes while she rang the bell and ran.

She snuggled in next to him as the children oohed and aahed over the bikes and other boxes.

The math-whiz youngest daughter counted each present. ". . .Eleven. . .twelve. I told you it would be twelve today. I wonder if we'll get thirteen tomorrow and—"

Phyllis shushed her. "Remember the song 'The Twelve Days of Christmas'?"

Both girls nodded.

"Today is Christmas, so there is no need for further gifts. It's Jesus' birthday, so let's go sing 'Happy Birthday' to Him and decide how we can surprise someone else next year on the twelve days of Christmas. Deal?"

The girls smacked palms. "Deal."

As the girls entered the house, Phyllis stepped out on the porch and looked straight at them, although Nick didn't know if she could see them or just sensed their presence. "Thank you, and God bless you. Merry Christmas!"

Nick's heart swelled with love for others, his Lord who had worked all this out, and for the best God-incidence in his life—the precious woman who knelt beside him. The one he wanted by his side for the rest of his life.

He pulled Carol to her feet. "Come on. We've got one more Christmas party to attend."

❄

Carol followed Nick to the truck, her breath coming in short gasps. She'd loved watching the sisters and their mom and believed the lesson the mother had taught the girls would stay with them for life. And now she was on her way to meet her own sisters for the very first time. Life couldn't get any better.

Nick was quiet on the way out to the Bellingham Plantation, probably moved by the touching scene they'd witnessed.

Carol fidgeted in her seat, slipping a rectangular-shaped package from her purse. She wanted to give this to Nick before they went in, before the hubbub of four sisters meeting for the first time.

He parked in the driveway to his house, out of sight of the main house, and pulled a square box wrapped in pink, his new favorite color, from under the seat.

She produced her box. "Great minds think alike."

"They must. Do you want to open first?"

"No, you." She handed it to him, getting tingles up her arm as her hand grazed his.

He tore off the paper to reveal a silver frame with a picture of the two of them taken by Aunt Molly, the only picture she owned of him. "I love it. I asked Aunt Molly for a copy weeks ago, and she kept putting me off. Now I know why." He kissed her. "It's my best Christmas gift ever. Thank you."

"You're welcome. Now my turn?"

He chuckled as he handed her the other box. "No wonder you love Christmas so much. You're a child at heart."

First, she rattled the box and then shook it. Next, she put her finger under the taped part and peeled the paper off in one strip. When she lifted the cardboard lid, she heard a tinkling sound like music. "I hope I didn't break anything."

"I don't think so. It's supposed to play music."

She lifted out a carved wooden music box, already playing the tune to "The Twelve Days of Christmas." "I love it, and it will always remind me of this special Christmas." She hugged him.

He nudged her. "Well, open the music box. I told you there's another gift since today's also your birthday."

Opening the lid, her eyes grew bigger than snowballs as they landed on an antique ring fashioned of a lavender stone surrounded by diamonds.

Nick looked into her eyes and began to sing.

"Lavender's blue, dilly dally, lavender's green,
When I am king, dilly, dally, you shall be queen.
Who told you so, dilly, dally, who told you so?
'Twas my own heart, dilly, dally, that told me so."

"Will you be my queen, my wife, my Christmas Carol forever and ever?"

Her arms flew around his neck. "Yes, yes. Oh, Nick, this is the happiest day of my life."

He slipped the ring on her finger. "The first day of our lives together."

They walked the short distance to the Bellingham house hand in hand, ready to face whatever the future held so long as they faced it together.

Rose Allen McCauley is happy to live in the beautiful bluegrass region of Kentucky on a farm surrounded by God's creation. She has been writing for over ten years and has been published in several non-fiction anthologies and devotionals. She is thrilled for this to be her first published fiction because Christmas books are her favorites. She has a growing collection of Christmas books, and this one will takes its rightful place among them.

A retired schoolteacher who has been happily married to her college sweetheart for over 43 years, she is also mother to three grown children and their spouses and Mimi to three lovely, lively grandkids! You can reach her through her website www.rosemccauley.com or blogsite at www.rosemccauley.blogspot.com

STARRY NIGHT

Jeri Odell

Dedication

This book is dedicated to my grandson Camden Dean
Odell. You are so precious to me, special in every way.
I know you'll be a good and godly man someday
like my hero. May you love Jesus with all your
heart, soul, mind, and strength.

"Where is the one who has been born king of the Jews?
We saw his star when it rose and have come to worship him."
Matthew 2:2

Chapter 1

Starr Evans turned the key and opened the small metal mailbox amidst rows and rows of other identical boxes. She pulled out several pieces of junk mail and an official-looking letter in an expensive linen envelope. Hmm? Maybe a job offer? She flipped it over and studied the return address. Brockman and Davis, Attorneys at Law, Monticello, Georgia. Georgia? Did she even know anyone in Georgia? Possibly the wrong mailbox?

She studied the typed address—Times New Roman. This law firm showed no creativity. The boring, common font very clearly spelled out her name. She laid the rest of her mail back into the box, partially hanging out, and used her index finger to open and half-mutilate the covering, pulling out the perfectly matched stationery from within. She unfolded it. Worry gripped her heart. Maybe this had something to do with her parents' deadly car accident. Surely no one was suing—at least not anyone from Georgia. She let out a long sigh, her gaze floating to the top of the page.

Dear Miss Evans. The knot in the pit of her stomach tightened. She closed her eyes, holding the page against her chest. *Please, God, don't let it be more bad news.* She stood there a moment, eyes squeezed tightly shut. How much more could she take? Then her dad's much-missed voice echoed through her mind. *The Lord never gives you more than you can handle. No matter what you face, baby girl, He's right there with enough grace to get you through.*

"Are you sure, Daddy? Are you absolutely sure?" Starr

whispered, gazing up at the smoggy Los Angeles sky.

This letter is to inform you that you are one of four identical quadruplets. . . .

Identical quadruplets? She glanced back at the address on the envelope. Perhaps she'd misread it. Nope. Starr Evans at this very address in LA, California. She sat down on the low landscape wall, sensing her legs might not hold her up much longer. Her parents would have told her if she were adopted. *Daddy was a pastor. He would not have lied to me. He just would not have.* They must have the wrong Starr Evans. No one in her entire life had ever mentioned adoption. *I cannot be adopted! But some poor unsuspecting soul may be.* Some other Starr Evans at some other address. . .

From her perch on the white mission-style wall, she returned her focus to the letter.

This letter is to inform you that you are one of four identical quadruplets born to Janice Lynn Bellingham, December 25, 1986. Janice expired December 28, 1986, from complications. The four infant girls were given up for adoption. Each child went to a different family. Along with your three sisters, you have inherited one hundred acres of land, which is now being used to farm peanuts, with a large antebellum home from your maternal grandparents, Charles and Emily Bellingham of Monticello, Georgia. There are two stipulations in the will. One, you and your three sisters must spend December 25, your birthday/Christmas day and night, at the plantation house together. Two, you cannot sell the property or home; it has to stay in the Bellingham family.

Could there be two Starr Evans with the same birth date? An uneasiness crept up her spine. She shivered. What kind of scam was this? She pushed her brunette hair behind her ear, securing it out of her face. Squinting her eyes, she continued reading.

> *Should you accept your inheritance, each of you will be responsible for a percentage of the taxes, upkeep, and related fees. Your adopted family is welcome to join you at the house for the holiday, if they so desire.*
>
> *Sincerely,*
> *Camden Brockman*
> *Attorney at Law*

Starr rolled her eyes and crumpled the letter, not even bothering reading to the end. Shaking her head, she rose off the wall, grabbed the rest of her mail, and relocked the box. "You're not getting fees out of me!" She stomped to her door, angry that things like that went on in this world. Thank heaven her parents had taught her to have a healthy skepticism of anything that sounded too good to be true. Just the thought of them made her heart ache. When, if ever, would missing them dissipate? When—if ever—could she think of them without the knife of pain slicing her heart, creating another fresh wound?

Opening her apartment door after her jaunt to the mailbox, she strode to the kitchen, shoving the junk mail and fancy fake envelope into her recycle receptacle. Then she carried the crumpled letter to her dad's old rolltop desk, where the shredder sat wedged between it and the corner. Straightening the wadded mess, she pushed it through the machine. "You wrote to the wrong girl, Mr. Attorney. Thanks to my daddy, I am no sap."

The chewing noise was music to her ears. She brushed her palms together as if swiping away some invisible smut that had been left behind by the offensive letter. Feeling heroic, she'd taken care of some violator who was out to sucker some unsuspecting soul into giving away large sums of money. *I wonder if I should have turned the evidence over to the Attorney General's office.* Glancing at the quiet paper-eating machine, she knew it was too late. The beast had finished its destruction of the evidence and sat quiet in its corner. She could almost imagine it licking its chops.

She wished the uneasy feeling would vanish as quickly and easily. Why was she the one they picked to scam? Was it coincidence, or was she targeted? Did they somehow know that her parents died and she'd inherited some life insurance money? All of her questions made her feel uneasy like her privacy had somehow been invaded. She chewed on her bottom lip. "I will *not* give in to the fear."

❄

"You've reached the recorded message for—"

Camden Brockman hung up the phone with a bit too much force and faced the elderly lady sitting across from his oversized hickory desk. He shook his head. "Emily, I've tried everything I know to try. I've heard from three of your four granddaughters, but we've got ourselves a rebel with this last one."

"Which one is not responding?" The white-headed woman leaned in toward him, her clear blue eyes searching his face.

"The third one—Starr."

"Ah, my little Starr. . ." Emily's voice broke, and she cleared her throat. Raising her chin, she continued, "I remember holding her so many years ago." Her gaze shifted away from him, and he knew she'd been carried away by time. "She was the fighter. She looked straight into my eyes, grabbed my finger, and held on for all she was worth. I said to Charles, 'This one will make it. She'll be fine.' And I knew in my heart she would."

Emily reached into her handbag, removed a perfectly starched lace hanky, and dabbed the corner of her eyes. "Starr was adopted by a pastor and his wife. They'd been married ten years, trying to conceive for nine. They were actually a southern couple—which of course was important to me. You know, we are different here in the South."

Camden nodded, though he more believed people were people, no matter where they hailed from.

"But when Starr was barely a year old, they whisked her off to California. California is no place to raise a child—at least not in my opinion."

Camden again nodded, though he knew millions of Californians would laugh at her biased opinion. It was probably not as much where you raised a kid, but how.

"Starr is spunky, and my first impression of her has proved correct over time. She attended Christian schools, was a leader, and won a full scholarship to UCLA, where she double-majored in graphic design and advertising." Emily patted the folder labeled STARR. "Her mother sent me biyearly reports, pictures, and all her report cards."

She hugged all four of the overstuffed folders against her heart. "They are all precious. I cannot wait to meet each of them. Somehow we have to get Starr here! Tell me what's been done to make that happen."

Emily Bellingham was a bit of a fighter herself. Starr must take after her grandmother.

He opened the folder lying atop his desk. "Upon sending the original letter, the other three girls responded within a few days. Starr's letter was not returned, but as I already informed you, she didn't respond either. I had my paralegal double-check the address, and it's correct. I re-sent the letter registered. She refused to sign for it, so we have our girl, but for whatever reason she's not interested."

Emily took in a deep breath, looking deep into his eyes. "She lost her parents in a car accident just over a year ago. Her mother's sister let me know. They still live in Alabama. I'd hoped the idea of a newfound family would thrill her."

"Maybe this is just more than she can handle right now." Camden felt for the girl. "Did she know she was adopted?"

Emily adjusted the silk scarf around her neck. "I don't think they ever told her." Disapproval laced each word.

"Wow." Camden let out a long, slow whistling sound. "That's a hard thing to read in a letter."

Emily squared her shoulders. "Will you call her, dear? I wish to leave her a message."

"Is that a good idea? Besides the letters, I've left three phone messages. She knows we're looking and obviously doesn't want to be found." An idea formed. "Why don't I fly to LA and meet her in person?" He had a hunch Starr needed proof. Lots of proof.

"On whose dime?" The shrewd businesswoman replaced the concerned grandmother. Emily Bellingham, though one of his wealthiest clients, paid him the least. You'd think the woman didn't have two quarters to clang together.

"The estate will pay. I won't touch a cent of your personal funds."

"Okay then. As long as you're not expecting a widow to pay for such an extravagance." She locked her gaze on him, making certain he understood that expense better not be billed to her.

"I'm just trying to help you out." Camden shrugged, hoping to send the unspoken message that he didn't care one way or the other—although meeting Starr intrigued him. He liked a good mystery and wondered why she wasn't interested in at least hearing what he had to say. "If you want all four of them present on Christmas Day, someone is going to have to chase down Starr. Letters and calls aren't getting the job done."

Emily's expression showed the briefest apology. "You are right, dear." She patted his hand. "You do what you have to do."

"Thank you." He glanced at his watch and rose. "I only have your best interest at heart."

Emily followed his lead and rose, too. "No first-class ticket, no five-star restaurants or expensive hotels." She punctuated her words with her index finger.

"Yes, ma'am." Camden grinned. As a well-raised southern boy, he'd never talk back or disrespect an older woman, or any woman for that matter. He opened first his office door and then the outer door, holding them as Emily passed through.

Returning to his office, he hit REDIAL. Once Starr's machine answered, he half-listened to the blurb, waiting for the beep.

"Do not call me again." He caught the tiniest hint of Alabama in those few words. "I have just survived the worst year of my life and have asked myself, 'Could things get any worse?' The answer is a resounding yes! You. You made things worse. I do not know who you are, Camden Brockman, except possibly some nutcase from Georgia, but I am not falling for whatever scheme you have going. I doubt seriously that you're even a real lawyer. Three identical sisters and a plantation in Georgia! Do you have some swampland in Florida, too? If you call me again—*ever*—I'll report you to the police." She shot the words rapid fire and slammed down her phone receiver before he ever got a word out.

So little Miss Starr was a skeptic. He punched in his assistant's number. "Figure out a way to clear my calendar next week, and book me a flight to LA; set up reservations at an *inexpensive* hotel." He assumed it would take at least a week to convince Starr he was the real deal and that she really did have three identical sisters.

Chapter 2

Good thing Mama and Daddy left me a tiny nest egg. The job hunt isn't going well." Starr sat at her breakfast bar perched on a high stool, Bluetooth in her ear, and fingers on the keyboard doing yet another job search.

"Not a great economy to find a job." Sandy, her best friend since kindergarten, stated the obvious. "Have you thought of changing your profession? Or at least the direction you're going with graphic design?"

"Not really." Starr replied absentmindedly, reading through the online listings for a graphic artist within the advertising industry. "But I do think I've applied for every job listed here and sent a résumé to every firm in the greater Los Angeles area."

"Could be a sign. You know the best thing I ever did was change career paths."

Starr could picture her friend's brunette head bobbing up and down. "I know resigning was the best thing that ever happened to you—"

"No, not resigning, but finding this new free me. I was a stress ball and am now so creative and energetic. I just want you to be free and happy."

"I loved my job. It did make me happy. It's all I really want to do. I can't believe I got laid off." Starr sighed.

"They say bad things come in threes, and now you have your three out of the way." Sandy aimed to cheer her up. Starr knew that, but sometimes Sandy's unorthodox approach to life drove the ever-pragmatic Starr crazy.

"I'm not superstitious, but you're correct in saying it's been the worst year of my life, starting with my parents' deaths, my breakup with Jason, and now losing my job. All of that is too much for anyone, especially in a twelve-month span. When I lost my parents, at least I had Jason. And when I lost him, at least I could throw myself into work. Now that's gone, too." She heard the self-pity in her words and hated it. *I don't want to be that person.*

"You still have me," Sandy reminded her. "And more importantly, you still have the Lord."

"You are right, of course. Thank you for putting up with me these last months. I'm grateful. It's just that I thought Jason and I were altar-bound. He was my forever person. No matter where God's path took me next, I imagined Jason by my side."

"I'm sorry, Starr. I know you guys dated a long time. We all thought you'd marry, but it wasn't meant to be."

Starr disliked that phrase. "Wasn't meant to be or was destroyed because Jason got on the wrong path far away from God's will? How do I reconcile God's sovereign plan versus the free will of man?" Starr rested her elbows on the front of her laptop and laid her head in her hands. She just didn't know. She'd believed—as had her parents—that Jason was God's plan for her life. Then he made a U-turn, filled his life with party-loving friends, started dating girls who didn't know Christ, and decided he'd rather make a lot of money than serve on a church staff with his administrative gifts.

"Starry, I can't answer your question, but I know a God who can. He's good, no matter how bad your year has been.

He's faithful, no matter how far Jason swayed from your expectations. And He will meet your needs with a new job. You're a tither, and He promises to supply your needs. As for your parents, they got a promotion. They are in heaven with God! Here on earth, we miss them like crazy, but they are worshipping the Lord of lords, the King of kings. What greater place to be?"

"You are right about all of it, and my head knows it, but my heart, my poor beaten and bruised heart, is struggling to accept it all. I feel like God is stripping me down to nothing, absolutely nothing."

"Maybe He is." Sandy's words were hard to hear—she'd barely whispered.

Maybe He is. Why, Lord? Why?

Starr decided now was a great time for a change of subject. "The nutcase from Georgia called again last night. I'd finally had enough. I picked up the phone and gave him what for. I don't think I'll ever hear from him again. He knows I've got his number."

"The thing I can't figure out—why did he say you had three identical sisters? I mean, sooner or later you'd want to meet them. How could he pull that off?"

"I don't know." Sandy's questions caused Starr to pause. Her heart pounded out a dance of fear against her ribs. Sandy was right. How could he fake three identical sisters? She'd been so convinced of the scam that she'd not thought through the implications of providing proof of her birth sisters. What if. . . Starr closed her eyes. Her mouth went dry. What if she were indeed adopted? Three sisters who looked just like her—dark hair and eyes a unique shade of violet. What if?

❄

Camden parked his blue convertible rental car in a space marked for visitors. He'd decided not to miss the beautiful autumn weather being cooped up in a tiny economy car, so he'd put the upgrade on his personal expense account. Leaving the airport, he'd typed Starr's address into the car's GPS system, and it had led him straight here. He glanced around the mission-style complex, wondering what kind of person Starr was and how she'd take the news. Her three sisters all proved quite different and quite interesting. Same package, but very different women.

He grabbed his briefcase from the backseat. Double-checking the apartment number, he'd remembered correctly. Letting himself through the black wrought-iron gate, he glanced around. The apartments appeared to be built in quads around a common area. He found building H and then rang the doorbell on number four. The screen was shut, but the door was open to the flower- and plant-filled courtyard.

"Come in." He recognized Starr's voice from his many encounters with her answering machine and the one personal contact where she had given him what for. He hesitated, certain he wasn't who she expected, but decided he'd better take advantage of the situation. Once she discovered his identity, he may be out on his ear in two point five seconds.

Pulling the black handle down on the wrought-iron scrolled screen, he pulled it open. Stepping inside, he assessed her apartment. Small. Tasteful. Not new or modern. Probably a lot of her things belonged to her recently deceased parents.

"I'm in the kitchen." She called.

He followed her voice and went through an arched doorway into what he assumed led to her kitchen. Sure enough, there stood quad number three. There was something about her that he'd not noticed in Holly or Carol. Something that drew him to her. Crazy, 'cause they all three were identical. He doubted he'd be able to tell them apart in a lineup.

Starr rolled dough at her counter in the small kitchen and hadn't yet glanced up. "Grab a soda or someth—" She stopped midsentence. Her eyes had grown wide when she noticed he was not whomever she expected. She raised the rolling pin from the dough and brought it toward her. He knew she was thinking *weapon*.

He raised his hands chest level, palms toward her. "Whoa. You invited me in. Now you're going to beat me over the head with that heavy wooden thing?" He spoke in a calm voice, thankful she was on one side of the counter and he on the other side and closest to door.

"Who are you?" Violet eyes were filled with fear.

"I'm not here to hurt you." Undecided whether he should tell her who he was—his name might actually prompt her to hurl that wooden rolling pin straight for his head—he kept his hands raised. "You invited me in."

"What's going on?" A brunette with shoulder-length hair stood a few feet from him. "I've already pressed the nine and the one." She held her cell phone up like it was a prized pistol. "Do I need to push the final one?"

Camden turned slightly to face the cell phone–toting tough girl. "Look, lady, I'm here on business." He pointed to the overstuffed briefcase. "I rang the bell, and your friend"—he tipped his head toward Starr—"invited me in. Now she

197

has a mind to beat me to a pulp with her rollin' pin."

"What business?" Her friend still had her index finger on the 1 on her cell's dial pad.

He cleared his throat. "I'm Camden Brockman, an attorney from Monticello, Georgia."

The friend exchanged a knowing look with Starr.

His gaze settled on Starr. Her face had lost all color.

Facing Starr, he prepared to state his defense with eloquence and speed. "Give me five minutes. If I were indeed a fraud, would I have traveled across the country, giving you an opportunity to have me arrested?"

Her eyes bounced from his to her friend's and back. "Five minutes and you'll leave?"

He nodded.

"Sandy, what do you think?"

Her friend gave a little nod.

Starr sucked in a deep breath and laid the rolling pin down, forgetting the pizza dough she'd been rolling out. She pointed at the counter separating the two of them. "Have a seat."

He climbed up on one of two tall rattan stools. Her friend settled on the second one. Starr stayed in the kitchen, keeping them separated by a breakfast bar and counter. He laid his leather satchel on the bar, keeping his movements slow and deliberate as not to alarm either woman. "May I?" He pointed to the bag's zipper.

Starr nodded. He opened the bag, unloading much of its contents on her bar. She leaned across the counter, watching closely. First he laid out his diploma, his driver's license, and his partnership papers. Starr picked up each one and examined it, then passed them to her friend, Sandy. No one said a word, and the silence wasn't golden but tense and uneasy.

After they'd each examined his paperwork, he broke the quiet. "Convinced?"

"You are probably an attorney, but that still doesn't make you legitimate." Those arresting violet eyes stared into his soul.

He smiled. "You are a hard sell, but what do I have to gain by lying to you?"

"You want money to support some peanut plantation."

What was she talking about? "Where did you get that idea?"

"The letter. The letter you sent mentioned all sorts of expenses that I'd need to cover."

Camden grinned, starting to see the writing on the notepad. "Did you read the whole thing or stop when you came across the mention of fees?" He pulled copies of the letter from the file to his left, handing one to each girl.

Starr's cheeks reddened. "Okay. I didn't finish the letter. I shredded it," she confessed.

He chuckled. "Would you read it now—to the end? Might change your opinion of me and the fees."

Both Starr and her friend were pin-drop quiet as they pored over the letter. All Camden could hear was the ticking of a clock from somewhere in the apartment. As Starr studied the paper in her hands, he studied her. Perfectly arched brow, long dark lashes, a smile any orthodontist would be proud of, a straight nose, high cheekbones. Clear, velvety skin. Perfection. She glanced up. His eyes darted away, but not before she caught him staring.

❄

"So my portion of the estate pays these fees?" Starr looked into clear blue eyes. The guy looked honest enough.

"Yes. You should never have to come out of pocket for a thing."

Starr grabbed hold of the counter as all the implications hit her. Thoughts swirled through her mind at warp speed. She moved to the small table for four resting in the nook at one end of her kitchen. Sliding into the chair, she rested her head in her hands. It suddenly felt like her entire life had been based on a lie—the lie that she was the daughter of Joe and Cindy Evans, and she could not fathom that.

Mr. Brockman and Sandy had joined her at the table, but neither said a word. Finally she raised her gaze to the sky-blue eyes of the attorney. "Are you sure—are you absolutely sure you've got the right girl?"

The attorney nodded, patting the file in front of him. "I brought lots of proof. We can take all the time you need sorting through it."

"Is this a joke?" She gazed around the room, looking for hidden cameras. "I feel like I'm being punked. Or remember that old show *Candid Camera*? My parents used to watch it. Is this something like that?"

Mr. Brockman shook his head. His compassionate eyes rested on her.

She popped out of her chair like a jack-in-the-box shooting out of his box and headed to her laptop on the breakfast bar. "I've never even heard of identical quads. Do they even exist?" She hit the return key, and her computer sprang to life. Typing identical quadruplets in her Google box, information on several sets popped up. Disappointment settled on her like a mantle of gloom. This was starting to feel much too real.

She returned to her spot at the table, with Sandy on

her right and Mr. Brockman on her left. Tears sprang up. "I didn't know. My parents never told me. Why wouldn't they tell me?"

Sandy rose and stood next to Starr, wrapping a protective arm around her shoulders. If only her friend could shield her from the painful truth. She spent several minutes with her head hung, trying to absorb this life-altering information.

"I have three sisters and a peanut plantation in Georgia. How bizarre is that?" She said the words aloud, hoping they'd sink in. "How did the three other girls respond, Mr. Brockman?"

"Please call me Camden. And they each responded differently, but the key is they *responded*." He grinned, and the kindness in his eyes assured her that he understood.

"Not like me, huh?" His smile prompted her to return it.

"Well, Holly had no idea that she was adopted either, so she stormed into town just a day or two after she received the letter."

"See, at least you aren't the only one." Sandy returned to her seat at the table.

"You are the only one, though, who chewed me out and accused me of being some sort of Georgia fruitcake," Camden teased her.

Her cheeks grew warm. "I'm sorry. I guess I'm a bit of a skeptic."

He nodded. "A bit."

"Start at the beginning. Tell me what you can about this new family of mine. You've met at least one sister. Does she look like me? What are their names? Why did our mother give us up?"

"Whoa." Camden held up his hand. "How about one

question at a time? And there are a lot of things I can't reveal until December twenty-sixth—as per the stipulations of the will."

She nodded. "Did the sister you met look like me?"

"Yes. I've actually met two of them. Their hairstyles are different, but their faces are your face. Same eyes. Same smile, yet each of you seems very, very different in your own way."

"Different—like how?" Starr decided to follow his humorous approach to this uncanny situation. "Alien-like?"

"Only you." He winked. "You all grew up very differently. One of your sisters grew up in a small town; one was adopted by a quite wealthy family; the third grew up on a ranch. As you can imagine, those externals formed very different women."

"And I'm the only skeptic?"

He nodded and grinned. "Sorry to say, you are."

She decided she liked this blond-haired, blue-eyed attorney very much.

"So." Sandy had those lines bunching up between her brows like they did when she pondered. "Are cases of this nature always so mysterious? I mean, waiting until the will is read seems so. . .so old school." She wrinkled her nose, showing her disapproval.

Camden gave her his full attention. "It was an unusual request, but I always do my best to oblige my clients' inclinations to the fullest extent possible. These stipulations were important to the Bellinghams—their last wish and deepest desire—priority stuff, and my job is to carry that out."

A man of integrity. Starr liked that. She glanced at the

bulging folder sitting in front of him on the table. "You'd mentioned proof, and though I do believe what you're telling me, can I see what you have?"

Camden pulled out four birth certificates, laying them in front of her. They were all born on December twenty-fifth. Tiny little things in the three- and four-pound range. Holly, Carol, Starr, and Noel. Sisters who came into the world together and shared a womb, yet had never met or seen one another. So much in common, yet nothing shared. Somehow it felt like another loss to her. Tears streamed down her cheeks.

❄

Starr was definitely the tenderest of the quadruplets. Her vulnerability tugged at his heartstrings, and an overwhelming desire to protect her surfaced. She obviously thought and felt deeply. She excused herself to wash up, and he and Sandy were left alone at the table.

"Can you even imagine what she is going through?" Sandy's brown eyes reflected the pain of her friend.

"No. I can't. Not at all." His heart ached for her. "But do you think in the end, this could be a good thing for Starr? She'll now have a family. It won't just be her against the world."

"I suppose, but we're like sisters. And she has a whole family of church members who love her and would do anything for her."

Camden wasn't sure that was the same as having a real family but didn't dispute Sandy's line of thinking.

When Starr returned she'd washed her face and reapplied a light dose of makeup. She smiled apologetically. "Please forgive me. I don't know why, but this news is really hard to take. I feel betrayed by my parents, which is so out of character for them. They were honest, hardworking, wonderful people." She reclaimed the chair she'd vacated. "Why wouldn't they have told me?"

"I'm sure they had their reasons." Sandy placed a hand over Starr's.

Starr shot up out of her chair again. "My pizza dough!" She went into the kitchen. "I'm sorry, but I think it's ruined. It's all dried out." Her gaze rested on Sandy. "So much for me fixing you dinner."

Camden rose and moved toward the little galley-style kitchen, stopping at its mouth. "Why don't you let me take you ladies to dinner since it's my fault that your plans went south?" He glanced from Starr to Sandy and back to Starr.

Starr glanced at Sandy, who shrugged.

"You know, I'd like that. It would give me a chance to ask you some questions, if you don't mind."

Camden nodded. "Ask away. If I'm free to answer, I will. I promise you'll know everything on December twenty-sixth."

"That's nearly three months away!" Starr protested.

"And it will fly by," he assured her. As they exited Starr's apartment, she turned and locked the dead bolt. He led them to his rented convertible, opening the passenger door and flipping the seat forward. Sandy climbed into the back and buckled. Starr took the front seat next to him. Once she was settled, he shut the door, looking forward to this week of spending time with her and getting to know her better.

Following Starr's directions, he drove them to a trendy sidewalk café. They were seated outside, and the weather was perfect. Once they'd all ordered, Starr focused on him.

"Where is this plantation? I never even asked."

"Monticello, Georgia."

Starr shook her head. "Not ringing a bell."

He smiled again. "It's the largest city in Jasper County, Georgia, and the county seat. Guess the population."

"Largest city," she shrugged. "County seat. One hundred thousand people?"

He laughed. "I thought those facts would mislead you. Two thousand five hundred people."

Sandy let out a whistling noise. "More people than that attend our church."

He glanced around the traffic-laden streets. "Small town USA. Much different than here."

While the waiter delivered their soup and salads, Starr asked, "Do you live there?"

"I do. My entire family, actually."

"Tell us about Monticello," Sandy urged. "Where is it in respect to Atlanta?"

"Sixty-five miles southeast of Atlanta, and about fifteen years ago, it was listed on the National Registry of Historic Places. Picture a quaint town square, dogwood trees lining two-lane streets, and stately homes. It's filled with charm and southern hospitality." He focused on Starr. "I think you'd like it. It's everything LA isn't."

"You make it sound irresistible. And to think I own a small piece of it. . . ." Her smile didn't reach her eyes.

"I hope you'll come on the twenty-fifth, even if you don't stay." Emily would be heartbroken if he couldn't convince Starr to come. "It's a chance to meet your sisters and get a glimpse of the life some of your ancestors lived."

"Do I have family that still resides there?"

He did not want to lie to her, but could not mention

Emily. He was bound by the attorney-client privilege. "I'm honestly not sure. There may still be some extended family in the area—maybe cousins or some older relatives of your grandparents."

"Did you know my grandparents personally?" Starr laid her napkin next to the salad she'd only picked at.

"I did." He nodded, pushing his own plate away. "They were an upstanding Christian family—active in both the church and community. Your grandfather was a deacon, head of the prayer ministry, and served for years on the town council. He was honest, forthright, and a leader."

He saw a longing in Starr's eyes. "I wish I could have met them before they passed. Tell me about my grandmother."

"She drove a hard bargain—an astute businesswoman who knew what she wanted and went after it. But always the epitome of a southern lady. There was a gentleness in her strength. She, too, served both in our church and in our community. She's a bit of a skeptic, too. Reminds me a bit of you."

"Reminds?" Sandy lifted a brow. "Isn't she gone?"

"Reminded." He'd have to be more careful.

"You said *our* church. Do you go to the same church that they did?" Starr studied him.

"Yes." Camden handed the waiter his company credit card. "My entire family is active there. It's a nice-size church. We are slowly creeping toward five hundred, which is a large church if you consider the size of our town."

Once the waiter returned his card and receipt, they sauntered back to the car.

"Would you ladies like to stop for coffee on the way back?"

"I'd love to."

"Can't." Starr and Sandy's answers came out simultaneously. Both girls giggled. Reminded him of his sisters back home.

Chapter 4

I'm not sure who said yes and who said no, but the idea of returning to an empty hotel room holds no appeal for me, so one of you has yourself a deal." Camden held the door open as they both settled into their original spots in the car.

"I can't," Sandy piped up from the backseat. "I'm expecting a call from Mike, which I don't want to miss." When she spoke of Mike, her voice took on a dreamy quality.

"Her boyfriend," Starr informed Camden. "He is out of town on business, and they have their evening date by phone. She never misses his calls."

"He's a lucky guy." Camden glanced over his shoulder and bestowed his very charming smile on Sandy.

How rare, a man who appreciates a good woman and a committed relationship.

"Thank you. I feel like the lucky one. Do you mind dropping me off? I live in the same complex as Starr."

"Not at all." His grin returned.

Starr studied Camden as he drove. He was the nicest guy she'd met in a long time, and that smile—oh that smile. . .

Starr climbed out of the car so Sandy could exit.

"It was nice meeting you." She hugged Starr. "Will you be okay?" she whispered as she released her.

"Fine," Starr mouthed. Sandy was her worrier and even more cautious than Starr.

"So where is the nearest coffee house?" Camden asked as she settled back into the front seat and buckled her seat belt.

"My favorite is about three blocks that-a-way." She pointed, and Camden steered the car that direction.

Once there he opened her car door and offered his hand to help her out.

Starr took his hand, trying to ignore the chemical reaction between them. "You are a true southern gentleman." She smiled up at him. *And tall.* This close he dwarfed her five-foot-three frame.

They entered the small independent coffee house. The aromas never failed to entice.

Standing at the counter, they each placed their order; then she grabbed a table for two near the corner while he waited on their order. The place was quiet tonight—not many tables were filled.

When Camden joined her, he placed her latte in front of her. She loved the huge coffee cups that they served their drinks in. They always made her feel like a little girl playing grown-up.

"How are you feeling?" Camden asked. "You've been hit with a lot to process today."

She nodded, not even knowing where to begin. The concern in his gaze touched her heart.

"Right now I'm numb. More questions than answers." She glanced up from whipped cream and caramel drizzle into a pair of eyes that invited her to share her darkest secrets.

"I'm here for a week—at your disposal if you'd like."

"A week? That seems like a long time. Aren't you basically done? You delivered the news I was unwilling to read or hear over the phone. Why a week?"

Red crept up his neck. "This is going to sound very presumptuous." He studied her face. "I thought you might need some time. I wasn't sure how readily you'd accept the news I brought."

"Why, I don't know why you'd think that." Starr shook her head and winked, a bit embarrassed by her own skepticism. "So you are staying a week on my behalf?"

He nodded.

"Not presumptuous, but very, very sweet. You are a kind man, and you obviously care about people."

Now the red climbed up his cheeks, highlighting his ears. "I just felt like the Lord wanted me to be here and help you sort through things. So here I am, if you want to utilize my assistance."

Starr laid her hand over his and squeezed. "Thank you. I think I will take you up on that, if you'll allow me to show you around Southern California. And that's me presuming that you've never been here before."

His eyes sparkled. "I haven't, and I would love that."

"Why don't you return your rental tomorrow, and we'll use my car. That will save your firm some money since you've gone to great expense on my behalf."

"If you're sure you don't mind."

"Not at all. Now, can you tell me anything about my sisters?"

"I don't know much but will share what little I do know."

She nodded, hungry for any snippet of info.

"The oldest quad is Holly Davenport, and she's a romance author from Mt. Vernon, Missouri."

"A real-live author? Not just one of those self-published people?" Awe wove its way through each one of her words.

"Yep. She was a nail tech, hairdresser, or something like that. Then sold her first book and quit her job. I'd say that's pretty real."

"I'm impressed."

"The second quad is Carol Wells, a history major at Mercer University in Atlanta. I believe she's in her last semester. I have met both Carol and Holly."

"Are they like me?" Starr sipped her latte.

"No ma'am, nor are they like each other. You three are all as different as the seashells on your California beaches. Similar packaging, but on closer inspection, you are all as different and unique as those shells. Come on the twenty-fifth of December, and see for yourself." He lifted his brows in challenge.

"What about quad number three?"

"She's a skeptic for sure. But also loyal, sincere, and just." He grinned.

She drew her brows together. "Sounds like me."

He chuckled. "You are number three."

She thought about his descriptions. They fit. "You know all that from one evening?"

He nodded.

"You aren't far off, but how did you do that?"

"I'm an observer of human nature. It's not that hard to figure out, if you pay close attention. Think about it. What have you noticed about me?"

Tall, blond, and very good-looking. She couldn't very well say that, though. Think Starr. Think deeper.

"You. . .you are kind. How many people would traipse across the country to track down some skeptic just because it was important to her deceased grandmother? You are thoughtful—staying a week to help some stranger through a hard time is pretty impressive."

The red ears had shown up again.

"You obviously genuinely care about people—your clients and people in general. How did I do?"

"As I said, it's not that hard. Watch and learn."

"How about my other sister?"

"Noel Brady. I know the least about her. Her family owns the Circle B Ranch, and she's a regular cowgirl, out riding and roping from what I can tell."

"Wow—a writer, a historian, and a cowgirl, an eclectic group for sure."

❄

He watched Starr as she processed all she'd learned. He didn't say it, but she was by far his favorite. Sweet, sensitive, skeptical Starr. Yep—he gulped the last of his coffee—why were there no girls like her in his part of the country? She could grow on him quickly like flowers in the spring on a dogwood tree.

"Now tell me about you and your family. You technically have the advantage, knowing far more about me than I do about you."

"Deal." He pushed his empty cup back. "I'm a Georgia Bulldog and come from a long line of Bulldogs. To go anywhere else would be no less than a sin, at least to my family's way of thinking." He winked.

"I come from a tight group of southern-born and southern-bred people. We live on the same ranch that has been passed down through the generations since before the Civil War. My grandparents, parents, my older brother, and I all have built homes on the place."

"Wow. You don't see that often out this direction."

"No, but it is still pretty common in the South."

"So you have an older brother. Is he a rancher?"

He shook his head. "A doctor."

"Would you like a refill?" The waiter asked as he picked up Camden's empty cup.

"Ice water would be nice, but no more coffee, thanks."

The waiter shifted his gaze to Starr. "I'm still nursing mine, but wouldn't mind a water myself.

"A doctor and a lawyer. Are there just you two boys?"

"No there are five in all. Gabe is the youngest brother, and he's in college, and Courtney is twenty-five and an RN. And the youngest is Cindy at twenty. She doesn't mind, though, because we all spoil her and watch her back. She's in college, too."

"Five kids." Longing filled the observation. "I wanted to have three brothers and sisters. Hated the only-child bit. Whenever I asked my parents about it, they just said, 'God only gave us one, so we all need to be content with that.' " She shrugged. "Four kids always seemed like the perfect family."

"I'm sure they were grateful for you."

She nodded. "Here is the irony, Sandy has three sisters—Elise, Becca, and Sarah—and I used to pray for three sisters as well."

"And now you've got them."

"Did you notice that all four girls in my biological family have Christmas names? Is that weird to you?"

"I can tell you that your birth mother named each of you, and since the adoptions were all private, that was a stipulation. She wanted your names kept the same."

Starr swallowed hard and pursed her lips. "So. . ." Her voice reminded him of a rough piece of sandpaper. "My mother named me? I mean my real mother?"

Camden nodded.

A tear slipped out, and she dabbed it away with her ring finger. She forced a closed-lipped smile and cleared her throat. Blinking, she fought more tears from slipping out. "Sorry."

"It's okay to cry. This is an emotional subject. And it's your life."

"That it is. My life—a whole set of strange new facts. I'm trying to figure out who and where the old me is."

He reached out and took her hand. "Nothing about you has changed. You're still you. You had two parents who loved you very much and, for whatever reason, chose not to tell you about the adoption. That doesn't make them bad or liars or selfish—they had their reasons."

Though she nodded, uncertainty etched itself across her face.

"Starr, you knew them better than anyone—did you ever see them act selfish or lie?"

She weighed his words, shaking her head.

"They were good people, and something caused them to believe that not telling you was the wisest choice. Otherwise, they would have told you."

She smiled, nodding. The uncertainty disappeared. "Thank you." She tightened her grasp on his hand for a millisecond and then let go completely.

"Guess I should get you home." He took a sip of his water and rose. Starr followed his lead.

He held the door for her and then followed her to the car.

"I can't remember the last guy who opened a car door for me." She settled in and buckled up.

"Really? That rarely happens where I'm from. A man could be taken out back and beaten for less."

"My parents were from the South, and you remind me a lot of my daddy. He was a good man. Thanks for helping me remember that." She stifled a yawn.

"No problem. I shouldn't have kept you out so late. Emotional exhaustion is the worst kind. Maybe you can sleep in."

"I'm on the worship team at church, so that won't happen tomorrow. But the good news is, I was laid off a few weeks ago, so I can sleep in on Monday."

Wow, lots of stressors in her life. Two deaths, a layoff, and now this. How much can one person take? Lord, will You be her all in all?

"Do you want to meet me at church tomorrow?"

"I can do that. What time?" He parked on the street in front of Starr's complex and turned off the engine, removing the key.

"You don't have to walk me in." She opened the passenger door and stepped out.

"As a good southern boy, I must. My momma'd have my hide if she heard I did anything less."

He took Starr's key and unlocked her door, returning it to her palm.

"Thank you."

"About church, I need a name and a time. I'll MapQuest it tonight from the hotel."

"Living in Christ and eleven. Have you seen the Pacific Ocean?"

He shook his head.

"Bring shorts and flip-flops. We'll have lunch and catch

some sand and surf." She closed the door, and he heard her turn the dead bolt. He whistled a praise song on the way back to his car. "Don't get too close. Can't mix business with pleasure, buddy."

Chapter 5

The constant buzzing roused Starr out of a deep sleep. With eyes still closed, she automatically reached for the offender. After several seconds, she hit the snooze button on her cell. Last time she'd looked at her phone, it had said three ten. Three ten! Now it was time to crawl out of bed and face the day.

Searching through her groggy mind, she grappled to remember why she'd set her alarm. Oh yeah, she'd seen her dad's lawyer yesterday at church and introduced him to Camden. Mr. Allen had invited them to come in early, and he'd go through her parents' file, searching for any kind of adoption information.

She smiled, thinking of Camden. They had spent the most wonderful day together yesterday. They'd had lunch down on the pier and then walked for hours, talking, sharing. Then they'd dined by the water at sunset.

He'd been careful to keep their relationship warm but businesslike. Starr had wished all afternoon that he would've taken her hand, but he never did.

The alarm reminded her she was still not up. Pushing up on her elbow, she opened her phone and dismissed the intruding sound.

After a quick shower and a rush job getting ready, Starr stepped out on the porch just as Camden drove up.

"Hey." Her heart quivered at his greeting.

"Hey, you, too."

He hopped on the ten heading into downtown LA.

Traffic crept at around twenty with occasional stops. "How does this not drive you out of your ever-loving mind?"

Starr laughed. "You get used to it."

"I assure you, I'd never adjust to this."

"My commute used to be an hour to an hour and a half. You adjust. It's a way of life."

"One way or round trip?"

"One way. My life consisted of eat, sleep, and work. I listened to the Bible on tape one way and prayed on the other."

"How long was your workday?"

"Twelve to fourteen hours. How about yours?"

"Nine-ish. And my commute is less than ten minutes. No traffic, no smog. Lots of trees, flowers, and blue skies."

"Are you trying to make me hate my life?" she joked.

"No, but I'm hoping you'll see there is a simpler way." He glanced in the rearview mirror. "You ever thought about moving?"

"Back to my plantation? Naw. LA is the hub for great graphic-design opportunities. I doubt Monticello has much use for advertising firms."

"Too true."

Starr thought she might have caught the briefest hint of disappointment. *Wishful thinking*.

Camden followed Starr's directions into the underground parking for Adam Allen's firm. "My first trip down here, I was so lost, but after this last year, I could find the place with my eyes closed."

"I bet." Camden paused and waited for her to enter the elevator. She hit the button for the sixteenth floor.

The receptionist had yet to arrive, but Mr. Allen was waiting.

"Thanks for squeezing us in this morning."

"My pleasure. I got here early and dug through your parents' entire file. They've been clients of mine for a couple of decades. Not one piece of paper in the whole folder indicates that you were adopted." He shook his head, his gaze fixed on Starr.

"However, if Mr. Brockman doesn't mind, I'd love to check over the documents he has."

Starr felt embarrassed for Camden.

"It would be my pleasure." Camden handed him the requested paperwork. "I knew Starr's grandparents personally, have visited the plantation, and made sure everything is in order."

"I appreciate that, young man." The older lawyer studied each piece of paper. It seemed like an eternity to Starr. She fidgeted in her chair, crossing and uncrossing her legs several times.

Mr. Allen closed the file. "After reviewing everything— but specifically the birth certificates, the will, and the papers drawn up for the private adoption—everything looks authentic and in good order."

His gaze moved from Starr to Camden. "Would you mind if I make copies for our files here in LA?"

"Not at all." Camden shrugged.

Mr. Allen headed out the door. "It'll only take a minute."

"Sorry we didn't get much accomplished here. Since your parents' deaths, have you gone through their personal effects? Pictures? Journals? Paperwork?"

"No. I know I probably should have, but I couldn't bring myself to actually do it."

"I understand." He sent her a reassuring smile. "If you

want, you and I can do that tomorrow. Or if you'd rather do it on your own, I'll give you the day off and entertain myself."

Never pushy. Always letting her decide how much of him she wanted. "I'd like the company."

"Then you've got it. Now what about the rest of today? Do you have plans?"

"No. What are you thinking?"

"San Diego. A quick drive down the coast, and we'll check out their beaches. See how they compare."

Starr nodded. Sounded like heaven. A drive along the ocean with the breeze blowing through her hair, sitting next to a man who, at the very least, had captivated her. Yep. As close to a perfect day as Starr could imagine.

When Mr. Allen returned, Camden took the file, and they shook hands.

"And you, little Miss Starr." He wrapped her in a fatherly hug. "Don't give in to the urge to be angry with your parents. They both adored you and wouldn't have hurt you for the world. Go to Georgia, and see what's there." He pointedly looked at Camden. "And as your attorney, I'd be happy to go with you on the twenty-fifth, if you'd like."

"I couldn't ask you to do that—it's Christmas. I don't think your family would think too highly of me, but thanks. And Camden will be there to walk me through any legal mumbo jumbo."

"Then you're going?" He studied her.

"I think so." She hadn't reached a final conclusion but leaned toward yes.

"Good." Mr. Allen nodded his approval. "Then you can make an educated decision about this new family of yours and whether or not it's time to leave LA behind."

Starr opened her mouth to protest, but Mr. Allen laid a finger across her lips and stopped her before she got a sound out.

"You've lost your parents, your job, and you and Jason are over. Who knows what God has for you?" With that he kissed her on the forehead and escorted them to the door. "See you next Sunday."

He again shook Camden's hand, and they were out in the hall heading to the elevator.

"He certainly has a way of controlling the situation."

Starr nodded. "That he does."

❄

Camden stopped for bagels and cream cheese the next morning. He'd started figuring out some of Starr's favorite things. When he arrived at her door, he had not only food but also a large mocha latte with caramel drizzle.

She opened the door before he had figured out a way to use his elbow on the doorbell. "Wow." She took the bagel bag from him and swung the door open wide. "I was just trying to figure out how to feed both of us with no milk, a slice of stale bread, and two eggs."

"Think no more. Problem solved." He carried the two coffees toward her nook but stopped at the bar when he noticed the table was fully loaded.

"That's everything my parents left behind as far as papers and pictures. I also found a box of my dad's prayer journals. I thought some of them might hold a clue, but it feels intrusive to read his innermost thoughts, even now."

Camden got that. "I'd feel the same way about my dad."

"Somehow it feels like crossing a line of privacy and

College of the Ouachitas

respect." Starr stared across the room at the stack of books and then focused on Camden. "But honestly, they are probably my best bet." She slipped up onto one of the two bar stools.

Camden took the other stool and blessed the food. He handed Starr her cinnamon-sugar bagel smeared with plain cream cheese and passed her latte over to her.

"This is such a nice surprise! Thanks again." The smile she wore made it worth the extra effort. "You are a great student of people. Jason never had a clue about any of my favorites. Could never remember if it was me, his mom, or his sister who liked what." She chuckled. Time had begun to heal, and looking back, he hadn't been the catch she'd originally thought. Jason had a lot of selfish tendencies.

"So, do you like roller coasters?" She cocked her head and bit into her bagel. Sugar and cinnamon glistened on her lips.

"What's not to like?" He winked.

"Okay. Knott's Berry Farm, Disneyland, or Magic Mountain?" The excitement in her voice reminded him of Courtney when she was about ten.

He thought for a minute. "I've done the Disney thing in Orlando. Don't know much about the other two. You a coaster girl?"

She nodded, eyes shooting off sparks of excitement.

"Where's your favorite coaster?"

"Magic Mountain." There was zero hesitation.

"Then we're there, tomorrow. Deal?" He held up his coffee cup.

She grinned. "Deal." And touched his cup with hers.

After a few minutes of silence, Starr asked, "So after

yesterday, do you prefer San Diego or LA?"

"San Diego. It seems cleaner, not as big, and less smoggy." He sipped his black coffee. "Of course that is a really uninformed observation. I'm sure both have their good and bad qualities."

They finished up breakfast and threw the bags and wrappers away. Both carried their coffees to her dining table. "Where to begin?"

He studied her and saw the trepidation. "Would you like me to take the journals?"

"Somehow that seems less invasive. Do you mind?"

He shook his head. "Not at all."

"The oldest one is on top. I figured you'd find more back then than in the more recent ones."

"What do you want me to share with you? Only references to the adoption?"

She nodded. "Someday, I'll read them for myself, but right now, they seem too close, too personal. I'll start going through the boxes of letters and such."

He took a seat at one end of the table and she at the other. She had praise-and-worship music playing quietly in the background. He lifted the top journal down from the pile. They were all brown leather and the same size. Camden noted her dad was a man of order and probably didn't embrace change. He liked nice things.

The journals went back to his seminary days. Camden read the firsthand account of his meeting his future wife. "Have you ever heard your parents' love story?"

"I have. They met in the seminary library. Sounds kind of dull, but both of my parents were academics, so it isn't as boring as it seems. Did he write about it?"

"He did." Camden returned his gaze to the journal and read aloud. "Today, I met a most interesting woman and cannot stop thinking about her. Cindy is her name, and with Your grace, I shall run into her again tomorrow."

Starr wore a sweet faraway expression. "He loved her. I always hoped for a man to love me with such intensity." She returned to unfolding papers and stacking them off to one side.

Her words, spoken with such honest sincerity, made him want to be a man who loved a woman that intensely. As he perused through journal after journal, he told Starr, "There are three things that I know about Joe Evans: he loved his Lord Jesus, he adored his wife, and he treasured you."

Chapter 6

That defines who my daddy was." She closed her eyes against the ache piercing her heart and took a deep breath. "Anything in there about me or my adoption?" Anticipation filled her gaze.

"Nothing specific." He laid the last book down, stood, and stretched. "After a couple of years of marriage, they started praying for a baby. Then the Lord blessed them with you. No explanation of where you came from or how you got there. One day you showed up, and every day he thanked God for you or something you did." Camden sat back down. "There is no mention of a pregnancy or an adoption. Just a constant daily request for a baby. Then constant praise and thanksgiving for you. You were loved—of that there is no doubt."

Tears streamed down Starr's face. Rising, she headed into the kitchen, where she grabbed a napkin and dabbed her cheeks. He followed her and wrapped her in his arms. It was at that moment she knew she was falling for him. Ignoring that still, small voice reminding her that they didn't stand a chance, she laid her head against his heart. The steady, solid beat offered comfort.

They came from two different worlds. Her life was in LA, and his was many miles away in Monticello. Besides, she felt certain he thought of her more as a sister than anything else.

"I'm sorry we didn't find anything concrete." His breath against her scalp sent tingles down her spine. "I know you were hopeful."

She had to escape those strong, solid arms before she said something they'd both be embarrassed by. She turned out of his hug and went to the fridge for a glass of water. "I was. I believe I'm adopted, so it's not that. I just wanted some understanding of why they never told me." She turned to face Camden and held out the glass. "Would you like some water?"

He took the offering, enjoying the cool liquid. "I'm starving. What do you say we get out of here for a while?"

Starr agreed, and after a quick makeup-repair job, they walked to a little sushi place about a mile down the road. Neither said much along the way. Conversation with Camden came easy. She loved how they could talk about anything and everything or discuss nothing at all, enjoying a comfortable silence.

After they were seated and had ordered, Camden broke the silence. "So, I've been dying to ask: who was Jason, and what happened? Do you mind me being so bold?"

She shook her head and shrugged. "Old boyfriend. Met in college. Dated too many years. Thought we'd marry. Joke was on me. He got bored with me and, in his words, 'the Christian existence.' Tired of existing, wanted to live."

"Wow. I'm sorry." Sincerity filled his expression and words.

"Don't be." She smiled, thinking about her recent discovery. "A few months ago that question would have brought tears, but time is a healer, even when you don't believe you'll ever heal. And the truth is, I can finally see God's grace in this. He was a great guy, just not the right guy for me." Focusing her gaze on his hand, she asked, "So what about you? No ring, so I am assuming you're single."

"Yes ma'am. I come from a pretty intense family." Camden paused while the waiter set their plates in front of them. When he retreated, Camden continued, "My focus was law school, and it started in high school. I needed good grades to get into college and excellent grades to get into law school. Not much time for a social life, and certainly no girl would have wanted a man with a self-imposed schedule like mine."

Starr giggled. "You sound like a barrel of fun. What about now?" She dipped her California roll into wasabi, a green condiment also known as Japanese horseradish.

"The past year and a half, I've been focused on my career and getting that off the ground. Thank the good Lord, I joined a firm where a senior partner was retiring, so I inherited a lot of clients from him."

Starr's mouth dropped open as the truth hit her. "So you've never had a girlfriend?"

"You say it like it's the worst thing ever." He feigned offense.

"I'm sorry. It's really sweet."

He rolled his eyes.

"Really. I mean it." Then she laughed. "Sorry. As my dad used to say, 'Not laughing at you but with you.'" She tried to get serious, but picturing him as a nerd tickled her.

"For you to be laughing with me implies I'm laughing." His eyes reflected a merry heart, but he kept his face serious. "And I'm not."

She placed her hand over her mouth. "Me either."

He grinned. "Let's see you eat like that."

After they finished their meal, it was growing dark. They sauntered back to Starr's.

227

"Let's call it a night. I don't think breaking off early would hurt either of us."

"I'm pretty pooped." Starr stood on tiptoe, placing a light kiss on his cheek. "Thanks for everything." A contentment settled over her, and she felt more peaceful than she had since her parents' deaths.

The next three days flew by for Starr. By Friday, when she drove him to the airport, she was convinced that she'd fallen for Camden, and in her dad's favorite terms—from his favorite hobby—she'd fallen hook, line, and sinker.

"We're a little early." Camden's comment seemed idle and meaningless. "Why don't you park, and we'll have one last cup of coffee."

"Sounds good."

She parked the car, and they walked side by side toward the terminal at LAX. He went to the kiosk and printed his boarding pass. Then they walked together to a little coffee stand and perched on two stools. He ordered for both of them, and he always paid. Her dad would appreciate that about him—that and a million other things.

"How do men do it? I mean, how can you fit an entire week's worth of clothes into one little carry-on?"

"It's all in the shoes," he joked.

Starr raised a brow, not following. "The shoes?"

He glanced down at her feet. "You haven't worn the same pair twice since I met you." Then he pointed at his joggers. "I, on the other hand, have been loyal to this pair the entire week."

"You've got a point." She smiled and sipped her really bad coffee drink.

He grew serious and studied her. "Are you coming in December?"

228

She nodded. How could she not? It was another chance to see him.

"Would you come a week early, so I can repay your hospitality?"

Her heart leaped at his invitation. "It's not necessary, but I'd love to."

He grinned. "Maybe you'll fall in love—"

I think I already have.

"—with the South," he finished. Glancing at his watch, he rose. "I'd better head toward the security check-in."

She slid off the stool and walked beside him. There were a million things she wanted to say, but nothing was really appropriate. Any feelings were on her part and her part only.

Starr felt a lump lodging itself in her throat. Well, she could forget saying anything now. She'd sound like a croaky frog. Maybe God was protecting her from making a fool of herself.

Camden stopped a few feet from the end of the line. He looked deep into her eyes and smiled. "It was a pleasure, Miss Starr." He sort of bowed from the waist like they did in the old corny movies her parents loved. He took her hand and kissed it.

"For me, too." The words sounded much smoother than they felt as she forced them past the tears balled up in her throat.

He wrapped her in a bear hug for the second time. "Take care. I'll see you around the eighteenth of December."

"Until then." *I'll be missing you. . .*

❄

He imagined himself pulling her into his arms and kissing those sweet lips. But instead he moved toward the line and

229

only dreamed of a good-bye filled with hugs, kisses, and regrets. One week. He'd known her one week. It felt so much longer. Maybe because it had been an intensely personal week packed with boatloads of emotion.

Normally a man moved by logic, not sentiment, he was shocked by the depth of his feelings. As he boarded the plane, he listed all the reasons he and Starr would be impossible. But then that phrase from a verse he'd learned years ago in AWANA popped into his head. *Nothing is impossible with God.*

That night as he crawled into bed, he picked up his cell phone. "Should I?" Every dating rule he'd ever heard popped into his head. Too soon. Appear too desperate. Wait at least three days to make contact.

But they weren't dating, so those guidelines didn't matter. He laid his head back on his pillow and hit number nine. He'd plugged her into his speed dial while in LA, since he was calling her so often.

"Camden, hi."

"Hello."

"I was hoping to hear from you so I'd know you'd made it home safe and sound."

His heart sailed at her words. "You were?"

"Of course. So what are you up to?"

"I'm heading to bed and just wanted to say good night."

"Bed? It's only seven," she chided.

"Ten here. Early golf game in the morning."

"Thanks again for coming, for staying, for everything. You've become a good friend."

Her words filled him with warmth. A good friend—he would take that. "I feel the same way. Would you mind if we kept in touch?"

"I was hoping for nothing less. Thank you. You are my one link between my old life and this new one. I just don't want to bug you or drive you crazy. I mean, you are the attorney. I'm the client. Does that include personal phone calls on your cell? The lines aren't clear. Am I rambling?"

He chuckled. "You said it before—you've become a good friend. Friendships usually include cell phone numbers, phone calls, et cetera."

"Okay." He could envision her bobbing her head in that cute way she did. "So if I call you from time to time, you won't roll your eyes and send me to voice mail?"

"Nope. What's on your agenda tomorrow?"

"I've got to get back to the job search."

"Tough economy to find one of those." He wanted her to remember it had nothing to do with her or any lack. "Have you thought about a career change?"

"I love graphic design. So no. But at some point I may be forced to rethink my whole life."

"Sometimes we all are. Sleep well."

"I will a few hours from now." She giggled. "Talk to you soon."

The next morning Camden put on a collared knit shirt and pulled his clubs out of his coat closet. Most Saturdays he, his dad, his grandpa, and Grayson all hit the greens and caught up on life. Today was no different.

Exiting his place, he walked to his parents'. Dad and Grandpa loaded their clubs into the back of Dad's Suburban. He and Grayson followed suit. The younger two settled into the backseat. Dad and Grandpa were discussing the stock market of late.

"I met a girl."

Grayson grinned. "Me, too, bro. Holly Davenport, one of the Bellingham quadruplets."

"No way!"

"You, too? The California quad?"

Camden nodded. That would be interesting if he and his brother ended up with identical wives.

"Man, they are so beautiful. Do you think any of the four will end up making a home here in Monticello?"

Camden shrugged. "Only time will tell, but I doubt it will be Starr. She's pretty set on staying in LA for career opportunities. What about Holly?"

"There might be a chance. She can write anywhere."

"Wish that were true with Starr."

Chapter 7

"I can't believe Thanksgiving is almost here. You are coming to my parents', right?" Sandy asked as she and Starr rounded a corner on their daily jog.

"Of course." They'd started running together when Starr lost her job. Sandy assured her she needed a good stress reliever in her life, and it was working.

Her phone beeped. A text from Camden. A grin split her face. GOOD MORNING. WISH I COULD JOG WITH YOU TODAY. INSTEAD, I'M HEADING TO COURT.

"Camden?" Sandy asked.

She nodded, fighting the urge to hug her phone against her heart.

"You two are worse than Mike and me."

"We're just good friends. You and Mike are more than that." But honestly, nothing brightened her day more than hearing from him in one form or another. Following each communication, she wore a goofy grin for hours afterward.

Sandy sipped some water from her camel pack. "I don't receive umpteen texts and calls a day. Every time I'm with you he texts or e-mails or calls."

And Starr loved it. She grinned bigger. "But you get that one long, sweet phone call in the evening. Mike is in meetings and seminars during the daylight hours." She decided to switch topics. "Two really important things God has taught me through this unemployment period is that I do have to exercise regularly in order to alleviate stress, and the Sabbath rest is really important."

"Our society as a whole suffers greatly in the area of rest. It's go, go, go. Once you get another job, will you have time to maintain your commitment to exercise and taking a real day off every week?"

"I have to. Once God shows me something, He expects my obedience."

"True."

Sandy led the way into their favorite little coffee shop. After they ordered, they grabbed a table for two.

Starr tapped out a quick text. GOOD MORNING TO YOU! HAVING COFFEE WITH SANDY. *And missing you.* She kept the last line to herself. She missed him like crazy, even though, as Sandy had pointed out, they were in constant contact throughout the day. She loved that about them. The little texts just filling each other in on the events of the day.

"Earth to Starr." Sandy grinned at her. "You are off in Camden land."

"Sorry." Starr tried to hide the constant grin and sip her mocha, which of course reminded her of Camden because they'd shared several the week he was here.

"Admit it, Starr. You've fallen for the guy."

"Hook, line, and sinker. But it would never work. To him, I'm a good friend, nothing more. He's a Georgia boy through and through, and small-town Georgia at that. My hope of a great job is limited to LA, New York, Chicago, and possibly a few other huge cities across the map. Monticello isn't even on the map." Starr once again recited the list of reasons that she so often reminded herself of.

"Go freelance. With the web, location matters little." Sandy was nothing if not practical.

"Bottom line is, he thinks of me as a friend—a good

friend, but nothing more."

Sandy grinned. "Yeah right. We're good friends, and we don't text a hundred times a day."

"What we have is really sweet. Sometimes I wonder if he may think of me like a younger sister. I know he worries about me because I don't have a family. And, besides you, he's the best friend I have." Her heart brimmed over with feelings for him.

Sandy's eyes were teary. "There is a lot to be said for friendship. It goes a long way in building a solid foundation for the future." Sandy was determined to turn this into a romance.

"Or you just have a really great friend for life. He's easier to share with than almost anyone I've ever known. And our nightly conversations—"

"Nightly conversations? As you measure it out, girl! How many rubs have I taken from you about my phone dates with Mike?" Sandy was now the one grinning.

"You are right, and I am sorry. But they are great, aren't they? I mean, he encourages me in the Lord and helps me find the strength to get through some pretty difficult days. I'm still struggling with the whole adoption thing. It feels like my life was all built on an illusion, not truth. I still don't understand why they never told me that I was adopted." Starr exhaled a long, slow breath.

"I don't get it either, but knowing your parents, they had a good reason." Sandy unknowingly gave her the same answer Camden had repeated endless times.

"Then I wonder about what other things they kept from me. Were there other truths they hid from me? I start feeling angry at them all over again."

"Starr, I don't think there were other secrets. They lived transparent lives."

"So we thought, but they had one big lie—me."

"Not a lie, but a choice. They never said you weren't adopted. They just never said anything."

"Omission is still a lie. How many times did Daddy say that to me? Anyway, when I get on one of these tirades, Camden keeps me grounded, and like you, he finds logical explanations for my questions without answers. And one of the best things about him being thousands of miles away is that we aren't distracted by the boy-girl thing. It's sometimes easier to confide in someone over the phone because you're not always trying to read them or their reaction. We've shared some of our deepest longings and biggest secrets. We laugh a lot. Sometimes I cry. We share self-discovery."

"I get it. I've been phone dating almost a year. And my relationship with Mike is miles deeper than I've experienced with any other guy. When you're far away, you talk, actually talk. When he's here on weekends, we talk far less. We watch sports, go to movies, run errands, but don't have the same intimate level of conversation we share during the week."

"So I'm not crazy? It is a different kind of connection."

Sandy nodded. "If he asked you to move to Georgia, would you?"

Starr shook her head. "I can't let myself even go there. If I start playing the what-if game, it would change the precious relationship we share now because I'd start having expectations, looking for signs. We are good friends, period. And I'm so grateful God brought him into my life. If and when I meet Mr. Right, my standards will be a lot higher than Jason, now that I know there are Camdens out there."

Sandy glanced at her watch. "We'd better hustle. I've got clients in an hour." Once they were back outside and headed toward their complex, Sandy continued, "I'm so glad you met Camden, too, and if you guys are never more than friends, so be it."

"Thank you."

As they parted ways, Sandy hollered, "I will, however, be praying for more."

Starr grinned, not sure how to pray for her and Camden. But one thing she knew for certain, she could not wait for the next three weeks to pass, so she could see him again.

❅

Camden waited impatiently down by baggage claim, rather pleased with himself. Both planes were scheduled to arrive on time, so his plan would be executed perfectly. *Lord, let this be the key to Starr's freedom regarding the adoption.* He stuck his hand into the front pocket of his jeans and clasped the ring between his thumb and forefinger. *And give me the perfect opportunity to tell Starr I want her in my future. I'm out on a limb here, Lord. I don't know if she has any of those kinds of feelings for me at all. This is the biggest risk I've ever taken.* Camden sucked in a deep breath. *Your will be done.*

Then he caught his first glimpse of her, moving toward him. His heart pounded. He touched the ring one last time. *Thy will be done.* He removed his hand from his pocket and opened his arms. She ran into them, and he held her tight.

"Welcome."

Her arms were tight around his neck. He knew that to all onlookers they appeared to be two lovers reuniting, but there were no kisses, only hugs. His lips longed to change that fact, but not today.

Her hug reassured him that she was as happy to see him as he was to see her. He needed that reassurance. After a couple of minutes, he loosened his hold.

"I have a surprise for you."

Starr's expression told him she loved surprises, which he already knew.

"What is it?"

"You'll know soon enough." He hugged her to his side.

The suitcases started rotating around the belt. They moved closer. "Let me know when you spot yours."

"That one." She pointed.

"The brown one with pink trim."

"Yep."

He grabbed it and set it next to her. "Any others?"

"That's it. What's my surprise?"

"Patience." Pulling the handle out on her case, he rolled it along behind them and strode toward the designated meeting place.

"Isn't that the way out?" She pointed to the large glass doors.

"Yep." He didn't move toward them but kept going until they reached a little restaurant. "Table for three."

"Three?" Starr glanced around. Nope, no one but the two of them.

The hostess led them to one of the round booths. Starr slid in, and Camden followed her instead of going to the other side, so she slid around to the middle.

"Is my surprise a person?"

He nodded. "But she—"

"She?" Was that a spark of jealousy in her tone? "Did you meet someone?"

Camden laughed. "I spend all my spare time with you. I don't have time to meet anyone." *Don't want to either.* "Anyway, as I was saying, she won't arrive for an hour or so. So in the meantime, fill me in on you."

Now Starr laughed. "Fill you in? We just talked last night for almost an hour. You're more filled in on my life than Sandy."

"You're right, but last night you'd mentioned something about what you've learned from God through this season, but then we chased a rabbit down some other path, and you never finished. That was what I wanted you to fill me in on."

She nodded. "Gotcha."

The waitress finally showed up. "I think we'll just have a couple of sweet teas and maybe share a slice of pecan pie." Then he focused on Starr. "That okay with you?"

Starr nodded.

He smiled. "Thanks for coming. It's good to see you in person." He squeezed her hand, wishing for so much more.

"Thanks for insisting," she joked.

Man, would he love to sweep her up and kiss those gorgeous lips of hers. Would she kiss him back? Slap him? Be appalled?

"What?" She scrunched her nose with the question. "Why are you staring at me with that funny look on your face?"

"Was I? Sorry. I was thinking that once our mystery guest arrives, we'll go have an early dinner and then bring her back to the airport before we head to Monticello."

"Someone is flying in to have dinner with us and flying out again." Her brows drew together. "That's crazy."

"It is." But worth every second. He had a feeling this was

Starr's missing piece of the puzzle. The facts would clear it all up, and life would make sense again.

"Okay, you wanted to hear my epiphany? My moment of truth? Even before the discovery of three sisters in my life, I'd been asking God the hard question about permissive will versus His perfect will. It has to do with the whole Jason thing. You know, what if Jason was God's will for my life and he chose a different path? What happens to me? Am I out of the loop for His perfect will?"

"I think we've all grappled with that one." Camden slid his glass to the edge of the table, and the waitress refilled it.

"God gave me the answer; at least I think He did. People do have free will, and their choices affect our lives."

He nodded.

"Take the drunk driver who killed my parents—he chose to drive impaired. His sin cost my parents their lives."

Camden nodded. "I've hurt people with my choices."

"We all have. Most bad or wrong choices, however, aren't so life-altering."

"Agreed."

"So here's my conclusion. Sin affects not just us but often many others whose lives interface with ours. The more grievous the sin, the greater its power to destroy."

Camden nodded.

"But the bottom line is Romans 8:28. If I keep walking with him, He will use my parents' accident, Jason's leaving the faith, and me discovering I'm adopted for my good. Somehow, these life-altering events will strengthen me and make me more like Jesus."

He reached for her hand, sending her a smile. "You're amazing." Oh man, did he want to hold her. *Thank You, Jesus.*

Thank You for giving her peace in the midst of so much.

"Those first two things were not His will, but they happened. And He will redeem them in my life. I just know that I know that."

"Preach it, girl."

Chapter 8

Starr stared at the woman the hostess led toward them. She couldn't breathe. Her heart pounded. Was she seeing a ghost? No, there were differences but huge similarities.

"Here you go, ma'am." The hostess stopped at their table. Camden rose.

Surreal. That was the only word that entered Starr's brain.

"Connie?" Camden offered his hand. "Camden Brockman. And this is Starr."

She faced Starr, smiling. "It's so good to meet you, dear."

Starr could barely nod her head.

"Starr, this is your aunt Connie. She flew in from Alabama to meet you."

Aunt Connie? She tried to remember. Did she have an Aunt Connie?

Camden slid in on one side of the booth, and this woman, who strongly resembled her mother, slid in on the other side.

"She knows your story—all of it." He grasped her hand under the table. She squeezed tight as if he offered her a lifeline of some sort.

Starr shifted her gaze to her aunt. "I'm sorry. I guess I'm dumbfounded. I didn't even know my mom had a sister. You sure look like her."

"We heard that all of our lives."

Camden rose. "Let me take you ladies to a nice dinner

spot. We can talk in the car."

Once Starr was out of the booth, Aunt Connie said, "Come here, and let me hug you." She threw open her arms wide, and Starr moved into them. A stranger, yet not.

They followed Camden and the suitcase to the car. Her aunt kept an arm draped around her shoulders.

"It's truly my fault that you didn't know about me."

"How so?" All Starr could think was *more secrets, more lies*.

"Let's wait until we get to the car; then I'll tell the whole story."

Starr felt numb. How many more stories were there?

Camden opened the back door of his Tahoe, and Aunt Connie crawled in. Starr waited at the back of his SUV with her luggage. After Connie was in, he returned and loaded Starr's luggage. She felt so dismal. When would the surprises end?

Suddenly, Camden pulled her into a hug. His arms felt like the last safe place on earth. She rested her head on his shoulder. While holding her, he whispered near her ear, "Remember the whole Romans 8:28 thing? This might be another occasion to put that into play."

She raised her head and looked into crisp blue eyes. Then he took her face in his hands and planted an innocuous kiss right smack-dab on her lips.

There was no time to respond or react. He took her elbow and led her to the backseat on the passenger side. "Why don't you sit back here with her? Easier to talk when you can look at each other face-to-face." He opened the door, and Starr scooted in.

Did he just kiss me? He acted as if nothing in the world were different.

243

"Starr, honey, I'm sorry for all of this."

She refocused on her aunt, filing the kiss away for later speculation.

"Your momma and daddy wanted a baby in the most desperate way, but month after month, then year after year, no baby came." Aunt Connie's accent was extreme.

"Finally, a chance to adopt privately arose, and they jumped on it. They were tickled to have you but mutually agreed they'd not tell you about your adoption."

"But why?" Starr loosened her seat belt and turned to face her aunt more directly.

"Your daddy was adopted, and as such really struggled with rejection and his birth parents not wanting him. They didn't want that for you but hoped for security beyond measure."

"I guess that makes sense." A parent would try to protect a child from similar pain and rejection.

"Well, the whole family, both sides, said they were wrong. After many discussions and arguments, they gave up and moved to California, cutting off relationship."

"My parents did that?" The information stunned her. "That is so out of character." Or was it? She no longer knew for sure.

"The whole brood was angry and would not promise to keep your adoption a secret. So moving away protected you."

"No wonder neither of my parents had much to say about extended family. Every time I brought it up, they managed to lead the conversation down a different path."

"They did try to reconcile several times." Her aunt dug through her purse and pulled out a tissue, dabbing the corners of her eyes. "But we all wanted our own way. By then some bitterness had rooted in some of our hearts. Now older and wiser, most of us wish we'd not made an issue of things. After all, you were their child, and they had the right to do as they wanted—no matter what we said or thought."

Starr only nodded. No words came.

"I guess life isn't cut and dry. It gets messy and complicated. When we're young, we think differently." Aunt Connie reached across the expanse of the backseat, patting Starr's hand.

The car had stopped. "We are here," Camden said from the front seat.

As Starr exited the car, she wished for some quiet alone time to process. Instead, she plastered a smile on her face and led the way into the fancy restaurant. They ended up having a nice visit, and Starr learned tons about her parents that she never knew before. A few hours later they returned Aunt Connie to the airport with promises to keep in touch and the possibility of future visits.

As they drove away from the airport, Starr said, "Now I have two families to get to know. How random is that?"

"Actually, you have three—mine."

Starr wondered if that was a multilayered comment with underlying meaning. She didn't have the mental energy left this evening to think it through. Her thoughts returned to her aunt. "What did you think about all my aunt had to say?"

"I think your parents did what they did out of a right spirit, not a vindictive one. You know, Starr, they were human just like all of us, and their motivation was pure—to protect you."

"I struggle to imagine them walking away from their own families."

"From listening to you, I think because your dad was a pastor, you expected a near-perfect man."

"In my eyes, he was. At least until lately."

"He's still the same guy you thought he was, just slightly more human. Give him grace, especially since you can't go back and get answers."

"You're right."

The rest of the ride to the ranch, Starr wrestled with that whole kiss thing. Was it a kiss? A friendly peck? What did it mean? She was too tired to delve into the deep subject, so they drove in silence.

❄

Camden had Starr text him when she was waking. He'd walk over to his parents' house and be there to introduce her to the gang. His mom had planned a big southern breakfast with biscuits, grits, and gravy. Those were only the sides. She also had eggs, bacon, sausage, and hash browns. By the time he arrived, his mom had a million tempting scents coming out of the kitchen. He'd expected Starr to sleep later since it was three hours earlier back in LA, but she texted before eight.

Starr came down the hall of the big ranch house a bit later. She'd showered and smelled like the fresh morning mist. Her face beamed. "I checked my messages last night." Her eyes danced. "I got a job offer! Not just a job, but as creative director!"

His heart fell. "Wow, congratulations." He thought of the little ring in his pocket. This sure put a different spin on things.

"I'll call this morning. They don't open until nine, so that's noon Georgia time. Can you make sure I'm somewhere quiet about then?"

He nodded and shoved his hands in the front pockets of his jeans. "Coffee?"

At her "Absolutely," he led her to the kitchen.

"Mom, this is Starr Evans. Starr, this is my mother, Eloise Brockman."

"Nice to meet you. I can see the family resemblance."

The petite woman smiled brightly and wiped her hands on her apron. "Welcome! Welcome! And it's really just Ellie." She came around the counter and hugged Starr. "It is so wonderful to meet you and have you in our home."

"Thank you. It's good to be here. I love your house, so warm and inviting."

"I always hope so." She focused her gaze on Camden. "There is still about fifteen minutes until breakfast. Why don't you give her a quick tour of the barns?"

Camden glanced at Starr with brows raised.

"Sounds great."

After they each had an oversized mug of coffee, they headed out the back door. Camden's thoughts were jumbled. If she took this job, the hope of a future would be over. He had to tell her how he felt. His stomach knotted. The risk was huge, but even bigger if he kept quiet. He hadn't planned to take the plunge this soon—more toward the end of the week. Her announcement forced him to rethink the situation.

He led her through the horse barn, stopping to introduce her to each animal along the way. He decided he'd do it now and get it over with. They'd either spend an awkward day together or a quite lovely one. Their entire future depended on Starr's response. He doubted their friendship would survive a turned-down proposal.

She stood at the last stall, petting a dapple-gray foal. He cleared his throat. "Starr?"

❄

When she turned, Camden was on one knee. He held a diamond between his thumb and forefinger. It caught the sunlight streaming through the barn door and winked at her. She leaned heavily against the stall, no longer sure she could stand on her own.

"This isn't at all how I planned for this to go. I thought we'd spend a wonderful week together and I would ask you on Christmas Eve, but this job offer of yours changes things up a bit."

Starr's heart pounded. She'd had no idea this was coming. What a choice—Camden or her dream job. She refocused on him.

"Somewhere in the past few months, I've fallen in love with you."

She smiled, knowing she'd done the same.

"You're the first person I think of at the start of each new day. You're the one I want to be talking to when I fall asleep each evening."

The perfect job or Camden? Was it really even a choice?

"I know we are only friends, and all these feelings may be mine alone. And if that is so, I understand. Most couples know they're both in love before the proposal, so this is a risk. I understand you may have zero feeling for me beyond friendship."

She shook her head and reached for his hand, pulling him up. He was worth laying down her dreams for. "I have so many feelings for you that I don't know where to store them all."

He grinned and brushed her hair off her cheeks. Then he kissed her, but this one wasn't an innocuous little peck. This was the kiss of a man who was staking his claim. And she kissed him back with everything she had.

When he finally broke off the kiss, he asked, "Is that a yes?" He looked pretty sure of himself.

"There has to be a question for an answer," she teased, feeling pretty cocky herself.

He held the ring up, still clutching it in his fingers. "Starr Kendall Evans, will you marry me? And share life with me? And have kids with me? And grow old with me? And love me always, because I know my love for you is a forever thing."

Her heart melted into a pile of mush. "I will." Her raspy voice brimmed with emotion. "I love you dearly. I don't even know exactly when it happened or if it's been there from the start." She ran a hand over his lightly whiskered cheek. "But in you, God has given me a family."

"Does that make four now?" His blue eyes twinkled.

She nodded. "But you're the most important one. The primary one."

"What about the job? Will you regret giving it up?"

She decided to toy with him. "No, I'm taking it. I can support you while you find a firm in LA."

The color drained from his face. She could see him putting together an argument in his mind.

She burst out laughing. "I'm just kidding."

He hugged her around the waist, picking her up and swinging her around. "You think you're funny, huh?"

"I did have you going for a moment."

"I don't want you to resent me down the road. I did some checking, and there are some decent advertising firms in

Atlanta." He shrugged one shoulder.

"Sandy also reminded me that in this day and age, location doesn't have to tie me down. The Internet is the *World Wide Web*, after all, and right in my own home. The possibilities are limitless."

He grinned, his arms still around her waist. "So you and Sandy discussed this possibility? What if I hadn't proposed?"

She grinned. "I may have had to ask you. You'll never know, but thanks to Sandy, I saw you and small-town Georgia as a viable option."

"Remind me to send her a thank-you note." With that the conversation ended, and a few tender kisses began. With Camden her world was bright with possibility, and her black nights had turned to mornings filled with love and joy.

Jeri Odell is a native of Tucson, Arizona. She and Dean will celebrate their thirty-eighth anniversary this year. They also celebrate three wonderful adult children and five precious grandchildren. Jeri holds family dear to her heart, second only to God. She thanks God for the privilege of writing for Him. When not writing or reading, she is busy working in the finance office of her church.

LOVING STETSON

Debra Ullrick

Dedication

This book is dedicated to my sister, Janice Swedberg.
Thank you for supporting me, for having my back,
and for telling just about everyone you encounter
about my books. You rock!
A ginormous thanks to my best friend and author buddy,
Staci Stallings. Thank you for all your support, your
expertise, and for the endless hours you spend mentoring
me and reading my manuscripts over and over.
I love you dearly, my forever friend.
Tamela Hancock Murray, thank you for being you,
and for being the best agent ever.
Thank you, Rebecca Germany, for believing in my stories.
Marjorie Vawter. . .you are one fabulous editor. Thanks!
Ricky Poo. Thank you for thirty-seven years of uncondi-
tional love, for supporting me, and for putting up with my
bizarre hours and many questions. I love you, hon.
Lastly, but definitely not least, thank You, heavenly Father,
for the gifts You placed inside me, and for making
this publishing journey possible.
Jesus, You Rock!

Above all, love each other deeply,
because love covers over a multitude of sins.
1 PETER 4:8

Chapter 1

Noel Brady's spurs chinked on the hardwood floor as she shuffled into the kitchen of her family's two-story Colorado Rocky Mountain ranch house in Grand County. Fresh-baked bread and cinnamon scents hung in the air. "Mom, you won't believe what came in the mail today."

Her mother looked up from attacking the lump of bread dough bundled on the butcher block. With the back of her hand she brushed away a loose strand of her graying blond hair and looked at the floor behind Noel. "No–o–e–e–el. Take off them muddy boots. How many times do I have to tell you that? Just look at the mud you've brought in. And I just mopped, too."

Noel wanted to roll her eyes at her own blunder but didn't because Mom would think she was rolling them at her. Even at twenty years old, out of love and respect for the parents who had adopted her and loved her, Noel still tried to do what she was told. But in her excitement she had forgotten to remove her Tony Lama cowboy boots. She looked down at them and then behind her.

Whoa.

Boy howdy.

She wasn't about to tell her mom that wasn't mud but a mixture of horse fertilizer and fresh cow pies from the barn.

She tucked the envelope into the back pocket of her Wrangler jeans and hustled back to the mudroom. With the aid of a bootjack, she removed her Tonys, and within minutes she had the mess cleaned.

"Thank you, Noel." Mom wiped her hands on her apron. "Now, what did you start to say?"

Noel pulled the envelope out of her pocket. "I got this in the mail today."

"What is it?" Her mom came over and stood beside her.

Noel handed her the letter.

As her mother read, a range of emotions bucked across her face. When she looked at Noel, concerns of losing her only daughter to her "real" family flashed through her eyes. But in a blink, she masked her true feelings as she had so many times in the past when she wanted to shield her children from upsets.

No way would her mother's worries ever come to fruition. As far as Noel was concerned, the Bradys were her real family. Nothing was *realer* than seeing her parents standing in the hot sun or wet snow as close as possible while she showed her prize steers at the Middle Park Fair and Rodeos, or staying up all night with her when she was sick, or crying with her over the loss of her favorite pets.

"Are you going to go?"

Noel put her arm around her mom and kissed her cheek. "Of course I'm going to go. But I'm coming right back. I can't be without my mommy." She hugged her and kissed her mother's cheek.

Her mom's mouth split into a wide grin. "Thank you, Elly girl." Her bluish-green eyes were moist with love.

"I love you, Mom."

"I love you, too."

"Well, I'd better get back out there, or Dad's gonna wonder where I've disappeared to again." She headed toward the door.

"Tell your father dinner will be ready at six sharp and to not keep you kids out there until supper's cold."

"I'll tell him, but I can't guarantee Dad'll listen."

"Won't listen to what?" her dad asked, stepping into the kitchen. He planted a kiss on Noel's forehead and then walked over and stood behind her mother. He slipped his tanned muscled arms around her mother's tiny waist.

Mom tilted her head back to look at him, and he kissed her smack-dab on the lips.

When their kiss ended, her mother slipped out of his embrace and playfully swatted his arm. "Behave yourself. I have to get this bread finished in time for supper. It's going to be ready at six sharp. And you'd better not be late, or you won't get any dessert." Mom shook her finger at him, but her eyes twinkled with a wink.

"Now, that's just downright mean, woman." His gaze roamed around the kitchen until it landed on a batch of freshly baked cinnamon rolls with lots of walnuts and almond-flavored frosting. Just the way her dad and siblings liked them.

Determination written all over his face, he headed toward the goodies.

Mom dashed between him and the counter, snatched a wooden spoon from the blue crock holder, and held it in front of her like a weapon. "Don't you even think about it, Tommy Dale Brady, or I'll wallop you with this here spoon." Once again, her mother's eyes sparkled in spite of her threatening look.

Noel laughed, knowing the woman was utterly harmless.

Her father whirled her direction. "So, you think that's funny, do you?"

Whoa. Noel spun and darted toward the door.

Her dad caught her by the waist and attacked her sides with his fingers, tickling her until she cried through a gaggle of giggles, "Uncle, uncle. Give, give."

"That'll teach you to laugh." He released her and gave her long braid a quick tug.

"Did you tell him your good news?"

His gaze darted between Noel and her mom. "What news?"

"Oh, I forgot." She tapped her fingers to her forehead, snatched the letter from her pocket, and handed it to him.

A lock of gray-streaked brown hair fell against his creased forehead. The same emotions that had crossed her mother's face earlier now crossed his. His attention reverted to her. The sparkle in his gray eyes vanished, and sadness replaced his smile. "Are you going to go?"

"Yes. I am. But, like I told Mom, I'll be back. After all, I can't be without my mommy and daddy." She leaned on her tiptoes and kissed her father's leathery cheek. "You're the bestest dad in the whole world." She dropped her heels back onto the hardwood floor. "I love you, Dad." With those words, she snatched two cold waters from the fridge and darted toward the mudroom. Noel slipped on her boots and headed out to the barn to tell Stetson her good news.

❊

Stetson Laramie glanced up from mucking the barn. "Hey, sunshine. How's my favorite brunette?" His lips curled right along with his heart. He layered his leather-gloved hands on top of the pitchfork handle and stared into Noel's lavendar-blue eyes. "Did you come to help me?"

Noel balked at the pile of soiled straw and tossed her

long braid over her shoulder. "Um. Uh-uh. No way, buddy. You're on your own. It's your turn. I had that mooey pooey job last week."

"Hey. Just what kind of friend are you, anyway?" He scooped a bit of the soiled straw onto the pitchfork and tossed it within inches of her boots.

"A very good one." She glanced at the muck and wrinkled her button nose at the offensive odor. "But not *that* good." She chuckled.

Stetson loved the musical sound of Noel's happy twitter. In fact, there wasn't much he didn't love about her. He pointed toward the waters in her hands. "One of those for me?"

"Nope. Why, did you want one?" Her eyes sparkled with orneriness.

He pointed his forefinger at her and raised his thumb. "Hand over that water or I'll shoot."

"Aaa. That gun wouldn't hurt a gopher. But seeing how you're such a good friend and I'm such a sweetheart"—she grinned and batted her eyes at him—"I'll give you one."

Every time she smiled like that, his body went to sweatin'.

She handed him a bottle. Her fingers brushed against his. Even through his gloves, her touch sent a current similar to that of a hotshot throughout his body. Beads of moisture formed on his forehead. He raised his cowboy hat and ran his shirtsleeve over the drops, then plopped his hat back into place.

"Can you take a break, Stets? I have something to show you." She reached behind her and pulled an envelope out of her pocket.

He yanked his gaze away from her perfectly curved hips

and thighs. "Sure." He jabbed the pitchfork into the mound of straw. "There's a breeze outside." He motioned for her to precede him. When she did, to keep himself from focusing on her backside, he unscrewed the water bottle lid and took a long, cool drink.

Each step Noel made, her spurs clinked. Her long, thick braid swished at her waist, and the sorrel streaks in her hair glistened in the warm September sunshine. When they reached the shade, she climbed the fence, sat on the top rail, and hooked the heels of her boots on the second rail.

Stetson sealed his water bottle and joined her. "So, what did you want to show me?" He watched every move she made as she opened the envelope and handed him its contents. "What's this?"

"Just read it—you'll see."

He scanned through the letter, shocked and amazed by its contents. His attention riveted toward hers. "You're an identical quad? Have you always known you were a quad?"

"Nope. Just found out today." She smiled, and then her eyes took on a faraway look.

"What you thinking about?"

"Just trying to figure out how anyone could give up their child."

Stetson swallowed hard. He didn't want her to see how uncomfortable her comment made him, so he started reading again. "It says, 'Along with your three sisters, you have inherited one hundred acres of land, which is now being used to farm peanuts, with a large antebellum home from your maternal grandparents, Charles and Emily Bellingham of Monticello, Georgia.'" While he was happy for her, at the same time his heart sank.

Noel had always been intrigued with the South. Would owning land there tempt her to move down there? And if she did, would he ever see her again? Those thoughts caused a stabbing pain to his heart, so he quickly plucked them from his mind and continued reading.

"That's what it says. Just think"—she stared ahead of her—"not only am I to inherit land with a large antebellum home on it, but somewhere out there, I have three sisters. Whoa. I just realized I won't be the only girl anymore." Happiness radiated from her smile.

Stetson shook his head. "Whoa, is right. I pity your poor brothers."

"Hey." She elbowed him in the side. "It's *me* you should pity. I'm the one they pick on and play practical jokes on all the time."

"Oh, you poor baby. Yeah right." He thumbed his hat off his forehead and rolled his eyes. "You've pulled your fair share of pranks on them."

"I have, haven't I?" She giggled and then shifted her weight toward him. "Remember the day before they were supposed to show their steers at the county fair? I spiked their tea with sleeping pills and then wrote 'kiss me' on their cheeks with a tagging pen."

"I remember." He shared in her laugh. "I also remember how every girl at the fair chased them. Even Mrs. Sorenson. Who'd a thought an eighty-year-old spry rancher woman would chase them down and kiss each one of them?"

"Were they ever mad! But they got me back big-time for that one."

"They sure did." Stetson laughed. "I can still see the shocked expression on your face when Stinky came to pick you up that night."

As was her habit, Noel wrinkled her nose. He loved how adorable she looked when she did that. "They said you wanted to take me out but you were too nervous to ask. Only it wasn't you at my door. It was Stinky. And trust me, he lives up to his name. I could have wrung my brothers' necks. I'd rather smell cow pies any day than Bobby. I don't think the guy ever showered or used soap. Phew-wee." She plugged her nose with her finger and thumb.

Stetson angled his shoulder to bump hers. "You didn't have to go, you know. You could have just told him there'd been a mistake."

"Yeah, well, I would have, but he was so excited, and I didn't have the heart to burst his bubble."

His gaze snagged on hers. "You always were a softy. Always siding with the underdog, and yet you are still popular." So popular she could have her pick from any of the guys around her.

The question that had dogged him for years resurfaced. He simply stared at a nearby badger hole while he corralled the courage he needed before looking at her. "Were you disappointed it wasn't me?" he asked quietly.

Shock cut across her face so fast that he wanted to rope back the words, but it was too late now.

Their eyes locked and held, until she broke contact by dipping her head, and her dark eyelashes fanned downward. "I was, actually." Her answer came out hoarse.

Like a frisky foal in the springtime, his heart crow-hopped.

His gaze dropped to her lips. Lips he wanted to feel with his own.

He tilted his head and leaned toward her.

Inches away from her face, he came to his senses and remembered why they could be nothing more than friends.

With a playful tap to her nose, he smiled. A forced one at that. "I don't blame you. That was pretty mean of your brothers to set you up with Stinky."

Without giving her a chance to comment, he moved away, pulled the paper in front of him, and asked, "So, what other shocking news is in this letter?" He pretended to read, but his mind was anywhere but on the letter. It was solely on her, and how close he'd come to kissing her.

❋

Noel's chest caved with disappointment. She'd felt as giddy as a high school girl when she thought Stetson was about to kiss her. But that was something she'd only dreamed about for the past five years. When he pulled away, she fought the urge to knock his cowboy hat off, yank his lips onto hers, and kiss some sense into him. And one day she would, too. She knew he cared about her, but something was holding him back. Someday she'd dally up enough nerve to ask him. But that day wasn't today. Today she had too much on her mind. Too much to think about.

The letter changed everything. The contents had excited her and scared her. Unanswered questions rolled through her mind like a tumbleweed chased by the wind. She understood her mother died in childbirth, but who was her father? Was he alive? Why didn't he raise them? Or any of her grandparents? But most of all, she wondered what it would be like meeting her sisters for the first time.

She jumped down from the fence, and Stetson joined her. She looked up at him, standing there quietly, watching her with those gorgeous olive-green eyes of his. What she would give if he would put his arms around her and hold her until the questions vanished from her mind. "Stetson."

"Yeah."

"Do you think they'll like me?"

"Who?"

"My sisters?"

"Ah El, how could anyone not help but like you? 'Course they will."

In that second her heart broke free. She looked up at him feeling every roller coaster emotion she'd felt in his presence for the last five years. "Do you like me?"

❄

Had she really just asked him that? Stetson struggled with his answer as Noel stared up at him with those wide innocent eyes. This was the first time he'd ever seen her look so vulnerable. He wanted to wrap her in his arms and kiss away every inch of insecurity he saw there. But his past wouldn't let him. Finally he shrugged. " 'Course I like you."

"No. Do you *like* like me?" Her eyes seemed to beg him to say yes.

And he wanted to. In fact, he longed to pull her to him and show her just how much he wanted to. Just how much he *like* liked her. How much he loved her. His kisses would leave her in no doubt of his intense affection for her. But his heart and lips would never know that privilege.

Again, his past had seen to that.

Chapter 2

"N o–o–el–ly, where are you?"

Noel turned toward the sound of Dustin's voice. "Coming." She shot a quick look at Stetson. On her way to the barn, she tamped down her disappointment at not hearing Stetson's answer whether he liked her or not. "Hey, what's up?" She managed to smile at her brother.

"Do you know where Stetson's at?"

"I'm right here."

Their attention shifted toward him.

Stetson's broad shoulders, slim waist, slightly bowed muscular legs, cowboy hat, and cowboy boot–clad silhouette in the center of the barn door sent shivers galloping through Noel's body like a racehorse on speed.

"Great. You're just the man I was looking for."

Me, too. Her heart sighed. Now she just needed to convince Stetson that *she* was the woman *he* was looking for.

"Dad wanted me to see if you and Noel would take the stock trailer to Mitch's place." Dustin met Stetson halfway. "Some of our cows got in with his, and we can't leave 'em there because he drylotted them."

Noel never understood how anyone could drylot an animal. When she'd discovered drylotting meant holding the cows in a pen with no food or water, it broke her heart. Well, no cow of theirs would go without.

She didn't even wait for Stetson's answer. "We're on our way." Out the barn she flew.

"Noel, wait up."

She stopped and waited for Stetson to catch up.

"Why don't we take my pickup?"

Seeing how the gooseneck trailer was already hooked up to his truck, she grabbed the sleeve of his shirt and yanked him forward. "Can't believe we haven't left yet." With that she darted toward his vehicle.

She placed her forefinger and thumb between her lips and whistled for Stub, her brother's blue merle Australian shepherd. Someday she'd get her own dog, but for now she just enjoyed babying her brothers' dogs. She'd pert-near had to beg Hale to let her take Stub today, saying she needed his Aussie worse than he did. Gathering cattle was hard work, and Stub was worth his weight in gold. Saved her and her horse a lot of hard work.

Stub came barreling through the pen, dove under the fence, and raced toward her. His docked tail wagged, and his front feet pranced. He was ready to go to work. Noel dropped the tailgate. "Load up," she ordered.

Stub jumped in the back, and Stetson's border collie followed suit. Noel rubbed Bozo and Stub behind the ears, slid in on the passenger side, and closed the door.

Stetson swung the driver's side door open and slid behind the wheel.

"What took you so long, hotshot?"

Stetson thumbed the brim of his cowboy hat up and tilted his head. "What's your hurry, nelly belly?"

"Who you callin' nelly belly?" She narrowed her eyes and scrunched her lips at him. The man had so many nicknames for her she couldn't keep up with them all. Secretly though, she loved them all. "C'mon. I don't want mister cheapskate starvin' our cows. Who knows how long they've been there."

"I see your point." Stetson started the truck, and down the lane they went.

A breeze entered their windows, swirling the stuffy air. The horse trailer rattled as it bounced across the rough road.

A quick tire drop in a huge pothole jostled Noel's body. Her gaze flew toward Stetson, who was busy looking out the window, instead of watching the road. Typical male. Her dad and brothers could read the brand of a cow grazing a hundred yards off the highway while traveling fifty-five miles per hour. She loved them all. Especially the hot cowboy sitting across from her.

Noel's mind drifted back to the question she'd asked Stetson earlier about if he liked her. She debated whether to ask him again, but judging by the relief on his face when Dustin had hollered for her, she decided not to. Still, there was no way she was giving up on this man. After all, brands were permanent, and her heart had been branded by Stetson years ago.

As they headed down the three-mile lane to the highway, she stared out the window and let her mind wander back to when she was fifteen. The day her dad had hired Stetson.

One look at him that day and she knew she was a goner. The tall, gangly, eighteen-year-old cowboy had two-stepped right into her heart. Whatever excuse she could muster up to be thrown together with him, she'd found it. And it had paid off. Well, sort of. She just needed to figure out a way to break the barrier that kept his heart penned; then perhaps she and Stetson would become a team. A married team.

She snuck a peek at him. How different he was now from the boy back then. His face had matured, and his body had muscled out. Plus, he no longer played the part of a brash, prideful cowboy. Accepting Christ two years after he'd arrived on the Circle B Ranch had definitely softened his heart. At first she'd been attracted to his outside, but now she was in love with the real him—the kind, gentle, caring man he'd become. A man whose arms she ached to be wrapped in, whose lips she desired to feel on hers, and whose sweet words of love she longed to hear.

"You're awful quiet over there. What're you thinking so hard about?"

Where was a blazing branding pot when she needed one? At least then she could blame her flaming cheeks on it. Boy howdy. Just how was she going to get out of this one? Lying wasn't an option, but telling the truth wasn't one either. "Um. . .I was thinking about when you first came to the Circle B."

"What about it?" he asked, glancing at her and then back at the gravel road.

"I was thinking about how much you've changed." Her spirit squirmed a mite. *Ah c'mon, Lord, cut a gal a little slack here; after all, I was thinking about that, too.*

"In what way?" His deep voice caused her heart to flip-flop like a fish breaking water.

"Well, for one thing, you're a lot kinder now than you were back then. And you're not so annoying or as arrogant."

"Me, arrogant? Never." His lopsided grin twitched.

Her eyes moved in a circular motion. "If I believed that one, then you could sell me some swampland down in Barber Basin to raise pet snakes."

"Well, it just so happens I own land there. How much you willin' to pay?"

"You're incorrigible, you know that?"

"Yeah, but you love me." He waggled his eyebrows at her. She sure did. Hopelessly, totally, and completely.

❄

The second the words left Stetson's mouth, he wanted to yank them back, but it was too late. From his peripheral vision he noticed Noel staring at him with the same longing he'd seen many times. The same longing he himself felt but knew he could never act on. Dwelling on it only made matters worse. That much he had learned.

He stopped at the end of the lane and looked left before pulling out onto Highway 40, heading south toward Kremmling. He finally worked up the gumption to ask Noel the question that had been eating at him since she received that letter. "I was thinking about something, small fry." He glanced over at her, flipped his right blinker on, and slowed way down to make his turn.

"What's that, stretch?"

"Stretch, is it?"

"Small fry, is it?"

"Okay, I deserve that one. Anyway, when do you plan on leaving for Georgia? How long do you think you'll stay?" His fingers ached from clutching the steering wheel while waiting for her answer. It was stupid to think he could hold her here and stupid to think he could ever let her go. And yet he had to.

"I don't know yet. It's all still so new; I haven't had time to absorb everything. I do know one thing"—she shifted in her seat—"I can't wait to see the antebellum house. I still can't believe I have relatives in the South. How ironic is that, since I've always wanted to live there, and now who knows? Maybe this is my chance."

271

"Do you really think you might move out there?" He swallowed the lump of dread clogging his throat. "Won't you miss your family?" *Won't you miss me?*

Stetson turned his right blinker on again and pulled into Mitch Parker's expansive ranch.

"Of course I will. But I have to say the idea of having blood relatives out there piques my interest. Can you imagine three more of me running around? Scary, huh?" She laughed.

The thought of three other women as beautiful as Noel running around wasn't scary at all. But it didn't matter how much they looked alike; his heart was sold out only to Nelly.

Stetson spotted the Circle B's cows in the west pen. True to Mr. Parker's word, they had no food or water. His blood boiled just thinking about someone treating an animal that way.

He started backing the horse trailer up to the pen. Not quite there, Noel jumped out and swung the gate open. In seconds he had it parked. On his way to the back of the trailer, he dropped the tailgate to let the dogs out.

Two short whistles and a finger-point to the right and Bozo ran behind the eleven head of Circle B cattle.

One long whistle from Noel and a finger-point to the left and Stub rushed around the cows. Both dogs worked back and forth, gathering the cattle and pushing them into the trailer. Hooves clanged and banged loudly as they loaded.

Mitch Parker charged in their direction like a mad bull. "It's about time you got here," mister cheapskate growled. The wrinkles in his forehead and the sagging circles under his eyes reminded Stetson of a bulldog.

Noel slammed the trailer gate shut and latched it. She stormed over to where he and Mr. Parker stood. "We got here as soon as you called." Noel stepped directly in front of the big man.

"Jim called you yesterday morning." He looked down at Noel and matched her glare.

"No one called yesterday. The first we heard of it was this afternoon, and we came as fast as we could." Fire shot from her eyes. "You could have at least given them water and hay. We would have given it back to you, and you know that."

One gray bushy eyebrow spiked upward. "Jim didn't call you yesterday?"

"Nope."

More wrinkles joined the others across his forehead. "Just wait till I get my hands on him. He's outta here." Mitch ran gnarled fingers over his whiskered chin. "I'm sorry your cows haven't had any water or food. If I had known that, I would have fed them myself. You can't trust anybody these days," he groused and stomped off in the direction from which he came.

So the seventy-two-year-old guy had a heart inside that stooped Amazon body after all. All this time they'd thought he was just being a cheapskate; instead, it was his foreman who deprived the Brady's cattle of their needs.

Stetson never did like Jim—a lousy drunk who was meaner than an angry badger. All you had to do was look at the bruises on his wife's arms and legs. Bruises blamed on horses, cattle, and fence posts that seemed to leap out in front of her. Everyone in the county tried to help her, but she refused to accept it and stuck to her story about the animals running her over and her clumsy feet.

"Stets, you okay?"

He looked down at Noel. "I'm fine. Let's get out of here before I do something I regret."

Chapter 3

"Hey, sis." Noel faced her brother Mark at the dinner table. "Mom said you got something in the mail today you need to share with us. What is it?" He plucked a piece of freshly baked, buttered bread from a thick slice and popped it into his mouth. His blond hair disappeared under the collar of his shirt. He was in desperate need of a haircut. She'd offer to give him one later.

Noel took a drink of her milk and then wiped her mouth off with her cloth napkin, which hinted of bleach and fabric softener.

"I got a letter from an attorney today." She glanced around the log table at each one. Shock, concern, and smiles stared back at her. The twins, Bailey and Dustin, continued shoving food into their mouths but kept their blue eyes locked on her. Mark, Hale, and Travis stopped their forks midair, their greenish-yellow eyes never leaving her. Her dad continued to slice off a piece of his rib-eye steak, and her mom smiled at her, but it never reached her eyes.

"It appears I have three other sisters. Make that identical sisters." Brows shot upward around the table.

"You mean there's more than one of you?" The smirk on Bailey's face showed he was only teasing.

"Yeah, and you'd better watch it, or I'll sic them on you." She pursed her lips at him and faked a glare.

Bailey held his hands up like a captured bad guy from an old John Wayne movie. "Don't shoot. Don't shoot. I take it back."

Everyone laughed, except for her parents and Stetson.

She put the napkin she'd been holding on her lap and leaned her elbows on the table. "According to the letter, my sister and I have inherited one hundred acres of land in Monticello, Georgia, with a large antebellum home on it."

"Woo-wee." Dustin whistled. "Land and a house. That's awesome, sis. So"—he popped a bite of steak into his mouth and spoke around the lump—"when are you moving?" He winked.

"Oh no. You ain't gettin' rid of me that easy."

Dustin snapped his fingers. "Shoot. I got all excited for nothing. Here I thought we were finally getting rid of her, and we wouldn't have to babysit the brat anymore."

"Brat?" Noel slugged him in the arm. "You'll never be rid of me. Besides, if I left, you guys wouldn't have anyone to pick on. And we can't have that now, can we?"

"She's got a point there," Hale piped in.

"Okay, you guys." Noel's gaze slanted toward her father's voice. "Let Newy get on with her news."

"Okay, so"—she shifted in her seat—"the thing is, Emily Bellingham, my maternal grandma, stipulated all four of us girls have to spend our twenty-fifth birthday together at the house." She looked over at her mother, who suddenly seemed interested in the food on her plate.

"What house?" Mark wanted to know.

"The one in Georgia, brainiac. What other house did you think she meant?" Travis, the youngest of her brothers, tossed a piece of bread at Mark, but it landed somewhere behind him.

"Pick that up, Travis," Mom ordered, shaking her head.

Travis hurried around the table, snatched it up, and then

sat back in his chair. "Go ahead, sis." Travis loved to take charge and possessed great leadership qualities.

"Thanks." She held back a smile. "Anyway, the other stipulation is we can't sell the house or the property. It has to stay in the family. We're supposed to meet at the attorney's office on December twenty-sixth to sign the papers to receive our inheritance."

"That's odd," Stetson said around a bite of potatoes.

Noel shifted her attention toward him. Those were the first words she'd heard from him since their earlier encounter.

"What's odd?" Travis asked. "That she has to be there on the twenty-sixth to sign the papers, or that they have to spend their twenty-fifth birthday together? Or they can't sell the property?"

"All of it," Stetson answered, jagged lines creasing his forehead.

"Why do you think it's odd?" Noel really wanted to know.

"Something doesn't sound right—that's all. Why would a woman, who you've never met before, force all of you to spend the day together? You may be biological sisters, but you're strangers. I don't like it. I don't like it at all. We don't know what kind of people any of them are. They could be criminals for all we know."

In that moment, Noel fell deeper in love with him. The man forever watched over her. Forever protected her. And forever kept her heart in a perpetual state of melted ice.

Stetson returned to his food. Eating as if he'd said nothing.

"Are you going to go?" She barely heard Hale's question.

"Are you, sis?" Concern laced Dustin's voice.

She looked around at each member of her family. Each one had stopped eating again, and they all stared at her with a sense of painful awareness in their eyes as they waited for her to answer. *Lord, show me how to handle this with grace.*

Her gaze landed on Stetson. His eyes lowered to his plate, but not before she noticed the shadow of sadness in them.

She wanted to leap up and wrap her arms around him, to comfort him. But that would never happen. He'd made it clear. Maybe getting away, moving to a new place, would help her forget him. She doubted it, but maybe it would be worth a try. Then again, she'd assured her parents she wouldn't. Maybe she shouldn't have done that. Ack. She didn't know. This whole thing had her confused. She sighed. "Yeah. I think I will. If I don't, I know I'll always regret it. Besides, I'd really like to meet my sisters. After all, I need someone to help me gang up on you guys."

The joke worked. They bantered back and forth for a few rounds, although Stetson remained quiet. After he finished his cinnamon roll, he excused himself and headed out the door.

Noel couldn't let him go like that. "I'll be back." She scraped her chair back, grabbed a light jacket from the mudroom, and swung the screen door open.

❄

The screen door squeaked as it opened and shut. Stetson didn't have to turn around to know who had stepped outside. He could feel her. Sense her presence wherever she was. Like he had internal radar where she was concerned.

Not wanting to risk her seeing what was in his eyes and

heart, he picked up his pace.

"Stetson."

He walked even faster.

Gravel crunched under her feet as she picked up the pace behind him, nearing him, until her hand snagged his arm, bringing him to a halt.

"Can we talk?"

His heart faltered. He didn't want to look at her, but the softness and pleading in her voice tore down his soul's barrier. *Run, Stetson, run.* He willed his feet to move, but his heart kept his feet grounded. Then she pulled him to face her.

Those lavender-blue eyes reminded him of the wild columbine flowers he'd seen while moving cattle. The very ones he had planned to pick and give Noel for her nineteenth birthday until he'd discovered they were Colorado's state flower.

He'd been disappointed because he knew she loved them. And at that time he wasn't sure if it was illegal or not to pick them. So rather than accept defeat, he had the flower-shop lady arrange a bouquet of silk columbines in one of Noel's favorite worn-out, discarded cowboy boots. Her bright smile when she saw the gift had been worth the effort. What he would give to never have to give it or her up.

"You okay, Stets?"

Pulled from his thoughts, he focused on her face, memorizing every feature because he couldn't help himself. He just knew that when she left he'd never see her again. Because either she wouldn't come back from Georgia, or if she did, he would have to leave the Circle B Ranch. His heart couldn't take being around her all the time, knowing she would never be his.

Then, as if it was the most natural thing in the world, Noel tiptoed, and her soft lips pressed against his and lingered there. Knowing it would never work and yet needing the comfort her kiss offered, Stetson wrapped his arms around her and kissed her with everything inside him—with all the love he'd kept tight-reined for so long.

Her sweet lips clung to his, matching his moves. Only when his lungs sought air did he raise his head. He tucked Noel's head against his chest, holding her tight against him. His insides trembled. "Heaven help me, but I love you, Noel. I love you so much." With those words he released her, ran to his truck, and tore from the driveway. In his rearview mirror he saw her shadow standing in the outside barn light staring after him. His soul moaned with agony. Things would never be the same again.

※

The next morning Noel quietly made her way down the stairs. Her eyes burned, and her lids were heavy from wrestling with her sheets all night. In the darkened kitchen, she headed to the coffeepot. It was already set to go, so she turned it on. Red illuminated numbers snagged her attention: 3:58.

One glance out the kitchen window, and she realized even the sun still slept. If only she could. She sighed heavily and rubbed her eyes. Sleep had eluded her, and she imagined it would continue to do so until she talked to Stetson.

After filling a Pro Rodeo mug full of coffee, she added a dab of chocolate syrup and creamer into the fragrant liquid and stirred it. She set her cup on the breakfast nook, plopped herself onto a barstool, and hooked her feet on the crossbars.

Hunched over the breakfast bar with her elbows on the counter, she held the chocolaty coffee to her lips and took a sip. She stared out the window, reliving the kiss that left her longing for more.

Barn lights cast their glow over the area where she had grabbed Stetson and kissed him. She still couldn't believe she had done that, and that he had kissed her back. And what a kiss. She sighed dreamily. It was everything she imagined and much more.

Her mom had taught her the difference between love and lust, and this definitely wasn't lust. However, having tasted of Stetson's sweetness, of his soft lips, and of the passion behind his kiss, she had to have more. She had to have him as her husband. But first, she had to convince him of that.

Noel sipped her coffee until it was gone and then peered at the clock on the stove. 4:15.

Stetson wouldn't show up for breakfast until 6:30. Well, she couldn't sit here doing nothing, so to help the time fly by, she flipped the kitchen lights on and started preparing the food.

Later, Noel ticked off her list:

Orange juice made.
Potatoes scrubbed and shredded.
Two–dozen eggs scrambled and ready to cook.
Fresh biscuits in the oven.

All that remained was frying the bacon and hash browns. "Boy, you must have gotten up early."

Noel stopped putting bacon slices in the electric skillet and turned toward her mother.

Mom surveyed the kitchen. "Wow. You've been busy. What's the matter—couldn't sleep?" She walked over to the cupboard, pulled out a mug, poured herself a cup of coffee, and sat at the table. "Come join me."

Noel glanced at the sizzling bacon.

"Turn it down; it'll be all right. You need to talk."

Leave it to her mom to sense when something bothered her. She often did, and the two of them would chat over a cup of coffee or a dish of butter pecan ice cream. She turned the dial down and fixed herself another cup of coffee before joining her mom at the table.

"Now, tell me what's on your mind."

Like usual, she had her mother's undivided attention. "I kissed him."

"And?" Mom's eyes sparked with interest.

Noel loved that she didn't have to explain who. Her mother knew she was in love with Stetson; they'd talked about it often enough.

"And"—Noel dragged out the word—"he kissed me back."

"Well, how was it?" Without taking her eyes off of Noel, her mother took a sip of her coffee.

"Oh, Mom. It was fabulous. But I don't know what to do. I love him more than ever now. He said he loved me, too, but then he ran to his truck and sped off."

"Maybe he's afraid."

"Afraid?" Noel frowned. "Afraid of what?"

"I don't know. Why don't you ask him?"

The sound of bacon popping drew her attention away

from her mother's question. She jumped up and turned the nearly burnt bacon over. Grease splattered onto her hand. "Ouch!" She sprinted to the sink and ran cold water over the burn.

Together they finished cooking, chatting the whole time. Six thirty on the dot, breakfast was on the table, and everyone was in their seats, except for Stetson. His chair sat empty. Noel turned to ask her dad if he knew where Stetson was, but a knock at the door stopped her. Noel jumped up and swung the mudroom door open.

Her heart hopped like a bunny, and her lips curled upward, until she noticed the dark circles under Stetson's eyes, his disheveled hair, and his unshaven face. She wanted to put her arms around him and tell him everything would be okay, but she didn't dare. "Morning," she said softly, moving aside to let him in.

"Morning." He looked past her.

Noel followed his gaze. Whoa. Each person in her family watched them like they were everyone's most favorite TV program. She widened her eyes and stretched her neck like a goose on the attack. *Hel–l–o–o.* They immediately turned back in their chairs.

"We need to talk." Stetson's breath brushed across her ear, and shivers skittered through her. Irish Spring soap swept through her nostrils. His hand was between them, and it brushed hers but did no more, and his nearness left her speechless. "Later."

She barely managed a nod. *You don't have to "catch me" later. I'm already caught. Do you want to marry me? I love you.* She blew out a long breath. Good thing Stetson couldn't read her mind, or otherwise he might bolt like a scared colt again. Too bad she couldn't take her lariat and dally it around his heart and hold it forever, as easily as she dallied her rope around a saddlehorn to keep whatever she had on the end of that rope from getting away. Maybe someday. But until then, she'd settle for another one of his yummy kisses.

Chapter 4

Later that morning, after winterizing the four-wheel-drive John Deere tractor, Mr. Brady sent Stetson and Noel to the BLM property to gather more strays.

As they rode, Stetson decided now was as good a time as any to have that long-overdue talk with Noel.

He glanced over at the woman he loved riding next to him. He battled the urge to rein her horse in and pull her onto his saddle in front of him and feel her soft lips on his again.

Every day that passed, he fell more and more in love with her. She was one of the sweetest women he'd ever met. Her love for people, her generous nature with not only her resources but also herself, had drawn him to her. But what roped his heart even more was her love for the Lord.

"Are you listening, Stets?"

"I'm sorry, buttons. My mind was elsewhere. What did you say?" he asked.

"I said," she drew out, "the more I think about the situation, the more I'm struggling."

"Struggling? With what?"

"Well, I know this sounds petty, but I just can't."

"Can't what?"

"I want to shake this feeling, but it seems like no matter how hard I try, I just can't."

"What feeling?" Why did women have drag things out? Why didn't they just say what they had to say? Frustration mounted within him. They split, each riding around a deep mud hole, before coming together again.

"I'm too embarrassed to even say it, but, well, you know." Her silence extended into minutes.

No, I don't know. Get on with it, woman.

"I guess I'm scared."

"Scared about what?"

"Well, after I read the attorney's letter, it got me to wondering about my biological father, and why didn't he take us?" Her hips rocked with every step of the horse under her. "I mean what kind of man walks away from his own children?"

Now Stetson wished she had dragged out what she had to say a little longer. The weight of a box of horseshoes dropped into his stomach.

"The more I think about him giving us up and separating the four of us, the angrier I become. The man oughta be horsewhipped. I have three sisters out there somewhere that I don't know. Twenty-five years of their lives were stolen from me. Unless that man died, too, there's just no excuse for what he's done. Even if he couldn't take us for whatever reason, why didn't he insist we be raised together? Boy howdy." She shook her head and blew out a long breath. "I'm having a terrible time forgiving him for what he did to us. For separating us. For abandoning us."

The talk he had planned out in his head a million times would never play out—not after hearing that. Telling Noel about his past was no longer an option.

"Did you hear me, Stets?"

"I heard you." His voice fell flat.

"Will you pray with me about this?" She looked at him with a plea for help in her eyes.

His heart sank lower than the deep mud hole they'd just passed. How could he pray with her when he himself had been guilty of that very same thing?

Last night, he had lain awake all night, wrestling his sheets and thoughts, wondering what to do about this whole mess. No longer could he ignore his feelings for her. Noel's kiss had seen to that. Her kiss had sent a massive fireworks display exploding inside him like the grand finale fireworks display on the cliffs outside of Kremmling.

All hope that she would not hold his past against him died, along with his plans of courting her. Old-fashioned yes, but he was an old-fashioned kind of guy. His heart clogged with remorse for what could never be.

"Are you okay, Stets?" Noel reined her horse, Cocoa, beside him. "Oh man, I'm sorry. Here I am going on and on, and you said we needed to talk." She pulled her sleeve back with her forefinger and looked at her watch. "Eleven thirty. We can stop and eat if you'd like."

Eating was the last thing he wanted to do, but they needed to talk about what had happened last night between them and how it could never happen again.

❄

While Stetson hobbled his horse, Mouse, Noel tethered Cocoa to an aspen tree, unzipped the cantle pouch on the back of her saddle, and removed the lunch she had packed for them.

Whatever Stetson had wanted to talk about, he never had a chance because all the way up here she had chattered like a magpie. She could only hope and pray the discussion included pursuing a relationship with her. If not, she would be humiliated for pushing something he didn't want. Then

286

again, last night, he'd said he loved her, and his kisses had definitely backed his words up.

She found a bare spot by the creek and sat down Indian-style. Her insides rolled and tumbled like autumn leaves blowing in the wind. One by one she sorted their food.

Stetson lingered by his horse, one hand draped over the grulla's mouse-colored rump, the other over the dun's saddle, staring over its backside. A sure sign he was as nervous as she was.

"You ready to eat?" she called, keeping her voice light.

"Yeah." He turned but walked like he was moving through a muddy watering hole. Her gaze followed his bulky frame as he sidled toward her. Uncertainty shrouded him. He sat down, pressed his back against a large boulder, and stretched his long legs out, crossing them at the ankles. Bozo trotted over to him after lapping water from the creek and shook the excess water off.

"Bozo. Down." Trained to stop and lay down immediately when Stetson said "down," the Border collie dropped in a crouched position. "Good dog." Stetson pulled a piece of dog jerky out of his pocket and rewarded the dog with it.

Noel handed Stetson his food and drink.

"Thanks," he said, never looking at her.

Her insides took a digger. "What? No nelly belly, short-stuff, half-pint, buttons, or munchkin? Just 'thanks'?"

He shrugged and popped open his pop.

"Okay, what's going on, Stets?" She waited while he took a long swig of his drink. Trying to look busy, Noel peeled back the corner of her plastic sandwich box and removed its contents. She bit into the sandwich, fighting to somehow look normal. Ham and mustard were her favorite, but today they tasted like aspen bark.

Stetson's distance ate at her like a blood-sucking mosquito. He looked everywhere but at her.

She quickly chewed and swallowed. "You're scaring me, Stetson. What's going on? You said we needed to talk. So talk already." She set her sandwich back in its container and laid it aside.

Time crawled by at the speed of a garden slug. She played with the fringe on her chinks, but what she really wanted to do was grab Stetson and shake him, force him to talk. Instead, she sat on her hands and studied his profile as he stared at the wide creek.

Today, even the hummingbirds flitting somewhere in the distance and the soft gurgle of the water lapping over the rocks didn't soothe her spirit like they normally did.

As the minutes continued passing—okay seconds, but they felt like minutes to her—mosquitoes buzzed around her, along with a bumblebee. The wait tore at her like a buzzard picking a carcass clean bit by bit.

Finally he faced her, his rugged jawline set, his eyes distant though only feet away.

She held her breath.

"I was thinking about what you said." His face carried the weight of the words he hadn't yet spoken.

Noel scrambled to recall what she had said to cause Stetson to think so long and hard, but she couldn't think of anything except his passionate kiss last night and now his frozen demeanor.

"You don't know why your biological father gave you girls up," he said as if each word hurt. "Maybe he thought it was the best thing for all of you. I mean look at your life,

Noel. You have two parents who love you as much as their own children. They provide a great home for you. And you live in one of the most beautiful places on God's green earth."

That's what he wanted to talk to her about? Noel didn't know whether to be relieved or frustrated. She had hoped for and expected something different, but perhaps he wasn't ready to talk about what happened between them last night.

"Don't you think you're being kind of hard on the man, especially when you don't know all of the circumstances?" He thumbed the brim of his hat upward. His green eyes were as dull as sagebrush, devoid of their usual sparkle.

She studied Stetson's face, waving away a persistent mosquito buzzing around her ear. "No, I don't. You have no idea what it's like to discover you have sisters out there you never even knew existed."

"You're right. I don't know what it's like. But how can you judge the man without even knowing all the circumstances? What if I did something like that? Would you judge me, like you're judging him?"

Judging him? What was Stetson talking about? Why did this matter so much to him?

"I'm not judging anyone." Noel's eyes narrowed. "All I said was I was struggling with anger toward him. How's that judging?"

"It became judging when you decided what he did was wrong without having all the details."

"How dare you! You have no idea what I'm going through. To all of a sudden wonder why you were given up. Why you were discarded like a worthless piece of garbage. To discover all your life you had three sisters who were torn from you. To suddenly feel abandoned. And to hate the man

289

who did this to you." Shocked at her own words, her eyes widened, and pockets of tears filled them. She didn't want Stetson seeing her cry, so she jumped up and walked to the edge of the creek bank with her back to him.

His presence surrounded her.

His large hands rested on her shoulders.

She stiffened, not out of anger but out of embarrassment for spouting out feelings she hadn't known existed. Feelings that made her feel as slimy as the moss on the creek rocks. After all, she had the best parents in the whole world, and she loved them dearly.

So why she was suddenly feeling this way, she didn't know. But she knew she didn't like it. She sniffed and swiped the tears from her lashes.

Stetson turned her around.

Noel kept her head down, too ashamed to look him in the eye. What must he think of her?

"Noel. It's only natural for you to feel that way." He tucked his forefinger under her chin and tilted her head up, but she kept her eyes downcast. "Look at me, marshmallow."

Her eyes darted upward. "Marshmallow?"

"Ha. Got ya to look at me." His smile liquefied her heart like homemade butter in a hot skillet.

Noel smiled. Stetson had a way of making her smile in the midst of whatever dilemma she was in. She loved that about him. But even his making her smile wouldn't take back the words she had spoken. A gamut of conflicting emotions swirled through her senses. Bitterness and anger were ugly things. Rejection was even uglier. And being robbed of her siblings was even uglier yet. "I can't stand the way I feel right now, but I hate him for what he did to us girls!"

❄

Stetson dropped his hands and stepped back. Seeing what she was going through, he wondered what his own little girl was going through. At that moment, he hated himself more than he ever had for what he had done. Would his daughter feel the same about him? Would she prejudge him, too, and offer him no immunity either?

Remorse trailed over him. "There are two sides to every story, cupcake." Sadness drove through his voice like horseshoe nails through a hoof.

Disapproval flashed from Noel's eyes.

Stetson couldn't handle being with her right now. He couldn't handle seeing how her being adopted had left her feeling abandoned and like a piece of garbage. Guilt ate at his gut. He needed to get away. He needed to get back on his horse, finish gathering the strays, and then get as far away from Noel as possible. He had some serious thinking to do. One way or the other, his future would never be the same.

Gathering his remaining lunch, he tossed it into the bushes for the animals.

"What did you do that for?" Her critical tone ripped through him.

He said nothing as he handed her the empty sandwich container, along with the other untouched ones. He headed toward his horse, unhobbled him, and swung into the saddle. Without looking at her, he said, "I need to be alone, Noel. I'm sorry. I'll meet you back at the truck." He whirled his horse around and gently spurred its side. "Come, Bozo." The dog leaped up and followed.

"Don't go, Stetson. I'm sorry I'm angry. I'll work on it. I promise." Noel's insecurity followed him through the pine trees. He wanted to reassure her it wasn't her, but he couldn't right now. His past had caught up with him in a way he'd never expected, and the devastating repercussions of it had met him face-to-face today through Noel.

Knowing that any minute now Noel would be right alongside him, hounding him to talk, he encouraged Mouse to go faster. He wound his way through the thick forest, putting as much distance between them as possible.

Chapter 5

Noel gathered the mess, tossed it into her cantle pouch, and zipped it. She shoved her foot in the stirrup and swung into the saddle. Movement in a nearby tree snagged her attention. There she spotted a black bear cub sitting high on a limb. She smiled and watched it play until reality smacked her.

Her heart raced, knowing the sow, the cub's mama, was sure to be nearby. While black bears weren't normally aggressive, Noel knew if you hung around their cubs, they might go into aggressive-protective mode to defend their cubs.

She needed to get out of there. She spurred her horse and turned in Stetson's direction.

Cocoa took a sharp step sideways. Noel grabbed the saddle horn and pressed her knees tight against the horse.

Mama bear came barreling out from behind a bush.

Cocoa reared and lunged forward. The mare tore through the trees, banging Noel's legs against them.

Noel pulled hard on the reins. "Whoa, girl, whoa," she spoke calmly even though her insides were anything but calm.

Cocoa stretched her neck out farther, straining against the reins, and continued to run.

Branches tore at Noel's face and arms. She shifted left, then right, dodging several branches, tugging on Cocoa's reins, but she couldn't get the frightened horse to stop.

Cocoa headed straight toward a low limb.

Nothing Noel did mattered. Her young horse wasn't stopping.

"Stetson!" she yelled, hoping he was within hearing distance. "Stetson! Help!"

Trees encompassed her.

There was nowhere to bail off.

Bracing herself for the inevitable, with her left hand she grasped the reins tighter and threw her right arm up to protect her face.

Pain cracked through her arm and neck.

She flipped backward over her horse's rump. Her shoulder collided with the hard ground, and her head smacked the base of a tree.

She lay there blinking, trying to assess her situation. She couldn't sit up because she couldn't use her arms. Her right arm was broken, and her left shoulder dislocated. She recognized this pain from the time the same shoulder had previously been dislocated.

Something wet skulked down the back of her neck. Noel didn't know if it was blood or sweat.

Through the fog of pain, she raised her voice to the level of a squeak and hollered with her last remaining strength, "Stetson! Help! Help me!"

❄

Bozo started barking and running circles around Stetson's horse. Stetson pulled on Mouse's reins, tilted his ear toward the direction of the faint sound, and listened.

He couldn't hear anything over his dog's barking. "Bozo, hush." Bozo's barking increased. Something was definitely wrong. His dog never disobeyed him. Pounding hooves hitched his attention. He shifted in his saddle and looked behind him.

Cocoa was heading toward him at a dead run.

By herself.

A rush of adrenaline sped through his body. Stetson whirled his horse around. "Hyaaa!" He leaned forward in the saddle and spurred his gelding. He caught up to Cocoa, reached out for the flailing reins, and pulled the lathered horse to a stop.

He glanced toward the direction Cocoa had come from, searching for Noel. When he didn't see her anywhere, he turned the horses around and headed back to where he'd last seen her.

His mind conjured up many scenarios about what he would find. None of them good. Noel was an excellent rider, and she had trained Cocoa well.

Guilt and fear rode with him as the four of them wove their way through the trees. Cocoa balked like a stubborn mule and fought him most of the way. Whatever had happened, this horse didn't want to go back.

"Stetson." Noel's voice was barely audible.

Stetson continued weaving the horses through the trees. Bozo took off running, barking up a storm. Stetson hurriedly dogged his trail until he spotted her.

A sinking feeling drove through him. Noel lay on her back, her left shoulder hung lower than normal, and her right arm was bent in the middle. He dismounted, dropping both sets of reins, and knelt in front of her crumpled body near the base of a tree.

Cocoa blew a fearful snort and took off again.

"What happened?" He looked her over. "Where are you hurt?"

"My shoulder and arm and head hurt."

"Can you move your neck?"

She rotated it in a circle.

He raised her head up enough to get a good look. Blood soaked her hair. "This might hurt"—he utilized the same gentle tone he used while breaking a young horse—"but I have to stop the bleeding."

She nodded.

He could tell she was trying to be brave, but pain wracked her face. Gently as possible, he supported her head and applied pressure to the wound. The sticky substance covered the palm of his hand.

Minutes later, Stetson removed his hand. Seeing Noel's blood on it churned his stomach. He scraped his palm across the weeds until most of it was gone. "Are you able to move?"

"I think so. Let's try."

Stetson placed his hand at the base of her neck and helped her lean forward. She dug the heel of her boot into the ground and shoved herself back against the tree into a sitting position. Every inch she moved, more pain scratched across her face.

Stetson pulled his cell phone from the clip on his belt and flipped it open. "There's no reception here. I need to go and get help. Will you be okay?"

"You're not leaving me here alone. I'll take myself down off this mountain if I have to."

Judging by the stubborn tilt to her chin, he knew she meant business. He grabbed two sticks and some rope, and untied his light Carhartt jacket from his saddle before kneeling on one knee next to her again. After splinting her broken arm, he fashioned a makeshift sling and secured her dislocated shoulder. He gently helped Noel to her feet, cringing when she yelped.

"You sure you don't want me to run and get help?"

"Yes. I'm sure," she said between gasps. "You know the ambulance can't make it up here. Besides, by the time you get down the mountain and call, we could be back at the truck and on our way."

"You sure you can handle riding?"

"No, but I will."

"Well then, woman, brace yourself, because this is gonna hurt." Carefully, he placed Noel onto the saddle, tossed the reins over Mouse's neck, and—using the stirrup—swung his body up behind her.

On the way to the truck, Stetson kept checking his cell phone. Still no reception.

Noel tucked herself against his chest. He leaned forward and noticed her lip was purple where her teeth clenched it. His heart went out to her. The last time she had dislocated her shoulder, she had tried to act brave, too, until she had passed out. He only hoped she didn't faint this time.

His horse stumbled. Noel's body stiffened, and a sob tore from her. Stetson hated this, but he had to get her to the truck and then to the hospital.

Over and over he kicked himself for leaving her like he had. If he hadn't been such a jerk, then none of this would have happened. Another pile of guilt dumped on top of him, reminding him why he didn't deserve someone like her.

When they got to the pickup and horse trailer, Stetson spotted Cocoa on the other side, grazing. After situating Noel in the pickup cab, Stetson loaded the horses and Bozo and then headed down off the mountain, dust swirling like a tornado behind them.

❄

Noel had to force herself to breathe. Boy howdy, did she hurt. Every bump just about emptied her stomach. The pain was unlike any she'd ever experienced. Stetson tried to comfort her, but all she wanted was her mommy. Even at twenty-four years old, she still needed her mom. Her mother had a way of making everything better.

"Mrs. Brady, this is Stetson. First let me say that Noel is okay, but she's had an accident." Stetson nodded and opened his mouth.

She heard her mother's frantic voice clear on the other side of the cab.

"She's—" He glanced over at her. "I don't know. I think she—" He nodded. "Yes, I'm heading there now. Okay, see you there." Stetson closed the flap on his phone and slid it into the holder. "Your mom said she'd meet us there." He glanced at Noel and then back at the road. "What happened back there, anyway?"

Noel drew in a long breath. "A bear spooked Cocoa. I couldn't get her stopped, and I hit a branch."

"It makes me sick to think about what you went through; how I almost left you there alone to go fetch help." Stetson shook his head. "I didn't know about the bear, or I would've never—" His tanned face paled. "I'm sorry, Noel. None of this would have happened if I hadn't left you in the first place."

"Don't go blaming yourself, Stets. You had nothing to do with this. That bear did. Besides, I should have never told you how I was feeling. I obviously upset you, and I'm sorry."

He said nothing, only rubbed and pulled at his chin with his thumb and forefinger.

Was that moisture in his eyes? It was hard to tell from

the side until a tear rolled down his cheek. Something was seriously wrong. She'd never seen Stetson cry before. Well, except for the day he'd accepted Christ as his Savior.

Noel wanted to grab his hand and comfort him, but she couldn't move. "Stets. Please don't blame yourself for this. I'll be okay. I've had worse things than this happen." Her giggle sounded strained even to her own ears. Nothing she could do about it now. She could only hope that somehow she could make him feel better. She'd do her best to try.

"Do you remember the time when that calf got stuck in the river and I jumped in to save her? Only I didn't see the barbed wire. That one got me twenty stitches. And a tetanus booster. The worst one was when I roped that crazy cow and she took off. I missed my dally. That one nearly cost me three fingers."

Stetson still said nothing. Was he even listening? She hoped so. She desperately wanted to cheer him up.

"Remember during calving season when we were sorting pairs and you asked me to run the gate the other way, only I forgot to raise the latch and ended up slamming my forehead against the top rail. I thought you were going to fall off your horse laughing. I saw stars for a long time."

A small smile curled his lips.

At least now she knew he was listening. "Then there was the time Dandy's legs went out from under him on the icy snow, and I took a digger. I sat there for a minute and then let out this loud war cry. Remember that? You thought I was seriously hurt and came rushing over to me. You looked so pale and frightened. Only got two stitches that time. And then—"

"Noel, I'm quitting. I'm giving your dad my resignation

when we get back."

"Whoa! What? You can't be serious."

His only response was a nod.

"Please don't go." She burst out crying. "You can't abandon me, too."

Chapter 6

Stetson paced the empty hospital chapel. Jingling spurs echoed off the paneled walls while Noel's words floated through his brain, forming storm clouds of confusion. Just when he'd figured out what he needed to do, everything changed with, "You can't abandon me, too." Is that how she felt? Did his daughter feel that way? His heart crushed under the weight of the past, knowing that he, too, might be responsible for someone feeling abandoned.

What are you doing? Stop it. You've been over this a million times. Let it go. You did what was best for her at the time. Children don't raise children.

He just hoped someday he would get the chance to tell his child that, but right now he didn't even know where she was, or who she was. That thought twisted his gut, but again, he needed to let it go. God had forgiven him, and he needed to forgive himself. But would Noel, once she learned the truth? Only time would tell. Until then, he would stay. Noel needed him. It was too late to do anything about his daughter, but it wasn't too late where Noel was concerned.

"Stetson."

He stopped wearing a hole in the carpet and in three long strides stood in front of Mrs. Brady. "How is she? How did the surgery go?"

"Noel keeps asking for you. She keeps trying to pull her IVs out. The nurses keep telling her she needs to calm down, but she isn't making any sense. She says she has to stop you from leaving. What is she talking about?"

301

Stetson shifted sideways and plowed his hands through his hair. He debated whether to spill all to Mrs. Brady, but then decided against it. Noel should be told first.

Pressure from Mrs. Brady's hand on his forearm caused him to look at her. "It's okay, Stetson. You don't have to tell me. But would you please go talk to Noel before she hurts herself?"

He nodded and then swallowed. Could he really do this? Could he face her? Could he do anything to calm her down, or would he just make it worse than he already had? "Yes ma'am. Where is she at?"

"Follow me. Only family is allowed in there. I need to let them know that you are family." She smiled up at him. "We love you as if you were one of our own."

As Stetson followed her down the long corridor, his heart wept tears of tenderness. He had no family. His parents had disowned him years ago—shortly after they found out what he had done. In fact, he didn't even know where they were or if they were still alive.

Thank God for the Bradys. He couldn't think of a better family to claim as his own. They had enough love and room in their hearts to fill a large indoor rodeo arena and then some.

Without one shred of doubt, he knew once he shared his past with them, they would still love him. After all, they had adopted Noel. They knew what it was like to be the fortunate recipient of someone's choice to give their baby a better life. That's what he'd done. Given his daughter a better life. One with mature, loving parents. Now, if only he had the same confidence in Noel.

He paused a moment at the recovery room door and

then slipped inside.

"Ms. Brady, you have to stop this, or you're going to re-injure your shoulder."

Seeing Noel hooked up to IVs and wobbly, fighting the nurses, Stetson picked up his stride until it landed him by her bedside.

She'd been so busy combating she didn't hear him come in.

"Noel." His voice was both firm and concerned.

Her sleepy gaze bobbled toward him. "You're still here." Her hands went limp.

Guilt pressed in on him as he stepped closer. "Yeah, I'm still here, doll."

Noel's shaky gaze turned toward the nurses. "Could you please leave us alone?"

"I'm not leaving until I know you're safe."

"I'll watch her." Stetson captured the brown haired, blue-eyed nurse's gaze. The nurse didn't look at all convinced. Her Jody Foster nose tilted, and one skinny eyebrow lurched upward before turning question-filled eyes toward the middle-aged nurse with the short blond hair and big puppy-dog eyes.

"I'll behave. I promise."

Both nurses glanced at Noel and then back at him.

"If you have any problems at all, we'll be right over there." Puppy-dog eyes pointed toward the nurses' station.

"Thank you. If I can handle a wild bull, I think I can handle her." He winked at Noel, who didn't smile at his attempt at humor.

Stetson watched the nurses leave and then turned toward Noel. The fear and uncertainty on her face made him feel like pond scum. He gently cupped her cast-free hand and gave it a light squeeze. Her half-mast eyes remained transfixed on him.

"Stets, please don't go. I don't want you to go. I can't bear the idea of you leaving." Tears slipped over her lids.

He grabbed a tissue from a nearby box and gently wiped her eyes. "Noel. It's okay. I'll stay as long as you want me to." Her body relaxed. "But I have something to tell you. And after I tell you, if you want me to go, I will."

Her lazy eyes bobbled open to their fullness. "There's nothing you could say to me ever that would make me want you to go. I love you, Stets." He watched as her eyes drifted shut and her breathing slowed.

His heart and soul wanted to believe her, but the past nipped at the heels of his conscience. There was no doubt in his mind that once Noel heard about the secret he'd been hiding for years, she would order him off the ranch immediately.

❄

Crisp air filtered through Noel's bedroom window. She still couldn't believe it had been six weeks since her accident. Today was the day she'd get her cast off, and if it was fully healed, she would be able to go back to work.

She missed working around the animals. Okay, she missed working with Stetson. But Dad had refused to let her work outside, said it was too dangerous and that he wouldn't risk her getting hurt again. Animals were unpredictable, to be sure, but she would have been careful. Still, it was nice to know her dad loved her enough to protect her and to say no. Warm fuzzies wrapped her in their embrace. *Thank You, Lord, for my awesome family.*

She glanced at the Tim Cox western art calendar hanging on the side of her dresser, facing her bed. Tomorrow was the first of November. The weather woman predicted eight to ten inches of snow for the high country, starting sometime this afternoon. The first snow of the season.

Noel slid out from under her covers. Old man winter frosted his way up her spine. Fresh air slipped in on a nippy mountain breeze, filling her nostrils. She drew in its freshness before she closed the three-inch gap in her window.

"Noel, are you up?" Her mother's voice sounded on the other side of the door.

"Sure am. Come on in."

Mom waltzed in and gave her a hug. "I thought you might like me to braid your hair for today."

She looked in the mirror at the ratty mane of hair. "Boy howdy, if Stetson saw me now, he'd run for the hills and never return." They both giggled like a couple of schoolgirls. "You sure you have time? I thought you and Dad were supposed to be in Vail at ten."

"It's only five. We have plenty of time. You sure you don't want me to stay and take you to the doctor?"

"Nope. I'll be fine. Besides, it'll give me more time with Stetson." She grinned.

"He's sure been hanging around a lot lately. Anything you care to tell me?" Mom's eyes held a wishful smile. Just like Noel's heart.

"Don't I wish. Trust me. You'll be the first to know if he decides to do anything other than herd cattle."

"I'd better be. Now park your little tushy in that chair." Mom pointed to the burgundy vanity chair. "We still have breakfast to get ready."

She scurried to obey. Seated, facing the mirror, she gathered a hair band and brush, and handed them to her mother.

Mom pulled the brush through her derriere-length hair, starting at the ends and working upward, careful to not hurt Noel as she worked through the rats.

Noel played with the elastic band, stretching it and releasing it.

Once that massive chore was finished, Noel watched in the mirror as her mother concentrated on pulling the sides and top together to make a French braid. What a beautiful woman her mother was. Noel wondered, if she had given birth to her, would she have gotten her mother's pixie face or her father's long one?

"So, did Stetson ever tell you what it was he wanted to talk to you about?"

Noel's hand stilled. Her gaze landed on her mother's in the mirror. "No. Not yet. I think he's afraid to tell me. Every time it seems like it might come up, he takes off."

"What did he say again?"

"All I remember him saying in the hospital was he had something to tell me and that once I heard it I would want him to go. Or something like that. It's all pretty foggy. I was kind of out of it."

"Just a little." They both giggled.

"Seriously, Mom, there's nothing he could tell me that would make me want him to leave. I love him. Why can't he trust me?"

"I don't know. But give him time. When he's ready he'll tell you. Right now, just be glad he's still here and he didn't leave."

"Believe me, I am." Noel pushed her bangs from her eyes.

The thought of Stetson leaving made her stomach squeamish. No matter what it was, or how bad it was, she would never ask him to go. In fact, if she didn't think it would send him packing, she'd ask him to marry her.

"There. All done." Her mother set the brush down. "Well, I'd better get breakfast started." She moved toward the door.

Noel stood and followed her mother. "I'll be down to help as soon as I get dressed."

Her mom moved into the hallway.

Dad stepped up behind her and slipped his arms around her mother's waist. "Hi, beautiful. You got a big kiss for your old cowboy?"

Her mother turned into her dad's arms. "There's nothing old about you, honey. And yes, I do." Their lips met.

Dad teasingly nibbled at her mother's neck and winked at Noel. With a smile, Noel returned his wink and then, wanting to give them privacy, quietly closed her bedroom door.

"Stop that. The kids might see you." A giggle accompanied her mother's words.

"So?" Her parents' conversation faded with the sound of footsteps heading down the hallway.

Noel leaned against the door. Someday she hoped for the same kind of marriage her parents had. Steady and strong and passionate.

She thought of Stetson and pictured herself married to him with a whole herd of miniature Stetsons and Noels running around. But first things first. He still hadn't even asked her out on a date, let alone to marry him.

Something held him back. She was certain it had to do

with their hospital conversation.

What secret did Stetson have that he thought would make her send him away? Her stomach twisted tighter than the braid in her hair. Whatever it was, she would get it out of him one way or another today.

Chapter 7

After breakfast Stetson and Noel headed to Steamboat Springs for Noel's doctor appointment. Out of the corner of his eye, he noticed Noel playing with the bottom of her braid. "You okay?"

"Stets." She looked over at him. "I want to know what you wanted to tell me. I mean, I don't get it. You said you loved me, and yet you've never even asked me out on a date. Is what you've been wanting to tell me keeping you from doing that? Or is it me? Or something else? Or what? Do you still love me?"

"Ah, sugar, of course I still love you." He reached over and clasped her hand, giving it a reassuring squeeze. He'd never told anyone about his past—he was too ashamed. Would he ever get the guts he needed to tell Noel about his past? The thought of seeing disgust on her face aimed toward him mashed the blood from his heart. Still, it wasn't fair to keep stringing her along like this. Tonight, one way or another, he would know.

"Let's see what happens at the doctor today. If you get your cast off, tonight we'll head over to Summit County and celebrate with dinner and a movie. How's that sound?" He looked at Noel's beautiful face and wide eyes, beaming like a morning sunrise.

"Are you kidding, Stets? Does this mean you're asking me out on a date?"

He gave a quick nod. "I am." The ramification of that settled on him like the low hanging clouds above them.

"Well, that is if it doesn't snow."

She raised her eyes upward and steepled her fingertips. "Lord, please don't let it snow. Please?"

Stetson laughed. "You're a nut."

"Yeah, but I'm a lovable nut."

"Yeppers. You sure are."

Stetson pulled the truck into an empty parking space in front of the clinic. After he shut the engine off, he ran around to Noel's side and opened her door. She hiked a brow and dipped her chin.

"Don't give me that shocked look, spitfire. I'd get the door more often if you'd let me. But whenever we're together, we're usually working, and you're out the door before I am."

"Okay, okay. I'll give you that one. I'll have to remember that and take my time from now on." She winked, and his heart winked back at her. "I kind of like you opening my door. Makes me feel more like we're a couple than coworkers."

A couple. In his dreams. And dream of her he had. His dreams included them being married, lying on the couch together after a day's work, holding each other, and kissing each other until the wee hours of the morning. In his dreams, they were definitely a couple. A couple in love. Tonight would be the deciding factor whether his dreams would become reality or end in a devastating nightmare.

❄

Noel lightly ran her fingers over the healed incision on her arm. "Well, that's it. Everything looks great. So"—she turned toward Stetson as far as the truck's seat belt would allow—"what time's dinner?"

Stetson glanced at the falling snow and then at his

watch. "Let's get over Rabbit Ears Pass first, and then we'll see what the weather's doing this evening, okay?"

"Hey, I'm not letting a little thing like snow stop me. I've waited a long time for this. Besides, we've driven that road a million times in the snow."

"I know, Noel. But we're supposed to get ten inches this evening."

"So?" She wasn't going to let anything stop her from having her first real date with him.

"You know how wet the first snow of the season is. Your dad would never forgive me if anything happened. *I* would never forgive me."

"You're just trying to get out of taking me." She crossed her arms and stared out the window.

"Look." He unwound her arms and pulled her hand into his again. "I'm not trying to get out of anything. Well, maybe I am. But I want to get this over with."

"Well, don't do me any favors, mister." She took her hand back.

"You're taking it all wrong, Noel."

"Am I?"

"Yes. What I was going to say was, I want to get this over with so we'll know if we can go on. Not get our date over with."

"Oh. Sorry." She sent him a cheeky grin. "Listen, Stets. I want you to know there isn't anything you could say or do that would make me want you to leave." This time she grabbed his hand, brought it to her lips, and kissed it. "I love you." The words slipped out before she thought about them. She held her breath, waiting for his reaction.

His chest rose and fell. "I love you, too, Noel. I can't help myself—I do. I just hope and pray you're right."

"Of course I'm right. I'm always right." She giggled.

❄

No date tonight. Nine inches of heavy, wet snow had seen to that. By the time Noel had finished cooking dinner, her disappointment had lifted—knowing there would be other opportunities to go on a date helped.

She headed to the den. "Dinner's on, guys."

"Well, it's about time." Mark rubbed his flat stomach.

Her five brothers and Stetson corralled themselves around the dinner table and bowed their heads.

"Father," Hale began, "thank You for this food. And thank You that Mom and Dad didn't try to come over the Trough road in this blizzard. Thank You that they're safe and warm. Bless this food, Lord. Please. After all, Noel made it, so it really could use Your blessing." All six of them laughed.

"Hey." She tossed a roll at Hale, hitting him in the cheek. "I'm a great cook. You could be eating Stetson's cooking."

Groans poured from around the table.

Stetson picked up his fork. "C'mon. My cooking's not that bad."

Dustin and Bailey coughed.

Hale and Mark shook their heads at him.

And Travis clutched his throat as if he were choking and then dropped his head onto the table.

Everyone laughed, including Stetson.

"Trust me, Stets. It is." She passed the platter of homemade fried chicken to her left, followed by the mashed potatoes, gravy, buttered peas, and fresh baked rolls. "I can still see the faces of those poor kids at church camp."

Church camp was held every year on their ranch. On

the average, about twenty kids showed up each year. And each child was given chores and responsibilities. Including cooking. Noel still thought her parents took that one too far. Especially after tasting Stetson's cooking.

"We were all starving, but man, who ever heard of mixing macaroni and cheese in with sloppy joes?" She couldn't help but cringe at the disgusting mix.

"Hey, give me a break. I was told sloppy joes and macaroni and cheese went well together. How was I supposed to know they meant separately? It was the first time I'd ever cooked anything."

"And the last. Oh, thank You, Jesus." Dustin's words gained another round of laughter.

"Noel's chicken doesn't sound too bad after all." Hale grabbed a piece of white meat off the platter before passing it on.

"What do you mean, it doesn't sound too bad? Noel's chicken's the best." As if to prove his point, Stetson picked up a leg and tore off a big bite. "She's a fabulous cook," he said around the food.

"That's just cuz you're hungry." Mark winked at Noel. "Trust me. If you weren't, you'd be choking on that there chicken leg."

She loved her brothers. They were so much fun.

By the time the food reached Noel there wasn't much left. She smiled, knowing they loved her cooking and that they loved teasing her. She wouldn't have it any other way.

Scooping up a portion of mashed potatoes and gravy onto her plate, she thought about the sisters she hadn't even known existed until two months ago, and she wondered again what they were like. Would she have as much fun with them as she did with her family? In less than two months, she would find out.

"So, sis, you looking forward to next month? Still plan on going?" Travis slathered his roll with butter and took a bite, and then focused his gaze on her. As did everyone else around the table.

"I was just thinking about that. Yeah, I'm still going. But I'm not sure how I feel about it all. One part of me is pretty excited and can't wait to go, but another part of me wants to forget the whole thing and stay right here."

"Well, tell the part of you that doesn't want you to go to shut up. I'm sure we can survive without the brat...um...you for a couple of months." Dustin winked and smiled.

"No, we can't." All eyes turned toward Stetson. Forks and spoons halted, and mouths hung open. "I can't."

Noel's heart and stomach pranced like a proud Tennessee Walker horse.

No one spoke.

The only sound in the room was the hot water circulating through the baseboard heaters as they prepared to kick on.

Stetson added a spoonful of peas and mashed potato mixture into his mouth and ate as if he hadn't said anything out of the ordinary.

She applied pressure to her knee to stop it from bouncing.

Dustin gathered the last of his gravy with his roll.

Hale suddenly became occupied with his coffee cup.

Silverware clinked against china plates.

Without another word, dinner was over in a matter of minutes. Everyone left the table and headed into the den. Everyone except Stetson and Noel.

Noel rose to clear the table.

Stetson stood but didn't move from his spot. "Can that wait? We need to talk. I can't stand not knowing anymore."

"Not knowing what?"

"Whether or not you will ever forgive me. If you'll still love me once you hear what I have to say." The paleness of Stetson's bronzed skin alarmed her, and a case of the nervous jitters flustered her soul.

She lowered the plate back onto the table. "We can talk in the living room. Is that okay?"

"That's fine." Stetson motioned for her to precede him.

Instead, she placed her hands in his and bowed her head. "Father, whatever is weighing heavily on Stetson, please give him peace, and help us to get through this together." *And give me the grace he deserves to accept whatever it is he has to tell me.*

Chapter 8

To knock the chill out of the spacious living room, Stetson added logs, kindling, and newspaper to the grandfather wood-burning stove; then he struck a match and lit them.

Flames curled the newspaper and licked at the kindling, igniting the aspen and pine logs before turning to ashes. If only his past sin could be consumed as easily.

Left in the ashes of time.

Not his daughter, but how she'd been conceived.

Stetson closed the door, which felt as heavy as his heart, and latched it. *God, give me the grace to go through with this. I need Your courage. Your strength. Help me to accept the outcome. Whatever it is.* He turned and faced Noel, who was sitting on the loveseat, playing with the end of her braid. A sure sign she was nervous.

He sat down next to her. Facing each other, knees touching, he slipped his hand into hers.

It took several breaths to get the words moving. "What I have to say to you isn't pretty. But let me start off by saying, Noel, I love you. I want a future with you. I know we haven't even gone on an actual date yet, but we've known each other for years. You're my best friend. My confidante. The joy of my life, and I don't want to lose you." His voice cracked.

He cleared his throat and pulled himself together before continuing. "I pray you can find it in your heart to forgive me. God has. I'm still struggling with forgiving myself. Especially every time I think about—"

He released her hand, leaned his arms on his knees, and clasped his hands together. Head lowered, he pinched back the tears that threatened to escape.

"Stetson, look at me."

One moment slipped into another before he finally straightened and locked gazes with her.

With the gentlest of touches, she tucked the tears that had managed to escape his eyes into the folds of her fingers. "It's okay. You can tell me." Her soft voice was filled with assurance. All he could do was pray she meant it.

He pulled a long breath to steady his nerves and then dove right in. "When I was fifteen, I met this girl at a rodeo. Her name was Kelsey. We hit it off right away. One night, while her folks were gone, she had a party in her parents' barn. Invited me and my buddies."

"She had a brand-new oval horse tank delivered and set up in the barn. Everyone brought a bottle of their favorite booze, and everything got dumped into that horse tank. Cowboy Kool-aid they called it. One drink led to another."

Stetson stood and paced the room. He stopped in front of the window and watched the snow fall.

Pure and white.

What he'd give to get his purity back. To offer that to Noel. But he couldn't.

Noel came up behind him and wrapped her arms around his middle, tucking her head into his back, holding him, saying nothing. Tenderness and love poured from her warm body into his, giving him the courage to go on. He turned in her arms and wrapped his around her. He clung to her and kissed the top of her head. "I love you, Noel."

"I love you, too."

He pulled back enough to look down into her face. "There's something about that night you need to know."

His knees almost buckled under him. He led her back to the loveseat and seated himself after Noel sat. *God, have mercy on me. Help me to do this.*

Stetson refused to look at her. Couldn't bear to see the love she had for him turn to disgust for what he was about to tell her.

"I woke up the next morning in Kelsey's bed."

He glanced at Noel, watched her swallow and take control of her eyebrows, which had started to rise.

She opened her mouth to say something, but Stetson pressed his fingertips against her lips to quiet her. "Please, let me finish."

Noel nodded, and he removed his fingers.

"Three months later I get a call from Kelsey. She told me she was pregnant and that I was the father."

Noel sucked in a sharp breath. Stetson didn't look at her for fear he would lose his courage.

"What—what happened to the baby?" she squeaked.

"When I returned, we—"

"Returned? Returned from where?"

"From joining the rodeo circuit."

"You abandoned Kelsey and your baby?" Her face paled. *God, help me here.* He ran his hand over his face and chin. She slid her hand out from under his.

Stetson searched her eyes. Confusion, distrust, and fear stared back at him. His stomach took a nosedive. He reached for her hands, but she tucked them securely around her waist.

"No. Yes. I mean when—"

She held up her hand to silence him. "Not now, Stetson. I need time to process this. I'm sorry. I'll talk to you later."

He watched her stand and walk away from him, perhaps out of his life forever, and he never got to tell her the whole story.

❄

Noel needed to talk to her mommy. Since her parents hadn't returned from their trip, the phone would have to do for now. With tears, she poured out the whole story and then sank further into her bed pillow and shifted the phone to her other ear. "I'm afraid, Mom." She sniffed.

"Afraid of what?"

Noel rubbed the end of her braid between her fingers. "Of Stetson abandoning me."

"Abandoning you? What do you mean?"

"What do you mean, what do I mean? He abandoned his child and girlfriend." Didn't her mother understand?

"She wasn't his girlfriend, Noel. You said he was fifteen years old when this happened. How was he supposed to raise a child when he himself was still one?"

"I don't know, Mom. I don't know." She shook her head, hoping to shake away the frustration and confusion tormenting her. "The thought of Stetson abandoning that girl and giving up his child makes me wonder if I ever really knew him. If I can ever trust him again. After all, if he did that once, what's to stop him from doing it again?"

"The Lord for one. Plus, he's not that immature boy anymore, Noel. He's a mature man now who loves God and desires to obey Him." She heard her mother sigh. "This isn't about him, is it?"

"What do you mean? Of course it is."

319

"I don't think so. Ever since you got that letter, you've been different. Not as confident or something."

Noel sat up.

She hadn't been the same, had she?

Slowly the realization came. She hadn't been the same because for the first time in her life, she felt insecure, wondering where she belonged.

Where she fit in.

And who she fit in with.

A weighty burden slumped her shoulders. "You're right. This isn't solely about Stetson. Oh, Mom, what do I do? I'm so scared and so confused." Needing the security of a blanket, she slipped lower into her bed and tucked herself under her flannel quilt. "This is the only home I've ever known. The only family I've ever known. And now I find I have two families. I feel torn.

"In a way, I really want to go and meet my sisters, but in another way I don't. Because I know once I do, things will never be the same. I'll want to be with both families." The second those words left her mouth, fear clutched her. "I didn't mean that, Mom," she blurted. "I want to be here. With my family. With all of you."

"Noel, honey, it's okay. You can love two families. When we adopted you, we knew one day you would want to find your biological family. And we're okay with that. Besides, we know you love us. And I know you have enough love inside of you to give to a million families. So, if you're worried about us, don't be. We'll always be here for you." Love flowed through the phone lines, wrapping her in its embrace. It was like a security blanket of love.

"That's right, sweetheart." She heard her father saying in the background.

A giggle of relief bubbled out of Noel. "Thanks, Mom . . .and Dad." Noel tossed the covers aside and stood. "Okay, Mom. I gotta go. I need to talk to Stetson. I love you. And tell Dad I love him, too."

"We love you, too, honey. See you tomorrow."

"Okay. Bye, Mom." Noel hung up and tossed the phone onto the bed. She slung open her bedroom door and darted toward the stairs. Planting her backside on the banister, she flew down the rail and into the living room.

Her heart sank. It was empty.

She raced to the den and peeked her head inside the door.

Dustin and Bailey were busy playing video games.

Hale and Mark were asleep, and Travis had his nose buried in a book.

No Stetson.

She hurried to the kitchen.

Her stomach cringed.

Her gaze trailed to Stetson's empty chair. Amongst the dinner mess was a folded piece of paper. She walked over and picked up the letter addressed to her and opened it.

My dearest Noel. I'm sorry. If I could go back in time, I would change everything. You never gave me a chance to tell you the rest. I would have stayed and made things right, one way or another. I didn't want to run, but Kelsey convinced me I'd better because her father was determined to have me arrested and thrown into juvenile hall on rape charges.

Guilt severed through her mind. She hadn't even given him

a chance to explain, or she would have discovered he hadn't really run away. But then again, she would have never gotten to the real root cause of her fear either. She continued reading.

The whole time I was gone, I kept in contact with Kelsey through a friend of hers. I sent her almost all of my earnings, except what I needed to live on.

She really had wronged him by not listening. Even back then, as a teenage boy, he'd had integrity.

In the meantime, Kelsey kept trying to convince her dad that she was the one who had lured me to her bedroom and that she was the one who had taken advantage of me and my drunken state.

Poor Stetson.

She hated what she was putting me through. Kelsey couldn't take it anymore. Knowing her dad would have his lawyer twist things around and even hire people to say they saw me seduce her, to put an end to the whole thing, she finally threatened to run away and never come back if her father didn't give up his ridiculous scheme. He agreed not to press charges under two conditions. One, if she agreed to go stay with his sister in the country until the baby was born, and two, we both had to give our consent to give the baby up for adoption.
 Just so you know, I didn't give the baby up to keep

*from going to juvenile hall. Kelsey and I decided we
were too young to be parents and that it would be best
for the baby if we gave her up. We wanted our daughter
to have a chance at life. A stable home. With two
parents who could provide for her and love her.*

The room swirled, so many things collided in Noel at
once. He had given up his child—not because he wanted to
but because he did what he thought was best for the child
considering the situation. After all, he had only been fifteen,
on the run, with no support and charges following him if he
didn't agree to the terms. What other choice did he have?

I hope someday you can find it in your heart to forgive me.

"Oh, Stets."

*I don't want you feeling uncomfortable in your own
home, so I'm leaving. Please tell your father I enjoyed
working for him.*

"No!" Noel cried out to the empty room.

*Tell everyone good-bye for me. Tell them I love them
and that I'll always be grateful to them for all they did
for me. Especially for showing me the way to salvation.
For introducing me to Jesus Christ. For loving me like
one of their own.*
    I wish you all the best.

*Love,
Stetson*

Noel dropped the letter and plopped down in his chair. She placed her head in her hands and wept. Never had her heart ached so cruelly. She had run off the only man she ever loved.

You idiot. Stetson trusted you, and you stampeded his heart right into the ground. Even told him there was nothing he could say that would make you drive him off. "Dear God, forgive me." She shoved the chair back, scraping it across the hardwood floor. Snatching up Stetson's note, she fled to the mudroom. Fast as she could, she dressed in her winter garb, and out into the blinding blizzard she fled in search of Stetson.

Chapter 9

What do you mean she isn't in her room? Where is she?" Stetson looked at the untouched dinner mess.

"That's what we'd like to know." Hale scanned the kitchen, too. "Noel never leaves a mess."

"What's for breakfast?" Travis entered the kitchen and glanced around, and then looked at each of them. "What's going on here? Where's breakfast? Did Noel sleep in?"

"Noel isn't here." Mark's voice didn't mask his concern.

"Not here? Where is she?"

"That's what we're trying to figure out." Hale turned to Stetson. "Did she say anything to you about going out?"

Guilt flooded through Stetson like a gully wash. He lowered his head and shook it. "This is all my fault."

"What's all your fault?" Hale asked.

Knowing he could no longer keep his secret from them, without giving them every detail, he explained what he had told her, her reaction to it, and the note he'd left.

The note. It had said he was leaving.

"Dear God, no. What have I done?" He ran to the door, rammed his feet into his snow boots, and laced them in record speed. "She must have gone out in that blizzard last night to try and stop me from leaving. I'm going looking for her." Out the door he flew.

Within seconds, Hale, Mark, Travis, Bailey, and Dustin joined him. They split up and went in search of her.

Hard telling where she went. Without any tracks, it

would be hard to find her. When he had left last night, the snow had been blowing so hard and the visibility so poor that he'd barely found his pickup. In fact, he'd had to guess his way home, even having driven it a million times.

Trudging through the deep snow, he made his way around to the west side of the house to see if Noel's truck was in its usual parking spot. It wasn't.

Stetson went to his pickup and got in. He started it up, turned the heat up full blast, and rolled his window down. He drove slowly toward his house, combing the area as he did.

Nothing.

He drove past his place and further up the road toward the bridge. Something shiny glistened in the sun. He headed toward it. Sitting at an angle at the edge of the bridge was Noel's truck. He shoved his pickup into neutral, rammed the emergency brake pedal, and leapt out. He slid most of the way down the hill, straining to see if Noel was inside.

Stetson reached the driver's side door and swung it open. Her pickup cab was colder than the outside. No wonder. The gas tank showed empty. "Noel. Newy, honey, can you hear me?"

Noel stirred under the heavy blanket draped over her. Ranch folks always kept what Mr. Brady called a "survivor kit" in their vehicles. The blanket that covered Noel was part of that kit. Good thing, too—no telling how long she had been without heat.

"Stets?" Her head wobbled as she rose toward him.

"It's okay, honey. I'm here. Let's get you home and warmed up." With the blanket tucked securely around her, Stetson lifted her out of her vehicle and carried her to his.

He placed her on the passenger's side and hurried around to the driver's side. *Lord, thank You for watching over Noel and for keeping her safe.*

The ride back to her house was riddled with guilt and concern. Stetson pulled in front of the massive ranch house.

Dustin came up to his truck.

"I found her." Stetson didn't bother hiding his concern at her condition.

"Is she okay?" Travis peeked around him.

"Yes. But I need to get her warm as soon as possible. Would you find the others and tell them?"

"Sure will." Dustin took off toward the barn.

Stetson carried Noel to the porch and tried to figure out how to open the door.

"I've got it." Bailey rushed up behind him and opened the door. "Take her into the living room. I stoked the fire in there so it would be nice and toasty when we found her."

"Good thinking. She's freezing. Can you make her a cup of coffee or hot tea? Something quick?"

"Already done. I'll go get it."

This family knew how to survive and what to do.

Stetson lowered Noel into the recliner in front of the wood-burning stove. He pulled up a chair next to hers and sat down.

Bailey came in and handed him the coffee.

Holding the cup against Noel's lips, Stetson patiently waited while she took small sips, which were better than nothing.

Before long, Noel had warmed up, and her foggy eyes had returned to normal. Once her brothers knew she was going to be okay, they headed outdoors to do chores, leaving

Stetson to take care of her.

"Stetson, I'm so glad you're still here." Her voice was low and soft.

"I had to come back." He took her hand and was thankful when she didn't pull it away. "After a sleepless night in the hotel, I decided running away wasn't the answer. I need to face the demons of my past head-on. Even if it means your parents sending me packing and you never speaking to me again."

"They won't."

"How do you know?"

"Because Mom already knows. She's the one who brought me to my senses." She snuggled her coffee mug to her chest. "I'm sorry, Stets."

"Sorry for what?"

"You trusted me, and I let you down."

"No, you didn't. I knew how you felt about adoption and a man giving up his child. I had to tell you the truth. I couldn't risk that dark cloud hanging over our relationship."

"That's just it. I don't feel that way about adoption. I'm extremely fortunate to have been adopted. I mean, just look at the wonderful parents I have. My problem was, after I got that letter, for the first time in my life I felt insecure and torn. Wondered where and who I belonged with. That letter dredged up a past I hadn't ever thought much about and made me feel abandoned. Why, I don't know. I only know it did.

"Then when you told me about your past, for some reason I was afraid you would abandon me, too. But I'm not worried about that anymore. I know you love me, or you wouldn't have come back. I don't care about what happened in the past. I care about the future." She smiled. "I love you, Stetson. I always will." She set her coffee cup down.

Stetson stood and pulled her into his arms. "Oh, Noel. You don't know how long I've longed to hear those words once you knew the truth." He captured her mouth and pressed her to him, binding their hearts and souls together. He pulled back and spoke against her lips. "How about dinner and a movie? Or even better yet, how about marrying me?"

"I suppose I could do that." She kissed him. "Would December twentieth be too soon?"

He yanked his head back and looked down at her. "Aren't you kind of rushing things a bit?"

Noel lowered her head. "I don't want to go to Georgia by myself. I would feel much better about meeting my sisters if you were there with me. The only possible way to do that is if we were married." She shrugged. "Thought it could serve as a honeymoon, too. You know, take in the sights. See the South at Christmastime."

Stetson tucked his forefinger under her chin and raised it. "The only sight I want to see at Christmastime is you." He winked. "Do you think you can plan a wedding that fast?"

"We sure can." Their gazes swung toward the door. Mrs. Brady's face glowed. Noel's parents barreled toward them with open arms.

"Welcome to the family, Stetson." Mrs. Brady hugged him and then Noel. "Just what I've always wanted. Another son."

They all laughed and hugged, and then Mrs. Brady did what she did best. Started mothering Noel. Wedding plans at Spur City were the last words he heard as he headed outside to help with chores. He couldn't think of a better place to hold a wedding. Her parents had built the 1800s town years ago to host parties, events, retreats, and youth camps. But their wedding would best them all.

Chapter 10

December twentieth finally arrived. Noel looked out the window of her dad's Ford Excursion as they drove through the snow-packed ranch yard, where SUVs were lined up to chauffeur their guests up to Spur City.

"Are you nervous?" Noel's dad asked.

"Nope. Excited is more like it. I still can't believe I get to marry Stetson."

"I can't believe *he* gets to marry *you*."

She smiled, thankful that God had placed her with such an amazing, loving family.

"When he asked for your hand, I almost told him no."

"What? Why?"

"Because." He glanced over at her and then back at the winding incline heading up to town. "I didn't want to lose my baby girl."

"I don't wanna lose my daddy. Besides, you're not getting rid of me that easy. Don't forget, Stetson and I will be living at his place."

"What about Georgia?"

"What do you mean?" She frowned.

"Well. What if you get there and love it? Then you may want to move there." Was it just her imagination, or had more wrinkles appeared around his eyes just now?

"Nope. Not happening, Dad. Ranching is in my blood. My family is in my blood. *This* is my home."

"You might change your mind when you meet your new

family." More lines appeared on his face, only this time it wasn't her imagination.

Suddenly it dawned on Noel what her father was doing. He needed reassurance. That she could give him, because she and Stetson had already discussed their future plans. "Well, they might be my new family. But quite frankly, I prefer my old family. Anyway, I can't leave. Who would keep the boys on their toes if I did?" They both laughed. "Seriously, Dad, I don't want to live anywhere else. Colorado is my home. I would miss my mountains too much. More than anything, I would miss you and Mom. And, yes, even the boys. Nope, sorry, Dad. Like I said, you aren't getting rid of me that easily."

His shoulders relaxed, and a small smile curled his lips.

Heading down the middle of Spur City toward the church, Noel smiled. The mercantile, barbershop, saloon, gun shop, Wells Fargo bank, Spur City post office, jailhouse, Rawhide Dining Lodge & Hotel, stagecoach stop, livery stable, and barn were smothered in twinkling Christmas lights. Lampposts wrapped with greenery and lights illuminated the boardwalks and street. Her brothers had done an amazing job decorating Spur City.

As her dad neared the church, wonderment danced in her eyes and heart. Christmas lights outlined the old barnwood A-frame church, including the steeple and cross, which seemed to reach toward heaven. Lights framed the double doors with the small cross-shaped windows.

Dad drove around the side of the building and parked in front of the side door. Noel grinned and shook her head. In the back window of Stetson's pickup, in bright, fluorescent-pink letters, were the words *Just Married*.

Rope streamers with cowbells tied on the ends dangled from the back bumper. Leave it to her brothers to use cowbells instead of tin cans.

After she and her dad gathered everything she needed from the Excursion, they stepped inside the dressing room. Heat from the wood-burning stove wrapped around them, zapping the chill from their bodies that the frosty outdoors had created.

Noel's cousins flocked around her, looking adorable in their floor-length emerald velvet bridesmaid gowns. The cherry-and-white-dyed fur around the neck and sleeves gave their dresses a warm Christmassy feel.

"Where's Mom?" Noel asked.

"Probably running around like a woman on a caffeine overdose." Dad chuckled and then left the room.

"I'm so happy for you." Trista roped her arms around Noel and gave her a huge hug.

"Me, too. I'm so–o–o jealous. I want a hot cowboy like yours." "Don't we all. . ." Cindy sighed. Dreamy romance softened Staycee's eyes.

"Congratulations." Anna gave her a brief hug.

"Keep Christ in the center of your marriage, and you'll be as happy as I am." Mary's eyes and smile sparkled with bliss.

"Thank you." Noel glanced at her relatives. "Okay, gang. I need help getting dressed or there won't be a wedding."

The girls scurried about, helping Noel get ready.

"How do you want your hair?" Mary asked, holding a brush.

"No braid today. Stetson likes it down." Her shiny, long mane ran six inches below her waist.

Her mom stepped inside and stared. "You look so beautiful, honey." Approval and love shone through her mother's eyes. "Well, you ready?"

Noel nodded. Hummingbird wings flittered through her stomach.

Her cousins lined up. One by one they headed out the door, holding their greenery-encased bouquets of red and white roses with foot-long strips of rabbit-fur ribbons. Her bouquet matched theirs, only it was larger.

※

Stetson stood in front of the church under an archway covered with pine-tree boughs. The air smelled like the forests he loved so much to ride through.

Mistletoe hung in the center of the archway, and Christmas lights, cowboy hats, boots, spurs, and other western ornaments decorated it.

Standing next to him according to their age were his dear friends Hale, Mark, Dustin, Bailey, and Travis. The thought of these guys becoming family made his heart smile and his insides two-step.

Across from him stood Noel's cousins, Staycee, Mary, Trista, Cindy, and Anna.

Family, friends, and neighbors filled the pews. But no one from his side showed up. Sadness tried to crowd in on Stetson, but today was his wedding day, and he wouldn't let anything rob his joy. His eyes scanned the room.

Scented candles in tin cans with old-west pictures embedded around them lined the windowsills of the rustic church. Each sat on a small rabbit fur, dyed red, green, and white. Stetson smiled, knowing Noel loved rabbit fur.

Christmas lights meshed each window. Spaced methodically on the end of each pew were large red, green, and white bows.

Todd, their worship leader, started playing his keyboard and singing a song he wrote for them about loving one another as Christ loved the church.

Stetson's breath hitched when his gaze snagged on Mr. Brady, rounding the corner with Noel on his arm.

Noel floated down the aisle toward him in a white velvet gown, with a white, fur-lined neckline and sleeves.

He wanted to lock eyes with her, but her white cowboy hat had some fancy lacy stuff draped over it that went about an inch past her chin and flowed longer in the back.

Mr. Brady handed Noel off to him. Their hands connected, and his heart rejoiced. The moment he'd dreamed of since stepping onto the Circle B Ranch was here. Noel was about to become his wife.

They stood facing each other, repeating their vows.

Before he knew it, the preacher announced, "You may now kiss the bride."

Stetson raised the lacy thing and draped it over her hat. Again his breath hitched. Noel's lavender eyes looked dreamy and overflowed with love. She was the most beautiful woman he'd ever known—inside and out.

He lowered his head, lovingly possessing her lips, and claimed his bride. Whoops and hollers echoed off the walls, but Stetson wasn't finished yet. Seconds later, he reluctantly stopped caressing her mouth and whispered against her lips, "I love you, Mrs. Laramie."

"Boy howdy. Do I love the sound of that," she whispered on a sigh. "I've waited a long time to be called Mrs. Laramie." She smiled. "I love you, too, Mr. Laramie."

❄

Early the next morning, after spending their honeymoon night at the Spur City Hotel, Noel said good-bye to her family. Trepidation, excitement, and uncertainty roped her emotions together as she and Stetson headed down the road to meet her biological sisters in Monticello, Georgia.

"I love you," she said with a contented smile.

He flashed her that infectious grin, the one that curled her toes inside her cowboy boots. "I love you, too, sugar lips."

Debra Ullrick is an award-winning author who is happily married to her husband of thirty-seven years. For over twenty-five years, she and her husband and their only daughter lived and worked on cattle ranches in the Colorado Mountains. The last ranch Debra lived on, a famous movie star and her screenwriter husband purchased property there. She now lives in the flatlands where she's dealing with cultural whiplash. Debra loves animals, classic cars, mud-bog racing, and monster trucks. When she's not writing, she's reading, drawing western art, feeding wild birds, watching Jane Austen movies, *COPS*, or *Castle*.

Debra's other titles include, *The Bride Wore Coveralls*, *Déjà vu Bride*, *Dixie Hearts*, *A Log Cabin Christmas*, *The Unexpected Bride*, and come January 2012, *The Unlikely Wife*.

Debra loves hearing from her readers. You can contact her through her website at www.DebraUllrick.com.

EPILOGUE

Jeanie Smith Cash

Epilogue

G rayson pulled up in front of a set of black wrought-iron gates. He got out and opened them and then pulled through. As he drove up the long driveway, a beautiful plantation-style home came into sight. Holly gasped, and Grayson glanced over at her.

"Oh Grayson. I had no idea the house would be anything like this. It's beautiful. Look at the grounds! It's gorgeous out here."

"Yeah, it's pretty impressive, isn't it?"

Grayson parked in front of the house, and they climbed out. Three other cars followed, and three couples stepped out to stand on the front walk alongside them.

Grayson could hardly believe his eyes. All four young women gasped as they stood looking at each other. The letter certainly had laid it out correctly. It was like looking at four clones. The girls looked exactly alike, right down to those magnificent lavender eyes. Oh, there were subtle differences in the way they wore their hair, and their outfits were different, but the young women themselves were identical.

The four young women stood staring at each other. Grayson shook his head; it was obvious they couldn't believe what they were seeing with their own eyes. He could understand that. It was a bit of a shock.

❄

"It's—"

"I—"

"This—"

"Whoa!"

Holly joined her sisters in laughter as they all started to talk at once. When they finally regained their composure, Holly said, "It's like looking in a mirror. I can't believe you all look just like me." She studied each face. There was no mistaking they were sisters. They were identical. "I'm Holly Davenport, and this is Grayson Brockman, my fiancé and Camden's brother. Hello, Camden."

"Hello, Holly."

"I wasn't sure I actually believed the letter. I had to come see for myself." One of the sisters took the hand of the man beside her. "But there is no doubt in my mind now. I'm Carol Wells, and this is Nick Powers, my fiancé. Nick is the manager here at Bellingham Plantation."

"This is amazing. I wouldn't have believed it if I hadn't seen you all with my own eyes." Another of the sisters introduced herself. "I'm Starr Evans, and this is Camden Brockman, our lawyer and my fiancé, who won't tell me a thing we don't already know from the letter we received." She smiled at him.

"Boy howdy! Amazing is an understatement! I still can't believe it, and I am seeing it with my own eyes. I'm Noel Brady, um, Noel Laramie, and this is my husband, Stetson Laramie."

After a good cry and a group hug, Noel said, "Why are we standing out here? I'm dying to see the inside of the house." She grinned.

Holly took hold of Grayson's hand and followed her sisters and their fiancés up the steps onto the porch. Camden produced a key and unlocked the door. The house was even more impressive inside. It fit Holly's idea of what a home set in the middle 1800s, during the Civil War, would have looked like. In the long foyer hung a chandelier from what had to be a twelve-foot-high ceiling. At the end of the foyer, a large sweeping stairway led to the upper floor. Dark cherry wood banisters ran the length of the stairway. Holly wondered how many children had slid down them throughout the years. They walked into a large living room where a fire blazed in a huge fireplace on one wall.

"Oh, look at this furniture. Isn't it beautiful?" Carol sat on a high-backed chair. The fabric was ecru, with a soft green and mauve floral pattern that matched the rest of the period furnishings in the room.

Holly smiled at her. "Yes, it is. This house is amazing. Not at all what I expected."

"I've never seen anything like this." Starr sat down on the matching chair next to Carol. They were separated by a small table upon which sat a beautiful glass lamp that matched the room's décor.

"Would you have ever thought, a year ago today, that we would find that we have three identical sisters and would be here spending our twenty-fifth birthday together?" Noel ran her hand across the smooth fabric on the back of Starr's chair before taking a seat on the sofa across from her two sisters.

Holly sat next to Noel on the sofa. She noticed that the four guys lingered in the foyer, visiting there in order to give the sisters some time together and a chance to get to know one another.

"Isn't the Christmas tree beautiful? It must be at least ten feet tall." Carol indicated the tree across the room.

Decorated in colored lights and a multitude of ornaments, it stood in front of a large picture window.

"Yes, it is, and look at the angel on top. Isn't she gorgeous?" Holly watched the colorful lights twinkling on the tree.

"Look, there are four large packages under the tree. Do you suppose they could be for us?" Noel grinned.

"That would be great." Starr grinned back. "But if they are, who could they be from?"

Holly glanced up as an older woman walked into the room. The woman gasped, and tears welled in her eyes, eyes the exact color as hers and her sisters'. Glancing from one to the other, Holly realized her sisters were every bit as confused as she was. Who was this woman?

The lady dabbed at her eyes with a handkerchief before she spoke. "Hello, my darlings. I know you are wondering who I am." She paused and smiled through a fresh bout of tears. "I'm Emily Bellingham, your grandmother."

Holly's sisters all wore the same shocked expressions on their faces, and she was sure it was reflected on her own. Noel, the more outspoken one of her sisters—as Holly had learned after spending the last hour with them—spoke up now. "Whoa, I don't understand. The letter we received made it sound as if our grandparents were deceased."

"Your grandfather is deceased, God rest his soul. I wanted to surprise you, so I asked Camden not to say anything about me still being alive."

"Well." Holly glanced at her three siblings and then back at Emily. "This certainly is a surprise, all right."

Holly and her sisters listened as their grandmother explained the reason they were put up for adoption.

"I desperately wanted to keep all four of you, but your grandfather thought it best for you to be raised by a young couple who could give you a family. The court wouldn't allow me to keep you without both of us being in agreement, and your grandfather wasn't in good health. He knew he wouldn't live long enough to raise you. He truly thought he was doing what was best for you. I requested that he draw up this will. It provided me with a house and an income for the rest of my life. I would have an opportunity to get to know you on your twenty-fifth birthday, and his will would provide an inheritance for you as well. I love y'all so much, it nearly broke my heart to give you up."

Holly and her sisters spent some time getting to know their grandmother. Emily shared with them that their father's name was Jonathan Lee Carrington. Janice, their mother, met their father when he was stationed in Atlanta. He was deployed for a year, and they were to be married when he returned. Two months after he left, Janice found she was expecting. Jonathan was killed in a helicopter accident three months later. "I wanted you to know your parents loved each other very much. Your mother loved all four of you and would have raised you had she lived."

"What happened to our mother, Grandma Emily?" Holly asked the question she figured they all would like an answer to.

"The doctor called it abrupto placenta; the placenta tore away from the uterine wall, rather than separating the way it was supposed to, and they couldn't stop the bleeding. She only lived three days after you were born. I have an album here with pictures of your mother and father I thought you would enjoy seeing. Y'all look so much like your mother.

There are a few pictures of your grandfather, too."

The girls spent an enjoyable few hours with their grandmother looking through the album.

Later that evening, they were joined by Holly's parents, her brother Lance, and his fiancé, Holly's best friend, Beth. Holly introduced them to everyone. It was so good to see her family and Beth. She had decided to forgive her parents, put the hurt and anger she'd felt toward them behind her, and go forward. She realized they had done the best they could for her, and they had been very good parents.

"Robert and Virginia, thank you so much for raising my granddaughter to be the sweet, loving Christian I can see that she is, even after only spending a few hours with her. She has shared with us what wonderful, caring parents you are. And Lance, what a devoted and caring brother you are. Beth, thank you for being such a good friend to Holly, as well."

"You don't need to thank us. Holly is our daughter, and we love her. We've never thought of her as being adopted. From the moment we laid eyes on her, she was ours." Robert looked over at Holly, and Virginia nodded her head in agreement.

Lance winked at Holly. "I couldn't love her more. She is my sister and always has been."

"She is more than a friend, Emily." Beth smiled. "I love Holly. She and I are sisters of the heart."

Holly smiled at her family and friend, all gathered in the music room. How blessed she was! The Lord had placed her in a good Christian family. He had sent Beth and Grayson into her life, and now He had brought her, her grandmother, and her three sisters back together.

"Grandma Emily, would it be all right if I played the piano?" Carol ran her hand lovingly over the beautiful cherry wood finish.

"Darling, I'd love to hear you to play the piano. I taught your mother, and she loved to sit down and play in the evenings."

Grayson sat next to Holly on the sofa and took her hand. She noticed that Nick had his arm around Carol. Starr and Camden, Noel and Stetson, and even Lance and Beth, were holding hands as they all sang Christmas carols.

"Before we go to bed, I have something for each of my granddaughters." Emily said at the end of the last song.

"Nick, would you please bring the four gifts from under the tree? The girls' names are on them, if you would please pass them out for me."

"Sure, Mrs. B, I'd be glad to."

Holly received her gift first but waited until Carol, Starr, and Noel received theirs before she opened it. She gasped, as did her sisters. In each box lay a beautiful, hand-crocheted afghan. Holly's was red, Christmas green, and yellow, while Carol found a navy, burgundy, and dark-green one in her box. Orange, green, and brown tones made Starr's afghan look warm and cozy. Noel's was navy blue, red, and yellow. All four throws displayed a soft ivory background.

Holly hugged her grandmother. "Thank you so much, Grandma Emily. This is lovely, and I'll cherish it always. It'll look so beautiful on my bed."

"Mine will look great in my house, as well, and I thank you for it." Carol also gave her grandmother a hug. "It'll be displayed where everyone who comes in can see it."

"This is gorgeous, Grandma Emily." Starr kissed her cheek. "It'll be so pretty hanging on my quilt rack. Thank you."

"Grandma Emily, words can't even express how much I appreciate this." Noel hugged the older woman. "It's so beautiful. I'll treasure it always."

Emily wiped tears from her eyes, and Holly had a hard time not crying with her.

"You are very welcome. I wanted y'all to have a keepsake that would remind you of me. I'm glad you like them. Merry Christmas and happy birthday, my darlings. Now I believe it's bedtime for me. Good night, my darlings. I'll see you in the morning." Emily hugged Holly and each one of her sisters before she left the room.

Holly enjoyed talking to her sisters after everyone else had gone to bed. Around midnight they decided it was late. They hugged and headed upstairs. Holly couldn't remember when she'd had a more wonderful Christmas/birthday.

The next morning Lance and Beth told Holly they had set their wedding date for June fifteenth, as she said good-bye to them and her parents. Holly was excited for them. There was no one she would rather have for a sister-in-law than Beth.

"Well, the time is finally here to finalize all of this." Holly held Grayson's hand as they walked up to the door of Camden's office.

"I know. It seems like it's been a long wait." Carol shifted her purse to her other arm and took Nick's hand.

"I wonder if Emily will agree to your proposal, and I'll still have a job." Nick reached to open the door.

"I think Grandma Emily will be pleased with our idea." Noel walked inside with Stetson and Starr.

Camden led them to his office, where Emily was already seated. They all sat down, and Holly said, "Camden,

Grandma Emily, before you give us the papers to sign, we have an idea we'd like to share with you. Carol, why don't you explain this since you and Nick will be more involved than the rest of us."

"Grandma Emily," Carol said, "since we won't all be staying here in Monticello, and the house is so beautiful, what would you think about making it a tourist place, so other people can walk through it and enjoy its beauty? I would love to be the guide and conduct the tours. Nick could stay on as manager and continue the production of the plantation, if you don't have an objection."

All four girls sat anxiously awaiting Grandma Emily's response.

Holly glanced at Nick, knowing he was concerned. His job rested on Grandma Emily's decision. After a few moments she spoke.

"I think that's a wonderful idea. I must say I'm proud of you girls for coming up with this. The plantation pays for itself now. When you start the tours, it will be making a profit. Camden, if the girls will agree to my terms, we'll add this to the contract they will each sign."

"I'll have Beverly add it to the documents if you come to an agreement," Camden said. "It will only take a few minutes."

"Good. Then let's go over this. The upkeep on the plantation and the manager's and tour guide's salaries will come out of the proceeds. The balance of the profits made will then be split equally between Holly, Carol, Starr, and Noel. Nick, if you still want the manager's position, it's yours, and Carol can conduct the tours. If at any time, Nick, you decide you no longer want the manager's position or Carol the tour-guide position, you may hire someone in your place.

"Is this acceptable to all of you?"

"Fine with me," Holly said.

Carol grinned. "I'll love being the tour guide."

"It's okay with me." Starr smiled.

"Sounds okay to me, too," Noel chimed in. "We won't be living here, so it will be good to have Carol and Nick taking care of the place."

"Nick, do you want to stay on as manager?" Emily asked.

"I love my job, so I'll be more than happy to keep it." Nick leaned forward in his chair.

"Well then, I suppose you'd better adjust that contract, Camden." Emily smiled at her granddaughters.

Soon Holly, Carol, Starr, and Noel signed the contract that would give them their inheritance.

Saying good-bye to Noel made Holly sad, but they promised each other that they would get together several times a year. She was glad that Carol and Starr would be living close by. The young women hugged each other and their grandmother, promising to keep in touch and to be at each other's weddings.

Holly waved at her sisters as Grayson drove out of the gates and headed back to his house.

"Things worked out pretty well." Grayson glanced over at her, and she smiled at him. "Are you happy?"

"Happier than I ever thought I could be." She smiled over at him. "The Lord has certainly blessed us. We now have three sisters, a brother-in-law, and a grandmother that we didn't know we had, and just think of all the weddings we'll be attending this year."

A Letter to Our Readers

Dear Readers: ·

In order that we might better contribute to your reading enjoyment, we would appreciate you taking a few minutes to respond to the following questions. When completed, please return to the following: Fiction Editor, Barbour Publishing, Inc., P.O. Box 719, Uhrichsville, OH 44683.

1. Did you enjoy reading *Christmas Belles of Georgia* by Jeanie Smith Cash, Rose Allen McCauley, Jeri Odell, Debra Ullrick?
   □ Very much. I would like to see more books like this.
   □ Moderately—I would have enjoyed it more if _____
   _____
   _____

2. What influenced your decision to purchase this book?
   (Check those that apply.)
   □ Cover   □ Back cover copy   □ Title   □ Price
   □ Friends   □ Publicity   □ Other

3. Which story was your favorite?
   □ *Christmas in Dixie*   □ *Starry Night*
   □ *Nick's Christmas Carol*   □ *Loving Stetson*

4. Please check your age range:
   □ Under 18   □ 18–24   □ 25–34
   □ 35–45   □ 46–55   □ Over 55

5. How many hours per week do you read? _____

Name _____

Occupation _____

Address _____

City_____ State_____ Zip_____

E-mail _____